THE FILE ON DEVLIN

When Lawrence Devlin's plane was reported missing in Afghanistan near the Russian border, it made headlines all around the world. To most people it seemed only a tragic accident. But one of the best operators of British Intelligence, Josh Canfield, had seen a Russian agent coming out of Devlin's London flat the night of the disappearance. The last person who had seen Devlin in Afghanistan was a British agent—but he too was now dead.

Josh Canfield was a hard-working journalist—a cover which suited Military Intelligence perfectly. When he was assigned to the Devlin case he started to follow Sally, Devlin's daughter, and found almost immediately that he was drawn to her in a way which had nothing to do with the investigation. However, the real secret of Devlin's disappearance lay in a well-guarded château in Switzerland, where his widow had gone into mysterious seclusion. But how to get Sally and himself into the château without alerting the opposition?

by the same author

THE TILSIT INHERITANCE
I KNOW MY LOVE
CORPORATION WIFE
BLAKE'S REACH
SARA DANE
DAUGHTER OF THE HOUSE
ALL ELSE IS FOLLY
DUST IN SUNLIGHT
WITH EVERY YEAR
THIS OTHER EDEN

PART I

ONE

Canfield first saw the posters in Baker Street; NOBEL WINNER MISSING. Before he had searched out the fourpence and reached to take the paper from the news-seller's hand, something told him that it would be Devlin, and it was. Lawrence Devlin, whom many people had expected would be given the Nobel prize for literature some years ago, and who had, last year, been awarded the Peace Prize, was missing somewhere in the northern regions of Afghanistan.

Canfield stood there on the pavement with the swirl of the rush-hour crowd forced to move around him while he read the brief bulletin. It was a late final extra, and the news was scant. Devlin had taken off from Mazar-i-Sharif, piloting his own small plane and heading back to Kabul. Between Mazar-i-Sharif and Kabul lay the great Hindu Kush mountain range. The plane had failed to arrive. It could have been, Canfield thought, the last of Lawrence Devlin's journeys. The thought struck him with more force and a greater sense of loss than he would have believed possible in someone who had encountered Devlin in person only once.

He had meant to walk through Mayfair to Arlington Street where he was expected for dinner, but instead found himself cutting over to Marble Arch, and starting along Bayswater Road. Canfield knew that Devlin had had a flat on the top floor of a house near Marble Arch since shortly after the war. He seldom used it now. Canfield also knew that this walk was made in the spirit of a pilgrimage and of a farewell. If it was also in the nature of a sentimental journey, he didn't mind admitting that either. Lawrence Devlin had been a kind of hero to him, and at thirty-seven, Josh Canfield had seen a lot of his heroes reduced to the size of ordinary men. But Devlin had kept his place—by all counts not an ordinary man. So Canfield made his pilgrimage, and he offered no excuses for it.

The cars and buses went by on Bayswater Road in numbers and with a rhythmic thunder that was new to London in this age of prosperity and demands to keep traffic moving. There wouldn't have been much, Canfield thought, that would now have been to Devlin's taste in this once leisurely thoroughfare. The noise was strident and the lights were harsh even through the mist that always seemed to accompany autumn dusk in London. Devlin had essentially been a man of remote places, of places where silence had endured for a thousand years; all the periods between his journeyings of the last five years had been spent with Elizabeth O'Mara Spence in that eyrie above their Swiss valley. The view from the famous terrace of the château of St. Martin would have offered Devlin more than the scene of the mist-shrouded spaces of Hyde Park, with the traffic roaring four storeys below him. But he had held on to this flat and the reason, Canfield guessed, could only have been Sarah Devlin, the one child of the marriage that had ended in the rubble of a bombed house in Chelsea, with the living child trapped for a day beside the dead mother. Sally Devlin had been with her father the only time Canfield had ever talked to him; the tenderness and the desire to compensate to her had been very evident. The daughter could have been the only reason for keeping this link with a city where Devlin now spent less than a dozen nights a year. The flat had been his past with Sally, but his present was with Elizabeth O'Mara Spence. For both women, probably, the past and the present had ended in a single moment in the wastes of Afghanistan. And, probably, at some future time the London County Council would place on this house their blue plaque to mark the fact that Lawrence Devlin, Nobel winner, had lived here from 1946 to 1963. Canfield glanced expectantly towards the house as he approached it, and it almost seemed strange that the plaque was not already there.

The front windows of the flat were dark; it looked to Canfield as if heavy curtains were drawn across them. But at the side, where the house rose one storey above its neighbour, a light showed at the slit where the curtains were parted. It was something of a shock to see it, and he wondered who could be there at this hour—on this day. It could have been a charwoman, except that Canfield's experience of charwomen told him that they didn't carry on with their routine when their employer's name was being headlined in the streets. It could have been Sally Devlin, making perhaps just such a visit as he was. He tried to picture her—Sally Devlin waiting, waiting through the hours or the days, or even the weeks before she would know what had happened to her father. If he were alive it could be a short wait; if he were dead it could be a long one, or forever. But as he watched the light, standing there in the swirl of the people on their way home or queueing up for buses, common sense told him that Sally Devlin would not wait here, in an empty flat. She did not live here any more. He began to feel foolish, gazing at a lighted window, and he was about to turn and go back to Marble Arch when the light snapped off. Then he saw a hand at the front windows as the curtains were pulled back. Without shame now he stood his ground and waited, wondering if after fourteen years he was going to see Sally Devlin again, and wondering if he would even recognise her. She wouldn't recognise him, of course, and he had no intention of speaking to her. But his curiosity was strong, and he waited.

But it wasn't a young woman who came to the front door and walked down the path of the tiny garden. The figures of two men, in heavy coats and wide-brimmed hats were silhouetted briefly against the light from the hall. Then the door closed behind them, and the purplish-blue glare of the street lights fell on their faces. As the first one fumbled with the gate latch, Canfield was assailed with a prickle of familiarity; he had had a long training in remembering faces; one of the men was Alexi Kogan, military attaché at the Soviet Embassy in London. The second man he had never seen before. They both carried brief-cases, fat brief-cases, and from the way they handled them, heavy ones. They crossed the footpath and stood staring at the on-coming traffic.

Automatically, Canfield glanced back at the door of the house, thinking that it was coincidental that they had come out only a second or two before the person who had been in Devlin's flat. But no one appeared there. As Canfield looked back to Kogan and his companion a car drew out of the flow of traffic; even before it stopped the rear door on the kerb side opened. Without a word the two men got in. It pulled back into the stream of vehicles again. Automatically Canfield registered the licence number and the fact that it carried no C.D. plates. Then he was annoyed with himself for being over-eager. Probably somewhere among the passers-by, or in the following traffic, there was the C.I.D. man who reported on Kogan's movements routinely. He didn't, he told himself, have to take his own job that seriously.

He glanced back at the house where Devlin had lived, but the sense of rapport was broken. The windows remained dark, as they did almost every night of the year. He began to doubt that he had seen the light at all. It didn't matter; it was nothing to do with him. Sally Devlin had not appeared, and the fourteen years had not been bridged. For a time he had been swept along, thinking of himself as the person he had been on the day that he had met Devlin. But his job and the present had obtruded rudely in the image of Kogan, and again Canfield was the person he had become. He thought he preferred the younger one. But the younger one was gone, and so was Devlin.

He raised his arm for a cab, and when it came he directed the driver to Arlington Street. The mist was turning to light rain.

II

There was talk of Devlin's disappearance over dinner at Arlington Street. Molly and Philip Ridley knew Canfield as an admirer and a student of Devlin's work, and he was pressed to talk about it, and he had to tell again, for the benefit of the three other guests, of that one meeting with Devlin and their hour's conversation.

Philip Ridley had seen a later edition of a different newspaper, and he added to Canfield's scanty knowledge. "I gathered from the story in the *Journal* that he could have been missing for some days already. He hadn't set any particular day for getting back to Kabul. No one there enquired where he was . . . Damned dangerous to fly that country in a small plane."

The talk drifted then to Elizabeth O'Mara Spence, and there were some stories about the O'Maras, good and bad, and then it was time for Canfield to offer to take home the girl the Ridleys had invited for him. Molly and Philip deplored what they called the bad luck of Canfield's marriage, and every six months or so they found yet another girl they thought would suit him. They meant well, and he didn't want to seem ungrateful for their concern; this girl was pretty, and too young, and when she asked him up for a drink he knew it could have been an invitation for him to stay. He liked her well enough, but he was past the stage of wanting to become involved for one night only and this would be a one-night girl. So he made an excuse about a long day, and he thought he did it well enough, but it must have sounded lame, because he sensed her hurt at the rebuff. So he went upstairs and had one drink, too quickly, and kissed her, also too quickly, and left. The only comfort he had in the taxi on the way back to St. John's Wood was the fact that he hadn't offered her the tired old lie about seeing her for dinner some night soon. He was past the stage, also, of those tired old lies, and he didn't want it on his conscience that she would wait for some time for a telephone call from him before she knew for sure that she would not see him again. He wished that he had a smoother way with women, or less conscience about using them, or that he could find a woman who could shake and jolt and worry him enough, so that love would not be a mere easement of need, but a total involvement. He had missed that with his wife, Linda, and had so far missed it with everyone else. Perhaps it just didn't exist. Perhaps it was his own fault—partly his fault and partly the fault of the job, which didn't permit of too much sharing. Himself and the job he did were a hell of a combination, he thought.

He listened to the one o'clock news, and there was nothing fresh about Devlin. But the train of thought was started again, and he found himself with the encyclopedia in his hands, refreshing his memory about the part of the world into which Devlin had vanished. As he read, it seemed more and more possible that Devlin could have been missing for some time without anyone being aware of it. It was a land to be lost in, a land of great empty spaces, high plateaus, desert in the south, sweeping up in the north east to the mighty Hindu Kush, the western tip of the Himalayan range. No railways, unsurfaced roads washed out in the spring rains, a quarter of the people nomadic, a country of camel caravans still; it was a land lost in time to the legends of Alexander and Genghis Khan, the land of the ruins of Balkh, with fabled Samarkand beckoning across the Oxus. He read off the lands it bordered—like a litany from the gleaming ancient past—Persia, the Soviet states of Uzbekistan and Tadzhikistan, the road out to Pakistan through the Khyber Pass, and even a long finger reaching up through the Hindu Kush to touch China. It was the kind of place to which Devlin had always been drawn.

Canfield thought it appropriate and right that it had been that kind of place in which he had himself encountered Devlin. He had been twenty-three then, a year out of Cambridge, fed up with the teaching job he had taken while he cast about for something that he wanted more. It had been the last day of his two weeks in Connemara, and he had climbed the hills behind Roundstone in the half-darkness to watch the sun cast its first light along the ridge of the Twelve Pins, to watch the Atlantic grow blue, then green, and finally to take on its early morning blue. It had been boggy up there, with many pools from Ireland's unending rain, and big and ugly toads had fled before his footsteps. But Devlin had been there before him, Devlin and his daughter Sally, climbing the other side of the hill from the white Georgian house down in the stand of pines, where they were staying. Devlin greeted him civilly, as strangers must do in lonely places. Canfield had recognised him at once, though Devlin had not volunteered his name. They had all three shared a piece of Devlin's raincoat as they sat for an hour and watched what the rising sun did to the magnificence of that wild landscape. He had shared Devlin's pack of cigarettes, and the girl, Sally, had got up and moved about, never out of earshot, but moving with the restlessness of a child. Canfield remembered that she had been a red-haired, white-skinned child, tall and too thin, boyish-looking with her flat chest in the violent green jersey, and the long legs encased in shabby corduroy trousers. She had had the pronounced boniness of her father's face, and his grey eyes with their surprising sweep of dark lashes. The two men sat and smoked, and Devlin had talked of other places, wilder than this one, where he had watched the sun rise, talked, not patronisingly, but as if he believed that Canfield was the kind of man who would one day see these places also. The girl, Sally, had followed his story as if it were a well-known, well-loved tale, prompting him, "Tell him about Tibet, Daddy—Daddy tell him about that place in China . . ." Canfield knew that most of these memories came from the years before the war when Devlin, then in his twenties, had been a foreign correspondent in the Far East for a London paper, and publishing his first novels out of that setting. Devlin's war years had been in the Middle East, with the R.A.F. as a flyer; the war had given him maturity and two decorations. The two novels published in the years just after the war had given him fame. Devlin was a man of high adventure and high courage. He had lived close to the heart of his novels; to Canfield he was already a man of legend.

Finally Devlin had stirred and risen. "Well, that about does it, wouldn't you say, Sal?" And then to Canfield he had added, "Why don't you come down and have some breakfast with us?"

Canfield had never really known why he had refused, except that he was acutely aware that a man like Devlin would be impulsively generous with his time; the past hour had possessed a kind of magic which Canfield was afraid might fade when they descended to the mundane world of food and other people. Devlin might discover that he had picked up a very ordinary, even dull, young man. He might regret his impulse; Canfield felt then that he would have done anything rather than let that happen. But he himself had regretted the decision ever since. He had never seen Devlin again.

In the years that followed he had sometimes wondered how much of a part that meeting with Devlin had played in what he had subsequently become. He knew that after it the thought of settling down permanently to teaching had become intolerable. He had taken a low-paid, somewhat precarious job in Fleet Street, had worked hard and talked as hard and managed to get himself sent to Korea as a correspondent. When he had returned to England he found the way inexplicably easier, and it wasn't until he had been touring European capitals for some months as a second-string political correspondent for the Croft newspapers that he began to suspect that he was being built up for something. When they finally approached him it seemed unreasonable, and they made it sound as if it would be unpatriotic, to refuse to do the errands they charged him with. He had a legitimate reason to be in many places, to interview many people, or simply to sit at pavement cafés writing his copy. In the beginning he was used merely as a courier, as a go-between, as a contact man, very often knowing nothing at all about the material or the information he handled. He never thought of himself as belonging to that darker world he served, he did not see himself as a part of a cloak-and-dagger organisation, because most of what he did seemed purely routine. He was aware that his editor at Crofts must have had pressure put on him, because Canfield was sometimes sent to unlikely places to write unlikely stories. At the back of his mind was always the thought that this had been the sort of apprenticeship Devlin had served, though he didn't believe Devlin had ever served any other master but himself. Canfield had married during this time, but the marriage had gone sour. Linda felt herself neglected because he was away so much of the time, and when he was at home, he salved his conscience over the betrayal of his first ambitions by writing two biographies, which had excellent reviews and sold a little less than eight thousand copies between them. Then Linda left him, and at the same time he realised that things were turning out very differently from the way they had been supposed to go. What had seemed adventurous became dully grubby; it began to look as if the innocence of adventure had gone for ever with the war, and that there no longer existed the kind of thing to which the ideal of Devlin had first inspired him. He was becoming a skilful writer, but that was all. And they were keeping him more and more in London. With experience had come some insight, and they were giving him other men's reports to evaluate.

"You have quite a talent for analysis, Josh," Willsden said once. He detested Willsden—or perhaps it wasn't Willsden, but Willsden's job he detested. "You're wasted in the field. But of course it helps to keep up the writing stuff. Makes an excellent cover. People start to wonder if a man doesn't have a job he can talk about."

So he worked for Croft Newspapers and for Her Majesty's Government, and he didn't realise how much had gone from him until the day they actually assigned him a tiny, dusty cubby-hole for an office in the vaguely import-export concern this particular branch masqueraded under. He hardly used it, but he wasn't expected to show himself there regularly. The other part of his life, Willsden said, had still to be maintained. But they thought of him as one of their regular men, and he knew that being regular in the wearying tangle of intelligence and counter-intelligence would be the death of the other side of him that had once hoped to be something like Devlin. He continued to write and to publish, to give his advice to Willsden when it was asked. In a spirit of revolt he wrote poetry which he knew would never be published. And by the time he was thirty-five he began to feel that he had missed out.

He thought, still holding the encyclopedia and remembering that hour on the mountainside, that he hadn't made very much of the feeling that had stirred in him that day. He hadn't committed himself strongly enough to the pursuit of being the kind of man he had envisaged then. He was haunted, even now, by the possibility of what might have happened if he had gone down to breakfast in that white house in the stand of pines.

III

The report was on Canfield's desk when he came into the office the next morning—that and half-a-dozen others. He went through them and came finally to the one on Fergus. Fergus had been murdered in Beirut a week ago; they had known the fact of his death almost at once, and the loss of the precious cypher he had been bringing with him. The details of it were now before Canfield for the first time, and from the pages of the report the name of Devlin came up to hit him like a blow.

Fergus had been a contact man, and his last meeting in Warsaw with a Soviet official stationed there had been the culmination of four years of patiently working on the man. Fergus was to have carried out with him the cypher key that they hoped they would be able to use for as long as twelve months before the other side discovered the leak, and changed it. During the time they had worked on the Warsaw agent, they had been placing money for him in a numbered account in Switzerland; within the next year he would use one of his frequent trips to Geneva to defect. That would probably mean the end of the usefulness of the cypher key. But for a year, even for six months, it was worth it. Fergus, who had been the representative of a heavy machinery firm in Birmingham, had travelled in Eastern Europe and the Middle East for years; at Beirut he had been scheduled to hand over the cypher. But Fergus had been murdered before that exchange had taken place. If he had carried the code with him, it had not been in the hotel room where his body and wrecked suitcases were found.

With a sense of dismay and doubt Canfield read the report again. Fergus, keeping to the routine he had followed for years, had dinner with a representative of a firm he had sold machinery to in the past, and then returned to the St. George's Hotel, where he was staying, and gone to the bar. Although the cypher would not be handed over until the signal came from Fergus that he considered it safe to make contact, he was already watched, and the watcher in the bar had seen Lawrence Devlin come to Fergus's table and ask if he could sit down. The two men had talked and drank for an hour, and had gone to the lift together. The watcher had noted that the lift stopped at the second floor, which was where Fergus had his room, and at the third and fourth. But there were other people in the lift, and the watcher wasn't able to report where Devlin had left it.

The next day a maid had found Fergus's body and the British authorities had been notified. It could have been murder for robbery, since everything of value was missing from the room; it could have been murder for the thing of real value that Fergus was to have carried. The British officials very much wanted to talk to Devlin, but Devlin had already left Beirut. He had given his destination as Baghdad. Baghdad knew only that he was heading farther east.

The part of the report that dealt with Devlin ended there. It had been compiled before the news of Devlin's missing plane in Afghanistan.

The report made no particular point of Devlin's meeting with Fergus. There was nothing strange in what Devlin had done—it happened hundreds of times a day in every big hotel all over the world. More particularly it happened to Devlin, because it was what he had always done. But Devlin had been there, at that precise time, and Canfield's mind kept returning to the sight of Alexi Kogan outside of Devlin's flat the night before. He sat and thought about it for a while, and then he lifted the telephone and asked to talk to Inspector Lester of the Special Branch.

They knew each other slightly from past encounters. "Lester?—any kind of report on anyone breaking into Lawrence Devlin's flat?" He gave the address, and waited while Lester put through the enquiry to the proper department. "That's the writer chap, isn't it?" Lester said when he got back to Canfield. "The one who's missing?"

"That's the one."

"Well, nothing's come in about the flat. Do you want the place checked?"

"Yes—might be an idea. Do it discreetly. No need to make a fuss. It may be nothing."

"May I ask *what* it may be?"

"No," Canfield said shortly, unwilling to be pinned down to the vague doubts that touched him. "Just an idea. Oh, and would you check if that address is one regularly visited by Alexi Kogan, military attaché at the Soviet Embassy."

"Right," Lester said. An hour later he was back to Canfield. "Don't know where you people get your information, but I wish we had it. The place was entered all right. Lock was picked, not jemmied—or they used a key. No one heard anything. It's a small place—just five flats, one to a floor. The regular charwoman Devlin has isn't due for two days, the caretaker says."

"Anything missing?"

"Hard to say. But it's been pulled apart a bit. Papers taken out of cupboards and spread on the floor. The caretaker chap seems to think there are some things missing. Can't be sure though. They'll have to get hold of the daughter and see if she can tell them. And the char."

"And Kogan?"

"There's no record of him having ever visited that building. But of course they can't be watched *all* the time." Lester's tone was slightly defensive. "When was he . . ."

Canfield cut him short. "Are you going over there now?"

Lester was mildly surprised. "This isn't something for Special Branch—or is it?"

"It could be. I don't know."

"I'd better see to it then—is that what you're saying? I understand Peterson's in charge of the case. I'll just tell him I'd like a look around. Anything particular I should know?" The question was politely put, but it was a demand.

"I'll meet you there."

There was the slightest pause from Lester. "Do you think you should? We're trying to get the daughter there as soon as possible. What am I supposed to say about you?"

Canfield hesitated for only a second. He shouldn't be going where he could be identified with authority of this kind. But he couldn't stay away. "Let her think I'm a finger-printing man. Just don't say who I am. She probably won't even see me."

IV

The constable at the door of the flat stepped inside and announced, "Miss Sarah Devlin, sir."

The three men turned to watch her, and she was something to watch, Canfield thought. He conceded that he could not even have imagined what a wonder the passage from child to woman could produce. He was glad she was beautiful; it would have seemed wrong if Devlin's daughter had turned out not to be beautiful, but fourteen years ago the outcome had been doubtful. He was glad she had pulled it off.

Peterson, although in charge of the investigation, was deferring to his superior. Lester advanced to meet her. "Miss Devlin—I'm Inspector Lester. I'm extremely sorry we had to trouble you at a time like this . . ."

"How do you do?" she said mechanically. She halted in her stride. Se had a beautiful walk, too, Canfield thought, and long beautiful legs. The red hair of the child had darkened to the colour of a rich cream sherry; she wore it almost shoulder length, cut straight around, and its shining curtain swung as she walked. She had the grey, upward slanting eyes he remembered, and they were fringed with the most sensuous sweep of lashes he had ever seen. She wore a white raincoat, carelessly belted; she was stylish, but somehow it seemed an accident of good taste rather than something cultivated. She was like Devlin in that respect also.

She scarcely looked at Lester—she certainly didn't pay any attention to Canfield or Peterson. She just stood there where she had halted, staring about her, seeming not to be immediately aware of what she saw, as if she fought a preoccupation. It would be, Canfield thought, a preoccupation with pain, and a sense of unbelieving loss.

"As you can see, Miss Devlin . . ." Lester was having a

bad time. It was difficult to talk to a person who really didn't see you—especially when that person was a beautiful young woman. She only half-glanced at him when he spoke, and then her attention went straight back to what had been familiar to her in this room, and must now be astonishingly unfamiliar—the open doors of the cabinets which formed the base of the bookshelves, the stacks of papers on the floor, the empty mantelpiece, a vacant pedestal. Canfield had seen her lips twitch, and she had thrust her air of preoccupation aside. When she spoke again her voice was surprisingly firm, and he realised that she had grown angry in the time she had taken to look about her.

"How could they be so rotten!—I mean, how could *anyone* be so rotten as this! To come here just after the news about him got into the papers—when they were certain he couldn't possibly be here."

"Have you some reason for knowing it was then, Miss Devlin?—we haven't been able to fix an exact time . . ." He was trying to avoid telling her how the burglary had been discovered.

She shook her head, and for the first time her eyes seemed to register more than the obvious facts of the room. "No, I don't know. I haven't any idea. I suppose . . . well, I suppose it could have been any time since Mrs. McCarthy, the char, was here. She only comes once a week when he's not here. No one uses the flat when he's not here, Inspector . . . I'm sorry, I don't remember your name. You'll have to forgive me."

He was in a hurry to forgive her; it was astonishing, Canfield thought, what an immediate and unearned advantage a beautiful woman enjoyed. "Of course, I understand, Miss Devlin. You have a great deal to contend with just now. Lester is my name. This is Assistant-Inspector Peterson, and —er—Mr. Canfield here is taking some notes."

She looked at both of them in turn. There was no flicker of recognition in her eyes as she acknowledged Canfield. It was fourteen years, after all, he told himself. He hadn't really expected it, and at this moment when he was on the job, he shouldn't have wanted it. It surprised him to find how much he wanted it.

She began to move about the room now, to move carefully, touching nothing, her glance running from the built-in cabinets at the ground up the height of the bookcases above; she paused before the mantelpiece for a minute; then she continued her tour of the room slowly, and the professional in Canfield had to stand apart and admire the control that did not permit her to cry out at each new discovery. The professional side of him was observing this girl very closely, and the other side of him was wishing that he didn't have to observe her in quite this way.

He supposed he was no different from most other men who would look at her and wonder why she wasn't married. Men always wondered that, didn't they?—and it wasn't their business. Perhaps she'd just had the good sense not to marry at nineteen and find out six years later that she'd grown up and now she wanted a different kind of man—which was what had happened to himself and Linda. He thought that if a girl had a father as famous as Devlin, the kind of man Devlin had been, she would do one of two things—she would either marry very young and try to break away and establish a life with another man, or she would wait around, and hope that somehow another Devlin would turn up for her. Either way was wrong. This girl had waited; he hoped she hadn't made the mistake of believing there would be another Devlin; he hoped she had just waited because that was the way things had turned out. She looked lonely, though, standing there.

He found himself wondering how she had taken her father's marriage five years ago to Elizabeth O'Mara Spence. How would a girl take her father's marriage to one of the most famous women of her generation, someone who also happened to be extremely rich? Canfield remembered the manner of the child on that Connemara hillside, the kind of proprietary air she had exercised over Devlin, confident and sure of his attention. It was true that she had spent most of her childhood alone at boarding and finishing schools, but over the intervening years Canfield had learned, from newspaper items and snippets of Fleet Street gossip, that Devlin had returned from whatever part of the world he had been in to spend holidays with her, and that she herself had flown to spend summers with him in the Far East, and there had been Christmases in places like Madrid and Rome—balm enough, surely, for any child's ego. She would have been about twenty-one at the time of her father's marriage to Elizabeth O'Mara Spence. That was old enough for her to have been able to let Devlin go—but how had she let him go? Canfield wondered about the confrontation of a girl of that age, and a woman past fifty—a woman like Elizabeth O'Mara Spence. It was strange now that he couldn't recall any newspaper references to such meetings.

Whatever the marriage had done to Sally Devlin, it had changed Devlin himself—you didn't have to be close to him to know that. Since the marriage he had published no fiction. All at once Devlin had seemed to put on the mantle of the reporter, which is what Elizabeth O'Mara Spence had pre-eminently been, and something which many people said he should have left to her alone. He had become the critic, almost the pundit, where once he had been the creator. Canfield knew he was not the only one who had regretted the change.

Anyone might have guessed that marriage to Elizabeth O'Mara Spence would have drawn Devlin towards the heart of the international political world where she had dwelt all her life, but Canfield doubted that many could have foretold that he would give himself to it so completely. His travelling and his writing both seemed to have lost their appearance of being undertaken almost on a whim; they became purposeful to a degree that showed through. He went, always accompanied by Elizabeth O'Mara Spence, where the trouble was, or where his wife, with her legendary "nose" for trouble, told him it would be next. The writings of these years had been about the places in the world where oppression and poverty had lighted the fire, and where the revolt was to come—Latin America, Africa, north and south, the Caribbean. The writings had force and bite, and a deep compassion.

What was almost as important, they found a huge audience. Canfield was thinking now of the *Letters from South Africa* which had first appeared in Whitney Spence's most widely circulated magazine, and which sold three million copies in a paperback edition. But the writer seemed almost as distressed and tormented as his subject, as if he were realising too late that he could never go back to the kind of lost innocence of the days of fiction. It was probable that it was the South African pieces more than anything else that had won Devlin the Peace Prize, but the award had certain political overtones, as if it were an accolade to be shared with the O'Mara family, and even, perhaps, with Whitney Spence. Canfield had thought then that, after all, candidates for the Peace Prize were few enough, and that the Nobel Committee was human, and the publicity surrounding Lawrence Devlin and Elizabeth O'Mara Spence had been immense. She had stood by his side at Oslo, and the pictures of them together had found their way into most newspapers in the world at the time, and had been a natural choice for the reviews of news stories with which most editors rounded out their year. It had been a popular award with the European press, even allowing for the slight residual jealousy most of them nourished towards Elizabeth O'Mara Spence. Canfield wondered how much of a satisfaction it had been to Devlin himself.

Sally Devlin had finished her tour of the room, and was back where she had begun, standing before the wall of bookcases and cabinets. As they watched, she dropped down on her knees before one of the piles of papers. There was an air of unsureness about the way she began to flick through the pile, as if she didn't know whether or not to begin the task. From the first pile she went to another and another. Then still on her knees she moved to the cabinets with their gaping doors, again tentatively lifting envelopes, taking a quick look at the contents, putting them back. All this was done in silence. Lester was a very patient man; he believed it paid off, and he didn't hurry her. Canfield's gaze rarely left the girl; the slim figure in the white raincoat whose shoulders now and then seemed to shake. She kept her face turned away from them, occasionally one hand was raised to it, as if she brushed a furtive tear away. It was a terrible day to have to make her come here and go through her father's things, he thought, when the news was still uncertain. It was as if they, he and Lester, were determined to kill that uncertainty in her mind, to make sure that Devlin was dead. By the time she got through here, most of the hope would be squeezed out of her.

Finally she sat back on her heels, and the shoulders registered an eloquent, defeated shrug.

"Perhaps you can give us some idea of what's missing now, Miss Devlin?"

She looked around at them; now that Canfield had had time to grow used to the beauty of the matured face, he was able to register the details more sharply. She had been putting on a good front when she had entered, a determined notion to get the business done with and not to let their sympathy break in on her optimism. When she had come in here she had not been ready to believe that Devlin was dead; but being here, touching his things, looking at his papers, had undone her. Her face was shadowed now with doubt and fear; it was possible to see that those wide eyes were held deliberately wide, fighting the weariness of a night without sleep.

"Missing?" This time she made a gesture of helplessness. "I don't know."

"You can't tell us anything?" Lester's tone was almost stern. He had been patient enough.

"Oh . . ." She blinked rapidly. "You mean the rest of the things, of course. I'm sorry . . . I was thinking about the papers. Well, to start with, there was the jade horse. Quite a small one, but lovely. And valuable, I suppose. And there was a Chinese bowl. I think that was *very* valuable. He used to laugh about it and say that the Chinese who gave it to him—it was sometime before the war—said that if he ever needed money badly, the bowl would be his money. He used to call it the family jewels." A weak smile flickered over her lips. "And then . . . oh, yes, there was an illuminated manuscript prayerbook. Fourteenth century. And a pre-Columbian clay figure . . . From Mexico," she added, as Lester had frowned a little in puzzlement.

"I imagine the insurance company will have a full description of all these items, Miss Devlin?"

"The insurance comany? Well . . . I suppose so. I suppose they *are* insured."

"Didn't Mr. Devlin value these things?"

"Why, of course. He cared about them very much. Most of them were gifts . . . he had many friends all over the world. And during the war he sent the things he loved most to Ireland for safekeeping. We lost a lot when our place in Chelsea was bombed. But these were the best . . ." She attempted a little joke. "I must say whoever it was had good taste . . . but I wonder why he didn't take the Braque and the Dürer? They're more obviously valuable than a rough little clay figure."

"Well, we'll have to look into that, Miss Devlin. Some thieves are very specialised. It may be a lead . . . Now, what about the papers there? Would you be able to tell if anything was missing? Manuscripts, for instance?"

"Manuscripts." Her tone checked, stopped being confidential and became dry. "No manuscripts, Inspector. They've already been given to Harvard."

"*Harvard*? But Devlin went to Trinity College, Dublin." Canfield had meant to keep his mouth shut all through the interview, but he hadn't been able to hold back the words. But it was too late. He could see the almost imperceptible shake of Lester's head, and the way her eyes focused on him sharply, closely.

"You knew that, did you? Well, he did go to Trinity. He didn't finish his course—went off to China, instead. But he always thought of himself as a Trinity man."

Now Lester was caught up. "Then why Harvard, Miss Devlin?"

"It was the O'Maras who went to Harvard, Inspector."

"I see." It was noncommittal, official again. "Anything else, Miss Devlin?"

"I can't be sure. Perhaps . . ."

"Yes?"

"Perhaps his notebooks . . . the notebooks for the novels. But maybe he moved them."

"They weren't given with the manuscripts?"

"I don't think so. But there's so much else I am not sure about. And I don't know how to check it."

Lester leaned a little towards her, the long body bending almost protectively. "Why not?"

"There was so much, that's why." She flung her hands out once more, wider, encompassing the whole wall filled with the cabinets, the mass of papers they could see on the floor and stuffed crazily on to the shelves. "He isn't a very methodical man . . ." Canfield noticed that when she talked of him the tenses changed from present to past and back again. "We're alike that way. You know, he travels a great deal . . . always has. He writes as he travels. He doesn't need to be sitting down at a desk in a study. So he just writes on whatever paper comes to hand. Longhand . . . in exercise books—that's when he's being *tidy*. More usually, though, it seems to be back of envelopes. I've seen him empty a whole suitcase of scraps of paper at the end of a trip . . ."

"Remarkable," Lester murmured.

"Oh, *he* always can make sense of them," she said quickly, as if she worried that her words might have been taken as criticism. "He would put them in order and have them typed up—quite often I did the typing for him—and somehow they all fitted together. When he'd sorted them all out, there would be a chapter! It wasn't so difficult once you got used to how he worked. But you see . . . he kept everything. He never threw anything away. He would make starts on things—short stories, articles—and then put them aside. He always says they're the things he'll go back to when he's too old to gad about the world . . ." Her voice trailed off. While she had talked about Devlin, explained him to Lester, animation had warmed her features and her voice. It wasn't optimism, because for those moments she had forgotten what had happened to Devlin, Canfield thought. She had forgotten that she was waiting. But the realisation was back that there might be no old age for Devlin.

She turned her face away from them, back to the cabinets. "So you see," she said dully, "I don't know . . . You'll have to ask him, Inspector. You'll have to ask him when he gets back."

She stayed and worked with Lester and Peterson through that afternoon, trying to make up a list of what was missing. Canfield stayed on also, though he knew he should not; when the finger-print men had left they moved on into the two bedrooms of the flat, and Canfield went with them, a little shamed by his own curiosity, but reluctantly fascinated by the sight of the girl going through each drawer and cupboard, checking with an intimate and careful slowness that revealed much to the men who watched her. Canfield thought she must be near to hating them as they stood there, strangers to her and to Lawrence Devlin, while she touched and fingered her father's possessions. He suspected that his guess had been right about Devlin not giving up this flat because it would have meant breaking a link to the past with his daughter. The girl seemed to handle his things with a kind of jealous possessiveness that defied anyone to take them from her. He noticed that she still held a pair of cufflinks in her hand the second time she went to phone Jackson Hayward, Devlin's publisher.

"Mr. Hayward?—Sally, here. Has anything come in?—any news?"

And from the shortness of the reply they could not hear, the news was negative. "No—I'm all right," they heard her say. "That's very kind of you—but I think I'd better be at home to-night. There might be news. He might be trying to get in touch with me. I'll ring you back if there's anything . . ."

By the time she was finished the dusk had fastened in on the city, and the roar of the evening rush-hour came to them strongly through the closed windows. She seemed tired and yet unwilling to leave. At six o'clock she made a final telephone call to Jackson Hayward. They were all back in the sitting-room with her then, and they could not pretend they did not understand what the conversation was about. When she put down the receiver her face was taut and white, and they stood there rooted, finding nothing to say. Her lips suddenly stretched in an unnatural smile; she swallowed, and her words came out high-pitched and shrill with the struggle to say them at all.

"Well—he'd hate to think of us working here like this all afternoon and leaving without a drink. I notice they didn't touch the drink cupboard. Will Scotch be all right?"

Lester moved uneasily. "Well, I really don't think we should, Miss Devlin . . ."

"Oh, come on, Inspector—have one for the road." It was close to being a plea. She was already bringing out the bottle and glasses from one of the cabinets. "My father's a great man for that last one for the road."

But when the drinks were poured she didn't have anything more to say. The three men made strained, awkward talk among themselves, while she stood before the window that gave a view on to the Park. Canfield, watching, could see the lighted room and the reflection of her face in the dark glass. A wind had come up and it thrust itself against the house, as if to invade the warmth and the light. She shivered suddenly and put down her empty glass.

"About when do you think, Inspector, the snows begin in Afghanistan?"

V

Against all the rules, and against his own sense of prudence, Canfield rode in the official car with Sally Devlin and Lester. Peterson went back to the Yard, and Lester offered Sally a lift; Canfield followed without Lester's invitation. It was a shock to hear her give the address in Maida Vale, and to realise that they lived within a half-mile of each other, and had probably done so for years. They were all silent as the car edged its way through the Marble Arch traffic, which didn't seem to move much better than in the old days before they had torn the whole place up and shuffled it about. While they waited in a solid jam in Edgware Road, Canfield, who was sitting beside the driver, glanced back and saw that she was lighting another cigarette from the end of the one in her mouth; he wondered if she always smoked as much as she had done that afternoon. There were many things he wondered about Sally Devlin, things he wanted to know, more than just wondered.

"Inspector?" She took a long draw on the cigarette, her tone speculative.

"Yes, Miss Devlin."

"When will you be finished with the flat—I mean, when can I put it back in order? Mrs. McCarthy will want to know."

"Oh, well—I'm not certain. No more than a day or two at most. We'll be interviewing Mrs. McCarthy, of course, in the usual way. I suggest you stay in touch with your father's solicitors, since they'll be dealing with the insurance company . . ."

"His solicitors?" She gave a faint shrug. "They haven't done anything for him for years. All his . . . his affairs have been moved abroad."

Now Lester himself began to search for a cigarette. He took some time about lighting it. "Well, I understand it's a firm of solicitors who handle the O'Mara interests in London. They have already been in touch with us and indicated they have Mrs. Devlin's authority to take possession of the flat whenever we say they can. I understand nothing is to be moved . . ." he paused awkwardly ". . . for the time being."

In the darkness of the car her face was shadowed from Canfield, but he thought her voice trembled on the verge of anger. "And who, Inspector, are the O'Mara solicitors?" She didn't like having to ask that of a stranger, it was suddenly as if pride as well as possession had been stripped from her.

He answered as casually as the could, as if he had not caught the implication. "Funston and Brown—Gray's Inn."

And after that they said nothing more until the car turned off Maida Vale where the Regent's Park canal emerged from its tunnel under St. John's Wood. The leaves of the trees that lined the canal drifted down into the thick oily waters; the street lights showed the old Georgian and Victorian houses with their fresh paint, and the glassy bulge of conservatories at the sides of some. Some were perfect houses, some ugly piles, all of them breathing the rather smug air of a newly fashionable district and high rents.

"Changed a lot, this part of London, since the war," Lester said. "It used to be up, in a very middle-class way, and then it went down, and now it's up again."

"Well," Sally said, "I'm on the edge of 'up' but I bought the lease when it was down. I've been house poor ever since. Thank you, Inspector—it's the place there on the corner. The gate in the wall on the side. I have the studio." Canfield thought she was making an effort to sound as if this was a routine social occasion; there were, they all knew, no rules for times when you are sick at heart.

The driver turned at Willett Road. They were almost in Paddington, and what she had said about the district was true. Fashion had already discovered all the gems farther up towards Edgware Road and was brimming over on to this old Victorian area. Many of the houses still showed flaking paint and a variety of cheap curtains at the windows. But the *avant-garde* of fashion had made its attack, and one or two houses in the row sported a coat of sparkling white paint and coloured front doors. In five years the rents would be trebled and most of the present population would have moved farther west. Sally Devlin had the detached studio of a house that faced the canal—a house with fresh paint. But the gate in the high wall she pointed to was a faded, unchic green and had a rusty iron knocker and a bell pull with the handle missing. Canfield got out before the driver and came round to open the rear door for her. She gave him a faint smile, but it was mechanical; he was one of the many people who had impinged on her that afternoon, and she never expected to see him again. "Thank you . . ." She didn't remember his name. Just as well, he thought.

Lester stood beside her on the footpath. "Thank you very much for your help, Miss Devlin. We appreciate it very much. If there is anything else, can Assistant-Inspector Peterson get in touch with you here?"

"Yes, —here, or at Tyne and Townsend. I'll be back there to-morrow—unless there's some news about my father."

Tyne and Townsend was a publishing firm that specialised in expensive art books; Canfield remembered that it was a subsidiary of Jackson Hayward.

Lester looked up from his notebook. "I take it you're not intending to go to Switzerland then?"

"Switzerland?—why would I want to go there?" she said quickly.

Lester realised he had blundered, and he had said more than he intended to. "I'm sorry—I was under the impression that Mrs. Devlin lived there."

The reply came bluntly, as if, having said so much she thought she might as well say it all. "She does live there—and I won't be going. Not unless they find . . . I've never met Mrs. Devlin. Good-night, Inspector."

The rap of her heels on the pavement was sharp, angry. Lester shrugged, and glanced, with raised eyebrows, at Canfield. Sally Devlin slipped her hand in the latch of the gate and swung it open. They could see a bricked path that led between sooty walls that cut it off from the neighbouring houses; there was a thick plane tree, planted about with ivy, whose leaves drifted down to stick damply to the path. At the end of the walk was the door to the studio, open, light streaming from it. They could see a man standing there, waiting. He took a few steps towards Sally and they met on the path. Before the gate to the street swung shut, the two men watching saw him take Sally Devlin in his arms and kiss her fully on the mouth. Canfield saw, in that instant, that he had been wasting his time wondering about the man, or men, in Sally Devlin's life. Then the street gate latched shut, and they were left only with the glow of the light from the studio skylights reflected on the nearly naked branches of the plane tree.

"Well," Lester said. He climbed into the back of the car. "Well—at least she has someone to console her."

"Yes," Canfield said. He followed Lester into the car, and slumped down in the corner, his head tilted back, his eyes half-closed. For some reason the scene he had just witnessed made him feel dissatisfied, reckless, as if he wanted to get drunk or do something out of routine. "How about," he said to the other man, "coming back to my flat. I feel like the other half."

Lester glanced at his watch. "All right," he said promptly. "Wife's at her Conservative meeting this evening. There'll be cold meat for supper, I expect . . ."

Canfield broke in. "Did you recognise that man—the one with Sally Devlin?"

"Can't say I did. Someone I should have known?"

"Not necessarily. His name is Halstead. Robert Halstead. He had his picture in the papers quite a bit about a year ago. He's one of these financial boy-wonders. The youngest director Hadley and Nichols have ever appointed to the board. At thirty-five he's more than a coming man. He's already there."

"Nice for her," Lester observed.

"Nice—yes. I suppose she's the type who lands on her feet. I mean—she's lost Devlin, but she's got Halstead waiting." He knew he was being unfair, but he didn't care. The scene had affected him very strangely.

"Why shouldn't there be a Halstead?" Lester objected mildly. "She's a beautiful young woman."

"So she should be," Canfield said quickly, as if it was nothing she could claim any credit for. "Her father was a very good-looking man."

"You think he's dead?"

"Of course he's dead. He has to be." He didn't say to Lester then that if Devlin was not dead, then the situation was worse. He leaned forward a little and spoke to the driver. "Round the next corner. Second house on the left."

VI

It was the high, square Georgian house left to him by his father, the only inheritance there had been. It had been badly shaken by bombing during the war, and when he had moved into the basement flat after Linda had gone, he had begun the job of remodelling and repairing, turning each floor into a self-contained unit. It had been slow and expensive, and although he had done a great deal of the work himself, he was still struggling to pay off the overdraft at the bank. It had long ceased to hold much interest for him, except as a task to be completed; his own flat was the last—because this was St. John's Wood the estate agents termed it the garden flat—and its state of half-doneness had stayed that way for a year because nothing and no one had convinced him that finishing it was urgent or necessary.

It was a surprise then to hear Lester say politely, as he took the Scotch from Canfield, "Thanks—nice place you have here."

"It's a bloody bore," Canfield growled back at him. He had never expected anyone to say such a thing, even out of politeness, and he didn't know how to take it.

"There are four flats upstairs," he added, because Lester looked surprised at his answer. "I've done a lot of the work myself—except the electrical stuff and the main plumbing—I have a tame contractor who'll put his stamp on what I do for a little consideration." He suddenly held his hands out towards the Inspector. "See those scars?—that's how many times the wrench slipped or the hammer hit the wrong place. I tell you, it's doing it the hard way." He threw himself down into an armchair which protested his weight, and took a long drink of his Scotch. Then he grinned at Lester. "The whole thing gets to be a bore when you suddenly realise how much time you spend worrying about the hot water. I've put up so much wallpaper that I count stripes at night instead of sheep. I'm fed up with being a landlord."

After a tour of the room Lester came finally to the chair opposite Canfield. Canfield knew that he had taken in the bookcases, begun and not finished, the general untidiness of the room, the little lighted space beyond the french window where he had attempted to make a rock garden that hadn't quite come off—he conceded mentally to Lester that he hadn't got the fine Japanese hand with rocks. The place was a mess, and he knew it. Everyone who came here said, or implied, that it needed a woman—especially the women themselves. And he thought to hell with that, unless it was the right woman.

Lester swirled his drink reflectively. "Well, Josh—what's it all about?" It was the first time he had ever called Canfield by his name.

Canfield told him about Kogan outside of Devlin's house; reluctantly he told him about the meeting between Devlin and Fergus, the train of speculation that had been started. He felt badly as he did so but there was no point in withholding it. By to-morrow all of this information would be in the hands of his superiors. If they moved further, or how they moved, would be their decision. But he felt bad because it was the first time he had ever instigated an action on his own; that it should have been connected with Devlin seemed to him an unnecessary irony. "Did something strike you as peculiar in what was taken from the flat?" he said to Lester as he finished.

"Several things—but what in particular?"

"As Sally Devlin said, they left behind a Braque and a Dürer. What they took was portable—portable enough to have gone into those two brief-cases."

"Yes . . . so?"

"I think they were interested in the papers. I have a feeling that the news about Devlin broke before it was supposed to. That *they* already knew about Devlin, but expected to have a clear run of the place for a while before anyone else knew. If they had been telephoned there that the news was on the streets there was a chance that Sally Devlin or anyone else connected with Devlin might have turned up there. They hadn't time to put back all the papers. They just stuffed whatever was small and valuable into their bags to cover up the fact that it was the papers they were interested in."

"Interesting," Lester said, but without conviction. "And where are the things they took?"

"Probably sitting in the Soviet Embassy right this minute —and you won't get a warrant to get in *there*."

"Interesting," Lester said again, maddeningly calm. "Any

proof that it *was* Kogan and his friend who took the stuff?—was his being there just conincidence. We'll be checking with the other tenants, of course. Any proof that Devlin really had anything to do with Fergus, or was that just a co-incidental meeting too?"

"No proof. Not a particle."

"Then we'll just have Peterson get on with his investigation in the usual ways."

"Do that—yes, do that. I hope you turn them up." Canfield tilted his glass and drained it. "Stay and have a bite with me. I'm not a bad cook when I've had enough to drink."

Lester blinked, and then nodded. "All right—I'll do that." He let his glass be refilled. "You know—you're a strange chap, Josh."

"What do you mean?—strange?"

Lester shrugged. "Oh, I don't know. This house—those books you write. Working for M.I. . . ." He didn't finish.

"*That* job is enough to send anyone round the bend. But I'm not there yet."

"You know, Josh . . . you ought to get married again. Eases the strain a little bit. This place needs a woman . . ."

"Mind your own business," Canfield said rudely.

Lester didn't take offence. He smiled slightly, and then, as if connecting the two thoughts, he said, "By the way, will you want to talk to Sally Devlin again?"

"No—leave her out of this. She's best left out of it."

VII

The gas fire had been lit, and all the lamps were switched on; she was grateful for the warmth and light that greeted her, grateful for Robert. She supposed she had known she would marry him on the day she had given him the key to the studio; he had never had to use it before. She had not talked with him since the news about Devlin; he had been in Hamburg, and had intended to be there all the next week; but she knew that unconsciously she had been counting on his coming back. She had grown to count on Robert very much.

"I've been trying to reach you all day," he said. "I even

rang Jackson Hayward, but for some reason he wouldn't tell me where you were."

"I think he was trying to spare me some phone calls . . . It was good of you to come, Robert."

He brushed it aside, typically getting to what counted. "Is there any news? What's being done about this?"

"No news," she said. "I spent half this morning at the Afghan Embassy trying to get some information. They knew nothing—just that search planes were being sent out. I don't think, somehow, there are many planes in Afghanistan." Her mouth sagged, and she submitted absently to him helping her off with her coat. "I looked at a map. There just are no roads. They said if they sighted a wreckage they would send out camels or jeeps. Imagine it—*camels*! I had the impression that they thought it very inconsiderate of him to go and get lost when their resources are so strained just to keep up with what they must do. And they kept saying 'But perhaps Mr. Devlin flew into Pakistan or Iran' and spreading their hands in that awfully polite way. It seems that he was a bit out of line just wandering about in that plane and not getting permission to be in certain places—or whatever he was supposed to do. I found myself apologising for him. It got a bit like Alice in Wonderland." She took a deep, sighing breath. "And then there was the news about the flat being broken into . . . it began to seem comic . . . it was just too much."

"Steady . . . steady!" Robert was looking at her in the way he had when he was trying to gauge whether or not she was joking. "What's that about the flat?"

She told him, jumbling the facts a little, and he asking questions to straighten them out. He was infinitely patient with her; while he listened he had led her to the sofa and gently forced her to sit down. She reached automatically for a cigarette. When he saw it he didn't say anything, just struck a match for her and held it. He was trying to make her stop smoking, but being very patient and subtle about that too.

He left her then with a light pat on the shoulder, and she could hear him moving about in the kitchen, which was a partly enclosed section of the ground floor of the studio. Her bed and the bathroom were on a wide gallery built half-way up the high back wall. She had left the gallery open so that the whole apartment could enjoy the great sloping skylights; she had the feeling that Robert thought the place rather odd, but he had never said so. She sometimes wondered why she was in Robert's life at all. She was too untidy for him, he didn't completely approve of the way she did things, or saw things, but was prepared to make allowances because she hadn't had the usual kind of upbringing. In small ways he was trying to make her over. Sometimes she thought she might let herself be made over just to have someone interested enough to want to do it.

Then she felt the chill of the glass in her hand. "I must send some decent glasses," Robert said. "You can't drink champagne from these things—it's like drinking out of a jam car."

Sally looked in bewilderment at the straw-coloured liquid in the glass, the bubbles rising and exploding like pale, exotic stars in a yellow sky.

"Champagne?" she said, resenting it. "Why this, Robert? I didn't know there was anything to celebrate."

"My dear Sally . . ." He often began sentences that way, and she was warned by it that he would lecture her a little, kindly but still firm. "Only the bourgeoisie think champagne is for celebrations. It's for any time when nothing else will do the same job. If I let you fill yourself full of Scotch to-night it would only depress you more—and to-morrow you'd feel worse. Drink it up—there's a good girl."

She sipped it obediently, wishing at the same time it was the whisky he had forbidden. It would have been a relief to feel the strength of it hit her empty stomach, and then to take more of it to dull the sensations of pain and fear that the day had held for her, the day and the long night before. But Robert knew about these things; he knew, for instance, by hearsay, that her father had been an erratic drinker—sometimes holding it well, sometimes giving in to it, and to euphoria or depression, a way the Irish often had about them. Her father, though, when it had mattered, had been able to take it or leave it alone completely; but Robert didn't know that. Robert didn't know everything. Robert didn't know that some of Devlin's best writing had been his own translation, his rendering, of what strangers had said to him in bars and street cafés all over the world. She remembered that Devlin had once said to her that he sometimes felt fraudulent about presenting his books as his own, because so much of them belonged to other people, people whose names he didn't even know. She looked down, and the glass was empty; she had come a long way on one glass of champagne. For the moment she had at least stopped thinking about the wreckage of a plane in an unimaginable wilderness; she had thought, instead, of Devlin alive. Perhaps Robert was right about the champagne, as he was right about so many other things. She held out her empty glass, and he was there, bending over her, anticipating her want.

"It was all insured, of course?"

"What?" Could he be talking about the plane?

"The things missing from the flat?"

"Oh—them . . . Yes, I imagine everything is covered. I hope they can get them back. He loved the little horse and the Mexican figure." It was like trying to fool the gods, she thought, all this talk about wanting back what was gone from the flat, when what she was begging for was the favour of Devlin's life.

Robert was writing in a notebook. "Who was the man in charge—Lester?—Peterson? I'll have the office keep in touch with them, and let you know what they turn up. No need for you to do it. And what was the name of the man you saw at the Afghan Embassy?"

She shook her head. "I don't believe I ever heard it properly. Some Muslim name . . ."

"Well, don't worry about it—it's never very satisfactory dealing with those second desk fellows. I'll talk to Hump Saunders at the Foreign Office. He'll know the best person to contact." He looked at her rather severely. "You know, Sally, you don't use your head very well. There was no need for you to go to the Embassy yourself. They can't do very much from this end, you know, and there are much better ways to impress them that one wants results. Why didn't you telephone me in Hamburg?—or at least get in touch with Miss Ritchards at the office? All this could have been done for you. I know several people in the right places in the F.O. and any number on Fleet Street . . ."

"So do I," she said, recalling Devlin's newspaper friends. "And I knew Jackson Hayward was taking care of everything. But *I* had to do something. So many people phoned here last night and this morning—including your Miss Ritchards. And I just couldn't stand being here and saying the same thing over and over—especially when there was nothing to say . . ."

He laid his hand on her arm. "I'm sorry, Sally. I really am sorry. I wish I had been here. I wish I had known last night."

"You do understand, don't you? I just had to go out. The Afghan Embassy seemed the logical place . . ."

"To-morrow," he said, "you must stay at Eaton Square. Simpson can look after you, and you needn't be disturbed." Eaton Square was where Robert lived in a luxury flat that was far too large for a bachelor, and Simpson, as he said, took care of him. She knew that if she married Robert she would be taken to live there, and Simpson would take care of her also, and nothing in the whole flat would be changed. It would absorb her and her belongings almost without a ripple. At times it seemed to her just a little like drowning—of course it would be drowning in champagne, but drowning just the same.

He said, "You must leave all these things to me now, Sally. I promise you you'll have news just as soon as it comes."

He sat and sipped his drink silently for a few minutes; he was planning, she thought, the ways he would make sure that everything possible was being done, was being found out. She looked at him and also thought that she really forgot at times how lucky she was—that was what everyone said to her. He was undeniably handsome, with a trim athlete's body, and a sure, neat way of moving. He was intelligent and generous, and he had already won a place for himself in a tough world which many other men had struggled for all their lives and failed to achieve. And it hadn't been handed to him, either—his father had been a small solicitor who had barely managed the money to send him to the right school. From there on, Robert had done everything for himself. He was an enviable young man—from a certain point of view he was even an admirable young man. He had everything, people said. He had everything until and unless—and here Sally's mind framed the thought for the first time—unless you had known Devlin's kind of man.

Abruptly Robert put down his glass. She started guiltily, as if he had read her thought. "There's one way," he said, "of getting the very first news—if there is any news. There's one absolutely certain source."

She answered him because she knew what he was going to say, and she could not avoid it any longer. "Don't you think I know that? *She* will have the first news. She wouldn't be Elizabeth O'Mara Spence if every news service wasn't at her disposal."

He sat and waited. "Well?"

"No," she said.

It was another minute before he spoke again. "Wouldn't it be a good idea if you went to St. Martin?—stayed with her for a while? It would look better."

She reached for another cigarette, wondering why it was he did not understand this. "It doesn't matter to me how it looks. It has never mattered."

He didn't argue. Part of Robert's skill was that he never dissipated himself in argument at the wrong time. So he merely nodded, and got up to go to the kitchen. The telephone rang and he ran lightly up the stairs to the gallery to answer it. She could hear his smooth, noncommittal words to whomever had telephoned. He was so diplomatic always—never blundering with words, except when he said something as he had just now, and never knew that she was shocked. She helped herself to the last of the champagne. It was characteristic of Robert that it was all done as well as the circumstances permitted. She didn't possess a wine cooler; the bottle was wrapped in a wet dish towel and set in a plastic kitchen pail into which he had emptied every ice cube her refrigerator would yield. He paid such attention to detail. She thought that if he hadn't been so brilliant in finance, he would have made a superlative personal Private Secretary to some Prime Minister. But no—that wouldn't have been enough for Robert. Robert would have had to be Prime Minister.

After that call was finished, he went on telephoning; he was getting down to the serious business of the evening. He often did this—about his own concerns. But to-night all the effort was for her. There would be no avenue of information or pressure—and there were many—which lay open to him which would not be tapped, either in friendship, or as a return for favours done. He would try everyone he could think of—everyone, that is, except Elizabeth O'Mara Spence. Not even Robert would do that without her consent.

Holding her glass in both hands, Sally leaned in closer to the fire, hungering for its warmth, her body rocking a little as if the pain had become physical. Wherever she turned, whatever path she sought to her father in the last five years, Elizabeth O'Mara Spence had blocked the way.

The woman that her father had married could only have been the product of her century and her country. She was an American, the most emancipated, the most aggressively intelligent, and, some people said, the least tolerable of her species. She had been born to a great deal of money, new Wall Street money, made by the speculative skill and daring of her father, Patrick O'Mara, the son of an Irish immigrant. The O'Maras, Elizabeth and her three brothers, had all been imbued with their father's fierce energy. With no need to make money, they had sought power. In a large measure they had achieved it.

Europe first knew the name during the ambassadorship of Patrick O'Mara in Paris during the Thirties. The appointment had been a reward for campaign contributions; he had taken himself out of the stock market before the crash, and could afford the luxury of playing diplomat. But the O'Maras rarely played at anything; he had acquitted himself surprisingly well. That residence in Paris had given all the O'Maras a taste for international politics which none of them was ever able wholly to get out of his mouth. But it had been, surprisingly, the only daughter, Elizabeth, who had been the first one to make the name stand for more than just money.

She had stayed on in Europe in the Paris Bureau of the Spence organisation, writing mostly for *Sphere*, which was Whitney Spence's newest magazine, and his favourite. Shamelessly she had used the political contacts engendered through her father's position to get the interviews she had wanted, and when that was not enough, she had used money. Other reporters still said of her that her success in those years hadn't merely been the famous " nose " for news, but also the ability to pay to charter a plane to where the news was happening. While she was still in her twenties the reports from Ethiopia and Spain were like so many trophies; but her real fame in the journalistic world came with her expulsion from Germany after she had published an interview with Hitler. By now she had the distinction of important enemies as well as important friends. That was the year she married Whitney Spence.

She did not depart the European scene, though, and Whitney Spence had had to make the best of a marriage carried on between Paris and New York—and between London and New York when the war made it necessary for Elizabeth to leave Paris. The war years made her a personality in the United States, where she had not lived for the last ten years—America heard her voice on N.B.C. every night from London. It was under her by-line that the Spence chain reported the conferences at Teheran and Yalta and Potsdam. By this time her brothers were catching up; the oldest was Governor of an important Eastern State, and Tom O'Mara was making his presence felt in the Senate. The net of the O'Mara influence was flung wide.

The divorce from Whitney Spence did not break her tie with the publishing empire; there was no public nor—so far as anyone knew—no private wrangling, merely an agreement to terminate the marriage. Whitney Spence kept his ace reporter and his valuable contact with the O'Maras. In a remark that was overheard and widely distributed in a rival newspaper chain, one of the O'Mara brothers had said, "I don't think my sister was ever really married to Whitney Spence—it was the relationship of a writer to a publisher." The remark was attributed to John, the youngest, the only one to follow his father into Wall Street. He was also the one supposed to have said, "I am completely satisfied to make money alone. It is the only thing that interests me." It was a remark the other O'Maras found hard to live down.

Five years ago, when Lawrence Devlin had married Elizabeth, the newspaper stories had been interlarded with such quotes. Sally had read all of them, and remembered all of them, puzzling to find the key to this woman her father had married, trying to find what qualities in these two people had sought and found an echo in the other. On the surface it was a very unlikely marriage. Devlin had never cared about money, had never saved it, and never had more of it than what the next book would earn. She knew the private questions that were asked on Fleet Street. "And what does Mrs. Spence want of Larry Devlin?" there being the decided feeling that the O'Maras never did anything that did not carry a built-in advantage to the O'Mara family. Apart from adding his fame to what they already had, it was difficult, Sally thought, to know what Larry Devlin could do for the O'Maras.

She remembered the shock of the wedding—the cable from Rome that preceded the newspaper stories by a bare few hours. And then a day later, her father's voice on the phone. "You'll like her, Sal. She's a wonderful woman. I know you'll like each other when you meet . . ."

They never had met. In the first year there had been excuses—which was a new thing for Devlin. They were travelling; then the château in the Rhône valley, which was Elizabeth's home in between her writing forays, was undergoing repair—they were wintering in Egypt, and Sally should spend her next summer holidays with them. That summer Elizabeth had to make two trips to New York, and Sally took the job with Tyne and Townsend, and her holidays never seemed to coincide with the periods that Elizabeth and Devlin spent at the château at St Martin. Devlin continued to visit London, but he was always alone, except for the one time that Elizabeth came with him and when they stayed not at Devlin's flat, but at the Connaught, which was where Elizabeth had always stayed. Sally had primed herself for the meeting that was finally to come, telling herself, and not quite believing it, that all the other mischances had been mischances only, and not deliberate actions. And then Elizabeth had suddenly gone down with a virus infection, Devlin said, and could see no one. Sally might have made herself believe even that if she hadn't seen a report in the paper of Elizabeth O'Mara Spence, as she was still called in the Press, having attended a reception for the Commonwealth Prime Minister.

Sally didn't tell her father that she had found out his lie—it was impossible to admit that lies were necessary between them. But the next time she hadn't been able to keep quiet. Devlin and Elizabeth were in London together, Elizabeth as the Spence representative to report a conference of African leaders. Devlin had phoned to ask Sally to come and meet Elizabeth.

"Tell her she can keep that invitation," Sally had said. "Tell her Sally's a big girl now and she knows when she's not wanted. Tell her—oh, tell her to go to hell." And then immediately she knew that she shouldn't have used those words: Devlin hadn't deserved that, and it wasn't her place to judge what Elizabeth deserved. "I'm sorry, Father," she said. "I've got no business saying things like that. . . . I didn't mean it for you."

"*I'm* sorry, Sal." He didn't attempt to excuse his wife. "It's just the way she is. It's this one blind spot she has—very odd in a woman like that, but there it is. I wish I could explain it to you better. It's hard for someone of your age to understand, but it's almost as if she were afraid to share . . ."

Sally had exploded into rude laughter. "*What*! . . . Elizabeth O'Mara Spence afraid of me! That's almost too funny to be a good story, Father. Just think of it—Elizabeth O'Mara Spence, adviser to presidents and dictators, is afraid of Sally

Devlin. Do you realise how funny that sounds, Father?" She knew she was distorting the truth, but she had been hurt and she needed to hurt back, even if it was Devlin who felt it, not Elizabeth.

"It isn't funny at all, Sal."

They had left it at that. Elizabeth avoided coming to London, so there was no further talk of meeting. Devlin came alone, and for a few nights at a time occupied the flat in Bayswater Road. Sally had moved to Maida Vale soon after the marriage, but for the time Devlin was in London her life centred again on Bayswater Road. She restocked the drink cabinet from Devlin's wine merchants, and sent an order to Fortnum and Mason for the paté and game pie he liked, and the English cheeses. There were fresh flowers on the tables where they had always been. They sat late over brandy before the fire and Devlin talked, and it seemed to Sally that it was a continuation of the traveller's tale he had been reciting to her since she had been a small child. Elizabeth O'Mara Spence slipped to the background and Sally was almost glad that the situation was as it was, because if Elizabeth did not admit her into the life she shared with Devlin, then neither did she, Sally, have to admit Elizabeth.

It was impossible not to be aware of Elizabeth O'Mara Spence, though. She did less writing now, but what she did carried more weight. Her name, coupled with Devlin's, kept coming up in the newspapers. Wherever Devlin travelled, she was with him, and he seemed to travel more than ever. These years gave stature to Devlin's reputation; no novels were published, but he seemed to have become the spokesman for the inarticulate, the universally voiceless ones. Sally had clipped a press photo of him taken in New York as he had spoken at a dinner on Human Rights Day, his lean face startlingly handsome above the white tie; the top table of that dinner had been a list of the prominent liberals of the whole country. It seemed that in Devlin, the O'Maras, always liberal, had found their own best voice. It was a free voice, too, which made it more valuable. No one owned Devlin, he owed nothing to anyone. The Peace Prize came as a crown to the honesty of that reputation.

Between journeyings, they stayed at St. Martin; the house-parties there were famous. Sally, flicking a magazine, found herself staring at her father photographed on a stone-flagged terrace, with a glimpse of snow on the distant mountains behind him. He was one of a group of people whose names were famous in international diplomacy. It was captioned CONFERENCE ON THE TERRACE. Elizabeth O'Mara Spence's hand rested on her husband's arm, and she leaned towards him as they talked. In five years there were many such photographs.

Sally and Elizabeth seemed to be stalemated in their hostility. Sally herself had grown tired of the subject, and her friends had learned not to talk about it. Letters came frequently from Devlin, and that was as much, she told herself, as she needed. They were ample, leisurely letters, mostly written from St. Martin, that carried several dates as they were set aside, then picked up again and continued. And her letters went back to St. Martin and waited for him to return from wherever the quest for material led him, or Elizabeth's urgings had taken them. Sally wondered when he would grow weary; he was fifty-seven and she thought that often, as he packed to leave once again, the deep quiet of that famous terrace at St. Martin must have been a strong temptation, even to a man like Devlin. But his last letter had shown no signs that he even recognised such temptations, much less thought of growing weary.

Elizabeth is retiring to a sanatorium near Zurich for a week or so—a new diet and a rest, she says. I begin to think that rest cures have taken the place of monasteries in this day and age. But she says she is not to be disturbed, so I am off—with no particular place in mind, though it will probably be the Middle East. I have an urge to wander a little, unencumbered; I have a need to taste the wilderness again. These Swiss mountains are magnificent, but strangely tidy . . . The letter rambled . . . *Your Robert sounds formidable . . . will he approve of me, do you think? . . . are you going to be happy, Sal?*

He had found his wilderness. She remembered the fear that had grown in her when she looked at the map after the news of his disappearance had come, the frightening, empty spaces, the names of places that belonged to legend, but not to the modern world. When the man at the Afghan Embassy had spoken of jeeps and camels, she had known that the rescue attempts must necessarily be feeble, and most probably futile.

Robert would know it was futile too; he was a good judge of probabilities, and a realist. The realities were a remote and almost impenetrable country, and snow and high winds on the Hindu Kush. The probability was that if he had survived the crash, Devlin had died that first night. She no longer wanted to weep, because weeping was too little a thing beside the weight of that thought. Never before had she felt her own body to be useless—too frail to bear a weight, too inarticulate to shout a grief. She wondered if it was this kind of knowledge that had driven Devlin so often in his life to seek out the primitive societies, where men were their bodies and little else. She rose unsteadily, and in doing it knocked the ashtray off the arm of the sofa. She stared down at the mess of ash and butts on the carpet and thought that Robert was right—it was a filthy habit.

He was still talking on the telephone. She went half-way up the stairs and stood there, looking at him. He covered the mouthpiece. "To-morrow I'll have an answering service put on this phone for a while—it will save you having to answer unless you feel like it; . . . oh, and I had Miss Ritchards pick up a few things from Fortnums before she came to meet me at the airport. I've put it all out on plates. Do just carry it in to the fire, there's a good girl. I'll be finished here in a minute . . ."

She nodded, and went back down to the kitchen, praying that it would not be the game pie she had always bought for Devlin. It was the game pie, and her striped tiger cat, Tim, had squeezed through the slit of open window, and was perched on the draining-board eating it. Very quietly she lifted him off, and gave him a smack, but not a hard smack. Then she cut off the end he had started to eat. She would tell Robert she had been too hungry to wait. Robert didn't very much care for Tim; Sally had the idea that the feeling was mutual.

VIII

The sound of the telephone jabbed into the silence, rousing Sally into full wakefulness. At the bottom of the bed Tim stirred in protest as she clicked on the light; it was almost three-thirty. She lifted the receiver.

"Yes."

"I have a call for Miss Sarah Devlin, Mrs. Lawrence Devlin is calling from Switzerland."

Her grip tightened; the room was chill, but in her thin nightgown sweat had broken on her body. "This is Sarah Devlin."

"One moment, please."

The wait seemed without end, though it couldn't have been more than a minute. She could hear the voices of the operators, and then for a while there was silence. She groped on the bedside table for a cigarette, but the lighter wouldn't work, or her fingers suddenly seemed to be without the strength to bring it into action. "Oh, God . . . he's been found." She didn't let herself think how he had been found. She turned her eyes back to the clock. When the the operator's voice came again, she couldn't believe the words.

"Are you there?"

"Yes."

"I'm sorry to have disturbed you. The call has been cancelled."

"What!—what do you mean?"

"I'm sorry—the caller has cancelled."

"No—wait just a minute! What did she say?"

"I'm sorry, miss. I don't have any other information. That's all I can tell you, miss. Good night." The line went dead. Sally held the receiver in her hand, staring at it in disbelief.

She put on a kettle of water to make tea, and smoked while she waited for it to boil. Tim had followed her into the kitchen, and automatically she had poured milk into his saucer. By the time the tea was made, the trembling of her hands had almost ceased.

"Why did she do it, Tim? Why would she do a thing like that? Nobody could be *that* cruel. She got as far as placing the call—if there were news, any kind of news, she would have gone through with it. But why cancel?—why begin if she never meant to talk to me? All right—so she's never spoken to me once in five years—but then, I've never spoken to her either. Why didn't I phone her?—why *don't* I phone her. If we can't talk now, we'll never be table to talk. . . ."

The endless one-sided dialogue continued as she sat and drank the tea on the sofa, her bare feet stretched to the warmth of the gas fire. Tim stayed curled beside her until the first light brought his usual restlessness, and then he jumped down, went through his elaborate ritual of stretching, and disappeared through the flap that had been specially cut for him in the door. She wanted to call him back, even to hold him back, but it was useless to do that with a cat. She was completely alone now, and even the sounds of the first buses starting seemed to emphasise her aloneness and the passage of time.

Finally she got up and went back to the phone. "I might as well *try* . . ."

The papers had said that Elizabeth was back at St. Martin from the sanatorium in Zurich. She didn't even have a telephone number for the château, but the Swiss lived up to their reputation, and she was through to St. Martin in a surprisingly short time. She realised then she had been counting on a delay so that she could prepare something to say to Elizabeth but she wasn't given the chance to say anything. She spoke in French to the servant who answered the phone first, gave her name, and asked for Elizabeth. It was some time before a man's voice spoke to her in accented English. "This is Madame Devlin's secretary."

Sally felt herself grow hot. "And this is Sally Devlin. I would like to speak to Mrs. Devlin."

"I regret that is impossible. Madame is unable to come to the telephone."

"But . . ." She closed her eyes and held back her anger; now she was reduced to begging. "Is there any news of my father?"

"I am extremely sorry, Miss Devlin. There is no news. We will communicate with you if there is anything. Good morning."

At ten o'clock she tried again, and this time she was told by the servant who had obviously received instructions, that Mrs. Devlin was unable to come to the telephone. Sally said to Tim, "Well—I tried, didn't I . . . ? If she won't—she won't. Nothing's changed. It's worse, in fact."

After that there was nothing to do. Robert had left her nothing to do; he telephoned her and told her that every source had been checked again that morning, and that there was nothing fresh. She was to come to lunch with him, he said, so that she wouldn't spend her time alone brooding. They would lunch in the directors' dining-room, he said, so that she would be spared a public restaurant, and the inevitable enquiries. Robert thought of everything, and she was very grateful, but he left her nothing to do for herself. She dressed carefully, and when it was time she walked the long way round on the other side of the canal up to Edgware Road to get a cab. But against Robert's instructions, when she got into the cab, she gave the address of the Afghan Embassy. She would be late to lunch, and everyone would have to have a second sherry while they waited for her, but at least she was doing something for herself.

When she got to the Embassy the same man she had seen the day before looked at her, shook his head, and spread his hands emptily.

She was half an hour late for lunch, and under any other circumstances Robert would probably have been furious with her. But he said nothing, and the other directors were very understanding. All through lunch they avoided any mention of her father's name, which seemed to Sally a pretty unnatural thing to do.

There was nothing fresh that Canfield, through their own special contacts, learned of Devlin that day—nothing except details, sent by the British Embassy in Kabul, of the search that was being mounted. There was an impossibly wide territory to cover, and Devlin had ignored custom by not keeping them informed of his movements; a long-time friendship with one of the ruling families of Afghanistan had seemed to excuse him from the formalities. Willsden had asked for information on anyone that Devlin was known to have had contact with in Afghanistan, but the results, they expected, would be slight. Canfield wanted to phone Sally Devlin, but there was nothing of hope he could tell her, and he was aware that yesterday he had far exceeded prudence in even permitting her to see him in the circumstances she had. So he did nothing, but it was one of the times when the dun colour of the background into which he was supposed to merge himself irked intolerably.

TWO

By the third day the story of the search for Lawrence Devlin had faded to a paragraph on an inside page, and Sally went back to her desk at Tyne and Townsend. There was nothing else to do. Robert had put on the answering service, and she thought that she owed it to him to let them answer, so that even that small activity was gone. Robert himself kept giving her the reports from his contact at the Foreign Office, until she asked him to stop. "Don't tell me if there's nothing—just if there's *something*." So that stopped too, and all that was left was a silence in which the whisperings of her imagination grew to a kind of unearthly shriek. She wished she could have taken refuge in the clamour of everyday life, but people were sympathetic and left her alone. Robert was too considerate and patient, and she missed his amiable bullying.

The envelope from Mrs. McCarthy was on the mat under the letter drop at the studio when she came home that night. It was bulky, and she felt the weight and shape of the keys as she ripped it open.

"*Dear Miss*"—Mrs. McCarthy had been Lawrence Devlin's char for twelve years, and she had been part of Sally's growing up. "*Its terrible news—just terrible. I cant believe it. Ive rung you up a few times but someone else answers. The police came to see me about the flat. I went there and looked round and told them what I thought was missing. Shocking isnt it? The police told me they would let me know when I could clean the flat again. Then yesterday I had a letter from some Solicitors. Funston and Brown their name is. They said they were making other arrangements about the cleaning and paid me three months wages. They asked me to return the keys but I didnt think it was right to give them to strangers. So Im leaving them with you as youll know best what to do with them. Id like to see you Miss some time when its convenient. I still cant believe it. A lovely man like that. Yours respectfully A. McCarthy.*"

Sally opened the drawer where she kept her own set of keys to Devlin's flat, and stood there for a moment wondering if she really was as careless as Robert sometimes accused her of being. The keys were nowhere in sight among the jumble of papers and string and playing cards and the remnants of a domino set. Finally she dropped Mrs. McCarthy's set down into the familiar chaos, promising herself she would search for them properly later. Probably Robert was right; the whole place needed a clearing out.

It had been something of a joke between her and Devlin, how the jumble of the studio had begun. The money from the trust fund that had fallen due on her twenty-first birthday had just about covered the lease of the studio and a few critical alterations, like putting in the plumbing. Devlin had come to inspect it on his first visit to London after his marriage. He had surveyed its empty spaces, with her clothes still in suit-cases and a kettle and one saucepan in the kitchen, and he had pulled a wry face. "We'll have to find you a chair or two to sit in, won't we, Sal? I'm too old to stand up every time I visit. Why don't you take what you need from the flat? And find somebody to put up some shelves and cupboards and things, and send me the bill. After all, you've got to have a few books around. There's a lot of stuff in the flat that could just as well be here as there. Make the place look more like home."

She had taken him literally. A carpenter had covered the high white walls of the studio with shelves and cupboards, the same kind that Devlin had at the flat. With a sense of luxury she ordered a long wardrobe, deep enough to take two rows of hangers, built against the back wall of the gallery; she had Devlin's habit of keeping old clothes, and it happily received her school raincoats and gum-boots, old slacks, dresses that might come back into fashion, tennis rackets and cardboard boxes. She had made her sweep of Devlin's flat, taking not just chairs and a sofa and bed, but also linen and china. Devlin's books appeared on her shelves and Devlin's papers filled the cupboards. He hadn't protested. "Gives me room to move at the flat again," he said. "But you know, Sal, we really ought to settle down some time I come over and clear out the rubbish. Half of this stuff I couldn't even be bothered reading again."

But they never had had that clearing out, and, taking his words as consent, she had continued to move more and more of his papers to the studio, fearing that one day he might carry out his threat. She had never sorted them; the empty cupboards had accommodated them all. In five years the accumulation of her own living and Devlin's past had become formidable.

"I really can't understand it," Robert had once said, surveying the chaos of one of the cupboards where she was searching for something. "Only the very poor ever hang on to every scrap this way, Sally."

She had shrugged and tried to laugh. "I suppose there are different ways of being poor."

She couldn't sleep that night; she couldn't even go to bed—and she had run out of cigarettes. She wished she hadn't told Robert that she felt all right, and wanted to have an early night. He might have been there with her, or he might have left her some of the sleeping pills he always kept on hand. Robert thought it was all right for him to take sleeping pills when he felt like it, but somehow he lumped Sally in with her father as being the possessor of that dangerously erratic quality the artistic temperament. Therefore she wasn't to be trusted with sleeping pills. At twenty-six it was depressing, she thought, not to be trusted.

It was too late to go out, but she went out all the same. She put on her raincoat and fished out Mrs. McCarthy's keys from the jumble in the drawer. Tim flashed out the door ahead of her, a swift grey shadow which blended almost at once with the darkness of the little garden.

It was foolish to walk so late at night but she didn't care. It had been raining, and had stopped, and the cold wind blurred the surface of the puddles, blue under the street lights. Edgware Road was deserted when she got there. There was no place to buy cigarettes. She turned in the direction of Marble Arch, walking slowly. She didn't hear the car behind her, heard nothing until the voice.

"You all right, miss?"

There were two policemen in the patrol car, and they scrutinised her carefully.

"Yes . . ." She brushed the hair back out of her eyes. "Yes—I'm waiting for a cab—to go home . . ."

"Never are many about this time of night, miss. We'll stop at the rank and send you one."

It came four minutes later. "Where to, miss?" It didn't seem odd to reply by giving the address in Bayswater Road.

By the time the cab reached the house she had stopped trying to make excuses to herself, had stopped trying to defend herself to Robert. Robert needn't know—no one need know. The reason for coming was simple. There had been no space and no privacy, no place to make a good-bye.

After she had paid the cab and it had gone, she looked up and saw that a light burned in the flat below Devlin's. It was a shock to see it; at the back of her mind there had been the conviction that the whole house must now be in darkness because the tenant at the top flat was never coming back any more. She stood there, looking at the light, and she knew that it had been the sudden certainty, reached about the time the cigarettes had run out, that he would never be back again that had brought her here. What else was there to do in the flat of a dead man at two o'clock in the morning except to say good-bye?

She let herself into the building with the front door key, and walked up the five flights of stairs to avoid the noise that the tiny lift would make. The stairs were lighted all the way to the top floor, so that she saw the notice as soon as she turned the last bend.

It was neatly typed on a sheet of paper fixed to the door with Scotch tape. ALL ENQUIRIES TO THE ABOVE. The engraved heading shone discreetly. *Funston and Brown, 46 Gray's Inn.*

The key shook in her hand as she tried to fit it to the lock. It glided uselessly across the metal disc. Unbelievingly she bent to look at it closely. The disc gleamed with the brightness of very new metal; below it a second lock had been added.

She turned and leaned back against the door, gripping the useless keys so tightly that it hurt. Her thoughts were an audible whisper. "You got here first! Damn you—oh, damn you, Elizabeth."

II

Robert's solicitors communicated at once with Funston and Brown, who pointed out that Elizabeth O'Mara Spence was Lawrence Devlin's wife, if not yet legally his widow; she held his power of attorney and had the right to make what arrangements she wished. In view of the recent burglary, they added with great reasonableness, such a precaution as changing the locks only made sense.

But what, Robert's solicitors demanded, about the property still in the flat which belonged to Miss Sarah Devlin? Miss Devlin, Funston and Brown replied, could visit the flat by arrangement, and remove her property; Funston and Brown's representative would take an inventory of any articles removed, and Miss Devlin would sign a receipt for same.

"No wonder they have money," Sally said. "If that's the way Patrick O'Mara made it. . . ."

"It isn't illegal to make money in the stock market," Robert replied. "And strictly speaking, Mrs. Devlin's within her rights. At least you'd have to go to a lot of trouble to prove she wasn't. It's very tricky until your father's declared . . ." He stopped.

"Legally dead," Sally finished for him. Since the night she had discovered the locked flat, the possibility of him being dead had become a certainty in her mind. The wreck of the plane had not been found, and the winter snows lay on the mountains of Asia. Devlin was dead, but the law could not, would not, state that it was so.

So by arrangement, as Funston and Brown had decreed, she went to the flat, and under the eyes of a deferential but quite unyielding man, who did not remove his raincoat nor unhook the umbrella from his arm, she went through Devlin's effects, as the Funston and Brown man persisted in calling them. There was very little she could claim unquestioningly her own—a box of toys put away on a top shelf, which she would send to a children's hospital, some text-books with her name on the fly-leaf, a stamp-book, a photo album which the Funston and Brown man argued over, and some letters written to her by Devlin more than ten years ago, discovered at the bottom of a hat-box. She signed the list, and the Funston and Brown man saw her off the premises, as if to establish who had the final right there. The day of choosing gaily, at random, without licence, from among Devlin's possessions, was over.

She was shaking with anger and misery at the wretched

poverty of this good-bye while she waited for an empty cab. Her arms were piled with what she had taken from the flat, and the driver came to help her settle them on the seat. She did not even see the man standing on the kerb who witnessed this; if she had, he was nondescript enough to have been the twin of the Funston and Brown man upstairs. London was full of men like that.

At the studio she laid out the things on the sofa, and sat smoking and looking at them. It was terribly little to have left. Then her gaze moved to the bank of cupboards against the wall, the cupboards crammed with Devlin's papers, thirty years of unsorted notes and fragments. She had plenty left. "Much more than Elizabeth O'Mara Spence even dreams of," she said to Tim, and then she put out the cigarette, not needing it any more.

To Robert that night she described the things she had taken from the flat. "That's the end of it, then," she said. "It's finished. What now? What do I do now? It's odd . . ." she added, "there's nothing really final. No funeral or anything. Somehow I think he would have been glad not to have had a funeral. He always hated them." Then a new thought struck her. "I suppose there's a will to be read some time."

"Not until . . ."

"Yes, I know . . . legally dead. How long does that take?"

"I'll find out." Then he added, quickly, so that she almost didn't hear him. "We'd better get married."

"Soon . . . not yet." He looked at her in a strange way, and she saw his lips tighten. But he didn't say anything more. She wished he had. He didn't know how close she was to saying yes to that because there was no more waiting for Devlin to come back. Robert could have made it happen if he had really wanted it then. That could have been the trouble—that neither of them was really sure. It only seemed sure when they lay in each other's arms—but she kept thinking of something Devlin had once said to her about marriage—that there was a lot of time spent out of bed, and that was where things could go wrong.

III

Canfield took a walk late that night, the night that Sally Devlin brought home the last gleanings from her childhood with Devlin. Without actually meaning to, he crossed Edgware Road, and headed down into Maida Vale. But by the time he reached the intersection with Willett Road, he was ready to acknowledge that he had meant to come here all along, had meant to turn at this corner, had meant to walk past the high brick wall with the door in it. Behind the wall, in the little bricked garden, he could see the light from the studio skylights reflected on the underside of the plane tree; there were fewer leaves left now. He stood there for a minute, and wondered if she would be frightened if he went through the gate and up the path and knocked. Then he saw the Aston Martin parked at the kerb; it was one of the long line of cars parked there—there was never any kerb space left free in London these days—but it was conspicuously expensive in the midst of the Fords and the Morrises. It belonged to Robert Halstead; he knew that as certainly as if it had been labelled with his name.

So Canfield turned and went back along the bank of the canal towards St. John's Wood. That was the beginning of the habit he formed that autumn and winter of crossing Edgware Road and walking down through Maida Vale. Very often he saw the light on the bare branches of the plane tree, and almost as often he saw the Aston Martin.

IV

Canfield had been reporting a Foreign Ministers' conference in Rome for five days for the Croft newspapers; it had been dull and rather pleasant because the work had been routine, and the autumn sun had been warm, and he had been able to do a piece which he hoped to sell to an American magazine; he had no task to perform for Willsden, and nothing to report. But the mild pleasure of the trip faded when he was summoned to see Willsden immediately he returned.

"Something you ought to see," Willsden said, handing the

report across the desk to Canfield. "It's just come in from one of our people in Switzerland. He's working with the disarmament conference. It concerns Devlin—or rather, Devlin's wife." To them she was still Devlin's wife; there had never been positive proof that Devlin was dead, and they still thought of him in connection with Fergus and the wrecked hotel room in Beirut.

Canfield read it swiftly; the agent was identified only by number. He could have been any one of the British delegation in attendance at Geneva, or he could have belonged to the delegation of any other Government represented. Canfield didn't ask; Willsden would have simply not replied. The identity of the agent was not important; what was important was what he had seen.

He had had a few days' leave and had spent it at Zermatt. On the way back he had stopped at Sion to visit the famous fortress church of Valère, and from there had driven on to St. Martin, intending to lunch and then continue on to Geneva. But the sight of the man he had recognised in the square made him decide to book a room for the night and to settle down to an afternoon of drinking Fendant, the wine of the region, and to collecting some information. The man he had seen he had once known in Australia under the name of Zotov, and he had been attached to the Russian Embassy in Canberra. He had left Australia just hours ahead of an expulsion order at the time of the Petrov case, and they had lost track of him. In St. Martin he went under the name of Hans Raedler. The locals knew little about him except that they remembered well the time of his appearance there. He had accompanied Elizabeth Devlin back from the sanatorium where she had been taking a rest cure at the time of Devlin's disappearance. He was known as Madame Devlin's secretary, but he had taken over the running of the château. The sight of him in the square of St. Martin was a chance one. He was rarely seen away from the château.

Canfield let out a low whistle. Willsden looked disapproving; professionals were never surprised by anything.

There was nothing more to the report. That part of the

Rhône valley was not the usual place for tourists, especially not in winter; the Geneva agent had not wanted to appear conspicuous by staying longer than one night, or by asking too many questions. But he was sure that it was Zotov who was in St. Martin.

"We'll have to have more on it," Willsden said. "We'll have to know more."

They had one advantage in dealing with the other side—about the only one, Canfield sometimes thought. There was no such thing as an ordinary, innocent Russian tourist; there was no such thing as a Russian who had decided to try another country. Wherever they were, they were there for a purpose. And now they were in the château of St. Martin.

"It doesn't seem possible, does it?" Canfield said. And yet they were always dealing in what did not seem possible. "But there has to be something going on." They looked at each other, their minds occupied with the one thought.

"I certainly don't like to think about it," Willsden said, speaking the thought. "The kind of people they've had staying at that place . . . Wasn't our own Foreign Minister there once? . . . isn't her brother a Senator?"

"He isn't just a Senator. He's Chairman of the Foreign Relations Committee," Canfield said. "And Jim O'Mara is Under-Secretary of Defence."

"Of course," Willsden added, "when you get a family with connections like the O'Maras, there is no area you don't touch. People in high places. St. Martin has practically been a rest-home for the NATO top brass. And him with a *Peace* Prize! I tell you, I don't like to think about it."

"It isn't true," Canfield said. "I don't believe that Devlin was a traitor."

Willsden blinked owlishly at him. "Any proof of that, old boy?"

"I just don't believe it."

"Very touching, I'm sure. But we'll have to have a little more than simple beliefs, won't we? I mean, if there should prove to be a real connection of the Devlins with the Russians, then there could have been serious leaks from St. Martin."

"Is the Geneva man positive that it really was Zutov? He couldn't be mistaken?"

"You read the report yourself. He's as positive as any man could be who only saw Zutov walking by him in the square. The Petrov case, after all, was ten years ago. But yes, we shall have to act as if the identification was positive. We shall have to take steps."

The steps they took, the guarded enquiries they made revealed the fact that the man who called himself Hans Raedler claimed to have been born in Leipzig. The surrender of Germany had found him on the west of the dividing line, and he had stayed there. The records and the history of Hans Raedler had disappeared into the maelstrom of war and defeat, and they could not check the Leipzig background. An application for a passport had been granted by the West German authorities in 1957; it carried the photograph of the man who was now at St. Martin.

They sent an agent from Berne, a man called André, to take a job as a waiter in Sion. He was a man with a well-developed Swiss passion for long walks.

V

Sally could not have said just when it was that she began to have the feeling that someone watched her. It was a sensation so slight that there was no precise way to name it. It was no more than if the air stirred behind her, but that faint stirring was cold and chilling to the spirit. It was nameless, it was nothing, but as the muted melancholy of the English autumn settled into winter, it began to seem as if it were part of her life, part of the season of grieving, something she must live with. It was a season of grieving and of shame for all of them that year; it was the autumn when a president died by an assassin's bullet, the autumn when the bitter aftertaste of a War Minister's lie in the House of Commons which had almost brought down Her Majesty's Government lingered and bred mistrust upon mistrust, a time when people seemed suddenly leaderless and bereft, when confidence was shaken. Her own private tragedy, Sally thought, was merged into the greater mood of unease; it was possible that the watchers, the searchers that she sensed, were only there in imagination because she too was bereft and shaken.

Looking back, she began to date the growth of this sensation, this suspicion, to a few days after she had brought back the last things from Devlin's flat. There was no disturbance visible when she got back to the studio from Tyne and Townsend, nothing to give her special warning; it wasn't until she went to pull out the photo album when she sat with her cigarette and coffee after dinner that she was struck by the conviction that it had been moved—somehow touched or disarrayed. She sat back on her heels before the cabinet where she had put all the things together—stacking them haphazardly on top of what was there already—and looked with doubt at the jumble before her. It was impossible to remember if the album had been on top or below the bundle of letters, whether it had been stowed at this angle or another; yet the feeling persisted that it had been touched, been opened. She drew it out now, and carried it back with her to the sofa.

The photographs began when she was a baby, sitting with her mother, playing with the first toy lamb, the first live kitten. Her father must have taken most of them, because he didn't very often appear himself. There were single snaps of him during the war in R.A.F. uniform, and snaps taken with other officers, some of them afterwards killed, and a few whom he'd kept in touch with after the war. He had never believed that men in peace could ever retain the closeness that the fear and boredom of war conferred on them. "It just isn't normal," he said. "And it's no damn' good pretending things haven't changed. They have—and who would want to go back?"

But if he had not tried to keep alive the war years, he had been faithful to his conception of a father—a rather conventional conception of a father she now realised as she lingered over the photographs that must have been taken during school holidays—some of them recognisably in London, at the Zoo, at the Tower. And as she had grown older and had been able to travel to where he was, the backgrounds grew unfamiliar—thatched roofs and a jungle crowding close, the wide veldt of Africa, the untouched purity of a lonely beach in the Caribbean. She smiled a little as she looked at these; sometimes it had been hard to keep up with her father—he had been demanding in his way, demanding a kind of maturity from her before she was quite ready. But to be Devlin's daughter had been different and sometimes perilously exciting. There wasn't much wonder she hadn't married when she was eighteen. She had never known when the next summons would come. That was what had been hardest in reconciling herself to the marriage to Elizabeth—the growing knowledge that there would never be another summons. Looking at the photographs she knew the truth of this for the first time, and wondered, now, if that hadn't been the first thing in which she had disappointed Devlin. He had asked maturity of her when she was very young, and when she was of an age when it might have been expected, she had failed him. It was hard to think now, that she could never say to him, "Look, I accept the fact that you're married. Let me in . . ." And then to hear the voice of the last five years answer back, "But it was Elizabeth's fault—it was Elizabeth who kept you out." She looked down at the faded photographs of the man in uniform and she could almost hear him saying what he had never said: "You were here first—if the first move had come from you the bridge could have been made. This is a conflict between women . . ." And she hadn't been quite enough of a woman.

She turned the page. There were some blanks here where photos were missing, as there were all through the book—places where they had fallen from their slots and never been replaced, lost, somewhere among all the piles and piles of paper that were Devlin's lifetime. Some of the blanks were of long standing, the paper beneath faded to a uniform colour with the rest of the page. Some had gone recently, the paper beneath dark and unfaded. She wished she could have remembered what the photos had been of—who had been photographed, herself or Devlin? And where? Where were the photos of the Canadian trip, one of the trips she hadn't been with him? And what year had that been? Hadn't there been one or two from Alaska? And had he ever taken photos on that journey down the west coast of South America, or had she simply pictured him there in her imagination, as she had pictured him wherever he had been in the world? Not a single picture in the whole album was marked with place or date. She looked up suddenly in a kind of despair at the whole wall of cabinets facing her, frighteningly aware of the jumble that they concealed. She was suddenly face to face with what a lifetime of congenital untidiness had done to her. The record of Devlin was filed in those papers she had so carefully preserved, or it was filed in her memory, which was now proving dangerously unreliable. She had saved the papers, but they, like the photos were unmarked and undated. Devlin was there, but illusive and fragmentary, and it was her fault.

By this she was reminded that she had promised herself she would find the second set of keys to the flat—the keys she had not bothered about because they had been made useless by Elizabeth's act. But now it was important to find them to prove to herself that she could not have been quite as careless as she seemed, something to prove that her father's possessions were a sacred trust and she had not betrayed it. She got up then and went over to the drawer; with one swift jerk it was out of its cabinet and the contents dumped on the floor. Immediately she could see that there were—exactly as there should have been—two sets of keys.

A wave of relief swept over her, and the telephone rang. It was Robert. They talked for a while. He had just come in from a late meeting; she could tell it had gone well. His mood was jaunty—that "I'm-a-match-and-better for the older men" attitude which both infuriated and awed her. He was so frighteningly on top of things; she had never known anyone who so much typified this country at this moment in its history—the young man's way of not looking back to past grandeur, of not wanting to burden the future by trying to be too big now; he would trade with the devil if the devil were a customer. And the books would always be in the black.

Again she wondered, as she often had done, why she was in his life. Perhaps she was Robert's sole concession to incompetence. . . . " Sally, you're not listening," he said.

She started upright. " Yes, I was," she lied. She stretched out her hand to take a cigarette, and then guiltily withdrew. Robert could always tell when she was smoking.

" Is there something bothering you?" he said. " Something else?"

What did he mean by something else? Was he bored by her grief for Devlin, impatient with brooding and introspection? She was jolted by the thought, and she said to him what she hadn't meant to say. " I don't know. I'm not sure . . . Robert, I have a feeling someone's been in the flat."

He didn't reply at once. Finally he said, " Why do you think that?" She thought the pause had been deliberate, as if he were allowing her time to grow calm, to reconsider.

" I'm not sure," she said again, defensively. " It's hard to say. Things seem to have been disturbed. As if someone's been looking for something."

" Is anything missing?" he said, making her get to the point. " Do you want me to get in touch with the police?"

" Oh, no." It was alarming to think that Robert would have the police here within a few minutes, and they would look with their polite blank faces at the jumble in the bank of cupboards, and they would ask " What is missing?" She spoke quickly. " I'm not sure anything's been taken. I just have a feeling."

" But nothing's missing?" he insisted.

" No—nothing that I know of."

" Then that's all right. You know, Sally, you mustn't let yourself . . ."

" I won't," she answered.

She tried not to, but she did. Each night when she put her key in the lock she found herself halting for a second, waiting, listening. There was never anyone there, never a real sign that anyone had been there. If there was a noise, it always turned out to be Tim as he jumped down from the sofa; beyond the purr of his greeting there was silence; no sound beyond the faint moan of the wind outside, the gentle rattle of the windows in their old frames, the little draught moved a curtain.

"He's right, Tim, isn't he? Robert's right—I mustn't let myself."

She never put into words what it was she mustn't let herself do or become or believe. But a change had come; that winter she settled down to the task, through the medium of the papers and books he had left with her, of setting Devlin's life in order —Devlin's life, and her own.

VI

The process of putting in order, of settling, of making an account, extended to the office. She went there on the morning after that first vague suspicion had begun, the first realisation that she had need to know her relationship with Devlin better, conscious that here also was proof of neglect, even indifference towards the things that had been Devlin's.

Tyne and Townsend was a relic of an earlier age that had come to life again with the new prosperity and the new trend towards sumptuous art books as gifts. The production methods were painstaking, and costly, and necessarily slow; the tempo of the house was geared to it. Sally and Mary Farrar, the girl she shared a crowded office with, were called editorial assistants; they wrote letters to printing establishments all over Europe, they checked sources, they wrote to great art collectors for permission to photograph works. The files of the books in progress, and those past, were stored in boxes that lined three walls reaching to the high ceiling. Looking with fresh and startled eyes at it all, Sally wondered if she had stayed on here, had liked her job, because the place had somehow reproduced the kind of disorder she had made for herself at home; here though, at least the material was filed and labelled, even if it was difficult to find once put away. She thought that when the winter was over, when she had made some progress with Devlin's papers, she would find herself another job. Then she remembered that probably she would marry Robert when the winter was over.

From the previous editor she had inherited a huge desk, once beautiful, now badly scarred with cigarette burns and scuff marks. It was double-fronted with drawers on both sides. There was trouble finding the key to the front left-hand side, but eventually it turned up with four others in the top drawer of Mary's desk, pushed far to the back. Mary shrugged. "None of those keys fit anything I know of—I expect the char found it lying round and tossed it in there. Some of these look old enough to open the Tower."

She waited until Mary had gone to lunch before opening the bottom drawer of the left-hand front. With a kind of sadness and shame she laid her hand on the manuscript; it was almost a year since she had even had it out of this drawer, the last chapters had just been thrown down upon the earlier ones as they had arrived, as she, absorbed in Robert, had not needed this proof of Devlin's thought for her. This had been the year of Robert, the year when she had been too restless and too absorbed to do more than her bare job here, and every other task had been let slide. It seemed long ago, that first meeting with Robert and the preliminary skirmishing. Neither had wanted to capitulate then, each was holding off. They had gone on having other dates, and finding, in the end, that the world had narrowed down to just themselves—or at least her world had narrowed down to Robert. With a sudden sense of surprise she realised that the restlessness, the agonised wondering over Robert was gone; was it always like this when a man and woman capitulate to each other—was there no more to know?

She didn't go out to lunch that day, but sat in the quietness of the empty room and thought a little about Robert, and more about Devlin, Devlin taking over as she flicked the manuscript.

This manuscript in an unspoken way was Devlin's pledge to her that things were as they had always been between them. It had started arriving shortly after his marriage to Elizabeth. It had come, a chapter or so at a time, unheralded and unexplained, as if it had no more importance than any of the letters he sent. It had continued to come, at irregular intervals, the last chapters more than three months ago. It was long—many sheets of Devlin's handwriting, and almost countless half-pages and related scraps of paper used as inserts, Devlin's usual method of writing. He had never mentioned publication, had acted as if what he sent belonged to her entirely, as did all the letters. There was nothing for or of Elizabeth in these pages, neither in subject matter nor in inspiration. Devlin had finally reached the point of writing about the Devlins, making a long, personal estimate of the family, disguising it as fiction but yet letting Sally know that this was her heritage. She knew that some day it would be published, but for the time being it remained between them, as he had meant it to. She knew from the state of the manuscript that no other copy had been made of it, and that Devlin had meant her to know this also, and to recognise its value.

Until the time of Robert she had kept up with transcribing it as it had reached her; but Robert had taken possession of her, and the manuscript was neglected. She had done no more than read the new chapters as they came, always marvelling at Devlin's sense of continuity when he was writing other articles at the same time; she had read them and put them in this drawer, along with the rest. She wondered how it was possible to take a gift like this for granted, but she had done it.

It was long, longer than she realised. The narrative had the amplitude of a writer who is taking his time, who sees no urgent need of publication; he had given himself time to feel it all, and to set it down as it had touched him. There were almost three hundred pages already typed, and as well as she could judge from the bulk of the handwritten pages, perhaps two hundred more still to be transcribed. She hadn't even been aware, in this preoccupation with Robert, how much the writing had speeded up as Devlin had approached the end. She felt that it was ended, although he had not said so. The family saga had reached the point in time when the young Lawrence Devlin had begun his journey into the world; what came afterwards belonged in newspaper clippings and files of reviews. Devlin hadn't been the kind to write about the years of fame.

Only one page was typed that first lunch hour. She broke out a new folder for it. The part of the manuscript already typed, and the original copy, she put in two big envelopes to take back to the studio, the envelopes neatly marked.

Everything was out of sight by the time Mary got back from lunch. She wanted no one asking questions about this manuscript—certainly no one who might report its existence to Jackson Hayward and through him, perhaps, to Elizabeth.

Devlin had not been in a hurry for publication; neither would she be. He had given it to her, and she would keep it until the time seemed right to give it up.

That evening she laid the two marked envelopes in one of the cabinets at the studio, surveying them with some satisfaction. It was the beginning, she thought, of the new régime. In time, all Devlin's papers would be filed and marked in this way.

VII

It was going to be a long, boring winter for André Duval at Sion. Although the reports from Berne never said as much, it was clear that Duval was restless. He hadn't expected the job as waiter to be permanent, he said. And there was nothing to report from St. Martin, so he had not even the feeling of having earned his money, which, as a good Swiss, he would have enjoyed.

"Nothing to report," Willsden said.

"That in itself is something to report," Canfield replied.

That was the departure; nothing happened at St. Martin. Raedler was rarely seen, Elizabeth was never seen.

"Visitors?" Canfield said.

"None. There hasn't been a soul near the place that Duval knows of."

"And there's nothing about her in the Press. Nothing. Not even in the Spence press." Canfield was checking that regularly. "It's as if she were dead too."

VIII

In Sally the feeling persisted and grew that the studio was

being entered and—she didn't know quite what word to put on it—searched or examined. She never had absolute proof of it, but she could not shake the conviction. She knew now that she could never say exactly that anything had been moved or stolen—how could she when she had never known the full extent of what was there? The manila envelopes full of Devlin's scraps of paper—there could have been two hundred of them, there could just as well have been three hundred. Some of them, put aside as long ago as twenty or thirty years from the appearance of the envelopes, she had never even looked into. No page seemed to have been headed or dated; she found many fragments that referred to nothing that Devlin had ever published, and seemed to belong to no period of his life that she could remember. It was all confusion; it needed much reading and much time, and she grew increasingly aware of her own naïveté in supposing that she had known all about her father's life. She had known him as a child knows a father, not as a woman knows a man. She was learning about a different man. Occasionally in the bundles of papers she came across letters from women she had never heard of, letters that no one but Devlin could ever have been meant to see.

The task was enormous, and almost defeating; but she went on with it because she was obsessed by the sense that she and someone else were in a kind of a race to reach the ultimate knowledge of this man that his papers could give. In her more logical moments she had to ask herself why?—and who? Elizabeth?—had Elizabeth sent someone here to take what she thought did not belong to Sally? If that was so, then what was missing? Where were the gaps? There were none. There came into her mind the suspicion that it might have been on Elizabeth's orders that Devlin's flat had been burglarised, and then she dismissed the idea as absurd. Elizabeth had had the right to change the locks on the door; she had the right to do almost anything else. When Sally thought about having her own lock changed, even having another one added, she dismissed that idea too. It would mean explaining to Robert why she did it. There was really nothing to explain. Would she tell him she was afraid? Afraid of what?

There were also Devlin's books to be gone through. They went back over a long period of time—some of them to his Trinity College days. He had had a habit when reading, of jotting comments on an envelope or any scrap paper handy—quite often questions which he asked himself and attempted to answer—and then leaving the paper forgotten in the volume. She found hundreds of them in the books on the shelves—she removed them, and by now had learned enough to mark on them the book they had come from; they went all together in a new and separate envelope. She also found that the dust on the covers and tops of the books had fresh smears.

When she asked the woman, Mrs. Bennet, who made a show of cleaning for her once a week, if she had been dusting the books recently, Mrs. Bennet looked at her in a way that was half amusement and half pity.

"Love you—no, miss! You told me—don't you remember? —not to touch them because of the way you had them arranged. I hope I know when to leave things alone."

The books had never been arranged, and both of them knew that. It was one more of the things Sally had meant to get around to.

Sometimes, when Sally got back at night, she almost caught the physical presence of someone—of a stranger—in the studio. She had felt it strongly on the night she had switched on the light and Tim had been there in the middle of the floor, his back humped and the fur standing on end. He had glared at her with his great golden eyes, and then spat.

"Tim?"

Immediately he was ashamed of himself. He ran to her, and rubbed against her legs, giving vent to one of his infrequent cries. She picked him up, holding him against her shoulder and stroking his head. "What is it?—What's disturbed you?"

He never did it again. But never again did he greet her with a lazy raising of his head from wherever he was sleeping. He was always fully awake and on the floor facing the door by the time she got it open.

And there was the afternoon when the fog had become so thick that old Mr. Townsend had sent all the women employees home in the middle of the afternoon. The bus crawled along Edgware Road; near the canal in Maida Vale the fog was a thick shroud. The street lights were like candles seen dimly and far away; their rays hit the folds of grey-yellow vapour and got no farther. There was a stench of acrid soot in the air, irritating the nostrils and throat, burning to the eyes—and yet it was cold and moist. Sally groped her way down to Willett Road from the bus stop, the façades of the houses lost in the woolly greyness, an occasional car passing slowly in the road, heard but not seen. The fog gave back muffled echoes of the steps of passers-by, who appeared suddenly and disappeared, like darker shadows moving out of the darkness. It was difficult to find the latch of the gate in the wall, and she slipped behind it and let it slam with a feeling of victory that she had fought and survived the blank baffle of the fog. A dark grey shape scurried before her up the path to the studio.

"Tim!" He did not stop; the fog swirled and closed between them. He waited, however, on the mat before the door. "Nice way to say 'hallo,'" she complained to him, nudging him gently with her toe. "Ungracious wretch . . ." She had the door open now, and the cat slipped in before her.

As always, the fog had seeped in under the doors and window-sills; it hung in the room like cloth drops on a stage, gathering thickly in folds under the skylights and in the corners. She tossed her coat and bag on the sofa and went to the kitchen to put on the kettle for tea. Tim hung about underfoot until she washed yesterday's saucer and poured fresh milk. She looked in the refrigerator speculatively. "Well, Tim, it looks like bangers and mash to-night. One thing's certain—I'm not going to fight my way down to the shop." Tim didn't stop—he was spluttering milk about him in a little spray as he lapped. He had always been an untidy eater. "You're worse than I am," Sally said. She took out the butter for her bread and slammed the refrigerator door.

Instantly she froze. The slam of the door seemed to have found an echo somewhere in the studio. Tim halted, looked sideways towards the french doors, his ears back. Sally laid down the butter dish and it clattered against the counter. " Who is it? Is someone there?"

The fog seemed to throw back her own voice at her. She knew that if she didn't move now, in another minute she would lack the courage to move at all. She walked around the counter and out into the middle of the studio, towards the french doors. It wasn't until she had almost reached them that she saw one of them was slightly ajar. The moist cold of the outside air seemed to reach for her.

" Ah! . . ." The cry seemed jerked from her as she slammed the door shut with the flat of her hand. Now she pressed against the glass, straining to see into the garden, but the fog hung six inches from the windows, and it seemed alive with shadows that had no reality. The footsteps she heard could have been on her own walk or from the street beyond the wall; the fog gave all sounds a false shape.

While she drank her tea, sitting on the edge of the sofa with her eyes fixed on the french doors, she told herself that she would be calm. There would be an explanation if she could find it. Yesterday morning, because the sun had shone fitfully when she was preparing breakfast, she had opened the doors—she always did this before the spring had come. It was a foolishly premature gesture of hopefulness. It was possible she had not fastened the door properly. Probably the same thing had happened before, but she couldn't remember it happening before. But Robert had always said her memory wasn't very good, and she should check things.

Either that, or Mrs. Bennet had changed her routine and had come to clean that morning. As she ran her finger through the dust on the sofa table it didn't seem very likely.

The other possibility was that someone had already been in the studio when she had entered.

Before she let her mind play on that, she went upstairs to

the telephone and dialled Mrs. Bennet's number. There was a wait while Mrs. Bennet's landlady went to knock on her door.

"Yes, miss?—what is it?" she said crisply when she finally came. Sally thought she sounded as if she had been dragged away from a warm fire and didn't like it.

"I'm sorry to disturb you, Mrs. Bennet. I just wondered if you had been here to-day?"

"What?—on a day like this? I should think not, miss. Catch me going out into this muck if I didn't have to! Is there something wrong?"

Sally told her about the door. "It wouldn't be the first time you've left it open, miss. Downright careless, if you ask me. *I* always make sure things are closed up properly. It's a matter of upbringing, miss. Some people are careless, some aren't, if you know what I mean. . . ."

"Yes, I do, Mrs. Bennet."

"Oh, and while you're on, miss . . . it's a good thing you rang. I've been meaning to speak to you."

"What about, Mrs. Bennet?"

"Well, miss—it's just this. I'd like to give in my notice. Shall we say two weeks, miss?"

"Your notice, Mrs. Bennet?—is there something wrong?"

"Well, that's really for you to say, isn't it, miss? I mean if you're not satisfied, it's your place to say so."

"What are you talking about?"

"Well . . . it's all those notes you've been leaving me, miss—those notes about did I move this, or did I touch that. Well, I mean . . . I've been trusted by some very high-class people, and no one has ever accused me of prying. I mean I don't go poking about in people's drawers . . ."

Sally leaned back against the headboard of the bed, closing her eyes for a moment, suddenly feeling helpless. "I'm sorry, Mrs. Bennet. I'm really very sorry. I didn't realise the notes sounded like that. It's just that . . . well, I've been going through all my things here . . . my father's things, and there's . . ." She had run out of words; there was nothing to say, there was no possible way to explain that possessions might be touched or looked at, but not stolen. She could hear Mrs. Bennet's heavy breathing; the woman waited with grim patience. "I'm sorry . . ." she repeated lamely.

"Well, really, miss—that doesn't sound very satisfactory, does it? It's all rather queer, if you ask me. But then you *have* been acting a little strangely lately—since your poor father was taken. Not quite yourself, if you know what I mean. Perhaps you'd be happier with someone else. Someone who didn't know you before and wouldn't know the difference. So shall we say two weeks' notice, miss? That will finish me up Friday fortnight. I hope you'll be feeling better soon, miss."

Sally dropped the receiver back into its cradle, and reached for a cigarette. "So you're not quite yourself," she said aloud, looking at her face reflected foggily, dimly in the mirror across the gallery. Tim had followed her upstairs and sat on the end of the bed. She beckoned him with her hand, and this being one of his less independent moments, he came to her. "Do I seem different, Tim?" She glanced back at her ghostly reflection. "I can't say you *look* different, my girl. But Mrs. B. thinks you've gone a bit off your rocker since your poor father was taken. Well, perhaps you have. Oh, God, Tim—perhaps I have."

For days after that Sally wondered if she should get in touch with Inspector Lester; the police had not turned up any trace of the things stolen from Devlin's flat—Robert's secretary checked regularly on that, and sent reports. But perhaps Lester should know about what was happening at the studio; there seemed somewhere to be a connection, since Devlin's papers were involved in both cases. But what was there to report—that she thought she had heard a door slam, and that there were smears in the dust on envelopes and books?—that it was possible a few snapshots were missing, though she couldn't have sworn even to that? It added up to nonsense—but perhaps he wouldn't think it was nonsense. She would say she wanted to talk to him informally; she would be very calm and make an appointment for a week ahead, so that he wouldn't think, like Mrs. Bennet, that Devlin's daughter had grown a bit queer since her poor father was taken.

When she telephoned, she was told that Inspector Lester was on leave, and would be back in three weeks.

After that she thought about the man who had been with Lester—not the assistant, but the other man. She couldn't remember his face—that had been the worst day of waiting, the one possible day when there could have been news that Devlin was still alive. She remembered very little now about that man except that he had seemed to know Devlin in a way the others did not, who had responded most noticeably to the disposal of the Devlin manuscripts. Who was he?—where had he belonged? Lester had never actually said.

She let the thought of the unknown man slip from her. And she had bolts put on the inside of the two doors of the studio. She said nothing to Robert, though of course he noticed them.

"It's about time, isn't it?" she said. "They should have been put on the day I moved in. I'm late . . . as usual."

He lifted the point of her chin between his fingers. "We'll get married," he said. "And you'll come to live in Eaton Square—and then you'll have Simpson to guard the door between you and the dragons."

She smiled faintly, but her glance went to the stacked shelves and cupboards. She had not yet fought her battle with the dragons for possession of herself and of Devlin; there were still things to do. She wasn't ready to move to Eaton Square yet.

In January, flicking through the pages of *The Bookseller*, at Tyne and Townsend, Sally came across the brief paragraph. *Jackson Hayward has given notice that the publication of the book by Elizabeth O'Mara Spence*, A New Wind, *announced last autumn, has been postponed. The book is a chronicle of the years of her marriage to Lawrence Devlin, and their travels together. Nobel winner, Devlin, disappeared in a plane disaster in Afghanistan last October. No future publication date has been set.*

To anyone in the trade, that simply meant that the book was not completed, and perhaps never would be.

For the first time, reluctantly, Sally sensed that she and Elizabeth O'Mara Spence had moved closer. Something personal spoke behind the bald announcement of the indefinite postponement of a book, something human. They did not share their grief—she and Elizabeth had never shared anything. But they might both have loved the same man. She thought about it that night as she lay in the darkness waiting for sleep, listening to the steady rumble of Tim's purr. She stretched out her hand and touched his ear, felt the little shake of his head, and then his settling back. "Do you think she loved him, Tim?" she said into the darkness. "Do you think she might really have loved him? Perhaps she's going a little off her rocker, too."

Canfield also saw the notice. It was added to the Devlin file. As he pondered its significance he thought that these last months must have been the one period of complete inactivity of Elizabeth O'Mara Spence's life, the one time since she had been a very young woman that she had been both still and silent.

THREE

The winter wore on. For Sally it was both too long and too short. It was too long; the crocus in the little scrap of garden beyond the french windows were late, the days only grudgingly lengthened. It was too short. Every evening not spent with Robert she worked on the stacks of envelopes, reading, sorting, trying to file. The days slipped by, the week-ends came around too quickly, she seemed to move at a snail's pace through the task she had set herself. And Robert was talking about when and where they would get married.

On the first occasion he had mentioned it she had answered

him casually. "Well—I just supposed we'd get a licence and go along to Caxton Hall some Saturday."

He had looked at her over the huge plush-covered menu of the restaurant they were dining in. There had been a change in Robert's choice of restaurants since Devlin's disappearance —they were elegant and expensive and impeccably discreet. Later, when the mourning period could be said to be over, he would go back to gayer and more social places, the ones in the news. There was always a great and observable rightness in everything Robert did.

"Well—I agree that under the circumstances we shouldn't be too gala, but I think a church wedding would be appropriate. After all, it's not as if either of us have been married before." She hid her face behind the menu. She knew that Robert never went to church except to attend weddings or funerals.

"I expect you mean St. Margaret's, Westminster. Something simple and expensive . . ."

He frowned. "I don't see what's wrong with St. Margaret's. The families would quite like it, I think."

"I don't have a family—except for an old great-aunt in Dublin who's blind. I don't think *she'd* add much sparkle to the occasion."

Robert had not replied; he had given his attention to choosing for them both, as he always did, and they had dropped the subject. But it kept coming back, and in a few weeks Sally knew she was committed to a wedding that, simple as it might sound now, would be on the front pages of all the Sunday newspapers. "Jackson Hayward will give you away," he said. "I'll speak to him, shall I?"

"I think that's one thing I can do for myself." If there had to be someone to give her away, Jackson Hayward would be the best. She thought of the fat publisher's good-natured irreverence, and knew that at least that quality would save the occasion from becoming too pompous. But it was not a wedding which she could have imagined Devlin attending. She had never seen him in a cutaway coat.

"I think June would be the best time," Robert said.

"June? Isn't that a little conventional?"

"There's nothing wrong with convention—in its place it saves everyone from chaos. It's almost time we put an announcement in *The Times*."

She hadn't realised until then that he was one of those people still left in England who believed that it was not possible to be born or married or engaged or dead until a notice appeared in *The Times*. She suddenly had a vision of Robert when he was sixty. He would have received a peerage by then, if the House of Lords hadn't been reformed out of existence—and it would be a hereditary peerage, too; Robert would make certain that his children inherited what he had earned. At sixty, he would be dynamic and on top of his world; he would be one of those tall lean Englishmen who grew more handsome with age. And she thought of herself, still struggling to keep up with Robert when he was sixty.

"And it's time," he added, pulling her back to the present, "that you got over this nonsense about Elizabeth O'Mara Spence. She certainly should be invited. This will be your chance to get to know her."

"Why? Isn't it rather pointless—*now*?"

He sighed, but was patient. "Look, Sally, you're a sweet girl, but you're also incredibly ignorant. You'll have to learn, when we're married, that we'll be mixing with a lot of people just because they can be helpful. One doesn't always have to like them. You've got to remember that one's own feelings aren't always the most important thing."

She almost laughed at him. "I don't see what any of this has to do with Elizabeth."

"The O'Maras are an extremely important and influential family. John O'Mara has just become president of Endicott Trust—that's about the largest bank in America. It could be extremely helpful to know him when our company makes its move into the American market."

She didn't feel like laughing any more. She suddenly had the sickening conviction that he believed that Devlin had married into the O'Mara family because Elizabeth could be helpful, that the Peace Prize had been thrown to Devlin because the O'Maras, strictly speaking, were not eligible. She felt as if she were drifting in a world where nothing happened by impulse, with a sense of joy; she had begun to wonder if there were any other kind of world, or had she only vainly longed for it because she hadn't grown beyond the stage of Devlin's fairy tales? She felt like a swimmer struggling helplessly, uselessly against the current. The distant shore didn't exist. It was easier to go with the tide.

II

So now she worked against time—against the time when Robert would take over, the day when the studio would be closed, and then the lease sold, and Robert would send all the papers into storage until the time was right for some approved biographer to examine and evaluate them. She worked now with a sense of desperation and guilt, because she knew she was hopelessly floundering with the material in her hands. She read and tried to file, but she didn't really know what she was filing for, or what she was searching for, either. She knew that what she handled most probably belonged to Elizabeth, as literary executrix, and that inevitably the demand would come to give them up. So she stayed up late at nights and smoked too many cigarettes, and every envelope opened added a fresh load to the burden of guilt and anxiety.

At the office, the typing of the manuscript went slowly. She did not dare work on it when Mary was with her. Word might get back to Jackson Hayward that Sally was typing a Devlin manuscript, and it, too, would be taken from her. She began to wish that Mary would have a love affair and begin to take long lunches. But Mary was not in love at the moment, and she was a very conscientious girl. Sally ate an apple at her desk, and typed, and locked up the manuscript pages as they slowly mounted. She did not, though, take them home. She did not put them in the envelope at the studio with the first three hundred-odd pages she had typed. She was beginning to feel that everything at the studio was vulnerable to the hand and the eyes of the imagined stranger. As the typescript at the office grew she took an old file box, and labelled it with the title of a book that didn't exist, and placed it among the other old ones on the highest shelf, where not even the title could be read.

It was a jolt the day that, with Mary out at lunch, she was transcribing the manuscript at what was quite a good rate, considering Devlin's handwriting, when the door opened and Jackson Hayward stood in the door. The Hayward offices, much bigger and grander than Tyne and Townsend, were diagonally across the road from each other, but Jackson Hayward did not often bother to cross the road. He regarded Tyne and Townsend as a profitable little concern that puttered along in its own way, and was best left to it.

"Heard your typewriter," he said. "Shouldn't you be out at lunch, Sal?" He was one of the very few men who called her by the name Devlin had used; she had known him all her life. He drew on the inevitable cigar; she regarded him fondly, and thought it a shame he got a little redder and fatter each year.

"Didn't feel like it," she said. "I thought I'd just finish up this . . ." Keeping his attention on herself, she released the paper from the typewriter and slid it into its folder. Very slowly, with seeming unconcern, she laid the folder on top of the manuscript. If Hayward came near the desk, if his eyes rested on the handwriting, he would recognise it.

But he kept his hand on the door-knob, as if it were holding him up. "I'd rather see you out," he said. "Even if it's just a walk down to look in the shop windows in Oxford Street. Can't have you moping and brooding," he added bluntly.

"I'm *not* brooding."

"Well, see that you don't. Dev wouldn't like it. And what's that Halstead fellow up to? Are you going to marry him?"

She spun around on the swivel chair. "I suppose you think you've got a right to ask questions like that?"

He didn't take offence. "You're damn' right I do. With Dev not here to ask them—yes, I do think I have the right."

"How did you know about Robert?"

He made an impatient gesture with his cigar. "He's a pretty well-known young man—and you're Devlin's daughter. The word gets around. They all say he's a brilliant fellow. Never do know much about these financial boys myself. Is he a sound man, Sal? Is he good enough for you?"

"Sound?" She nodded her head slowly. "Yes—yes, I'd say Robert was very sound. And as for being good enough for me, I spend all my time wondering just how I'm going to measure up to him."

Hayward gave a little snort. "Just look at yourself. That's all a man needs. As soon as a girl starts thinking something else she gets herself all mixed up." He examined her carefully. "Well—I suppose I can leave that to you." He added then, casually, as if he had not come for that express purpose: "You all right for money, Sal?"

She nodded quickly. "There's the trust fund, remember? There was a second one when I was twenty-five. It isn't a lot, but it buys the little black dresses to wear to Robert's expensive little restaurants."

"Well—marry him, and let him pay for the little black dresses. But seriously, Sal, if you need money . . ." She shook her head again, but he went on. "There's royalties for Dev piling up. Can't touch them, of course. There'll have to be some disposition after a while. Not sure about Swiss law, but Elizabeth O'Mara will have quite a say. She may be entitled to most of it, but I'm sure there must be a provision for you. But I could always advance you if you needed something."

"The trust fund—it's enough."

"Yes, well . . . good thing Dev set it up. I made him, you know. He never thought about things like that. But, God love him, that's the way he was. Well—I must be off. Don't mope, you hear? I'll see you soon—I'm just across the road, you know."

And then he was gone. Sally didn't return to the manuscript; the visit had strangely unsettled her. She realised that it was a long time since she had talked to someone who also had loved Devlin.

III

Canfield thought it was odd that he should see them both in the same day—his ex-wife, Linda, and Sally Devlin.

Linda was driving a Bentley which was meshed in a traffic jam in Bond Street, crawling a few feet at a time; walking, his progress kept pace with her all the way down the street. He had had many long looks at her, but she never once glanced towards the throng of shoppers on his side of the street. It was more than five years since he had seen her.

She looked wonderful, he thought. She had been a good-looking girl, and she had grown into a beautiful woman. He judged the Bentley, and the sleek coiffeur, and concluded that the man she had left him for was doing better than even she could have expected. He thought of himself, still writing his pieces for Crofts, of the two books that hadn't made any money, of the assignments from Willsden, and the eternal repairs to the St. John's Wood house—and he also concluded that Linda had been a good judge of the things that mattered these days. At Piccadilly he had turned one way, and the Bentley the other. He had bid her a silent good-bye, and hoped it would be as many years before he saw her again. As he walked along Piccadilly he was surprised at his sudden sense of freedom. He had seen Linda, and he had bid her good-bye. She was gone now, completely, and he was unaffected by the parting.

It had been another matter when he had seen Sally Devlin that evening in the Crush Room at Covent Garden. At the last minute he had decided that he wanted to hear Callas as Tosca. There had been nothing left except the most expensive seats, which was more than he wanted to pay, but he paid. At the interval he had glimpsed Sally through the crowd, talking to a man he recognised as Lord Letwood, the chairman of I.S.C. In a moment Robert Halstead had joined them, followed by a waiter with a tray of drinks. Canfield edged closer, sometimes the press of the crowd between them blocked his view and he caught only fragmentary glimpses of her. They played a kind of hide and seek, except that Sally didn't know she was playing it. He made one attempt to break away, going to the bar and ordering a second Scotch. By the time he had it, the warning bell had rung. The room started to empty. He saw all of her now, and it became impossible to take his eyes away. She was not as he remembered her that afternoon in Devlin's flat; she did not wear her air of grieving abstraction, her face was not shadowed with weariness. He found himself just staring, fascinated by the sight of her, the glow of the white skin against the sheen of the dark sherry hair, the black dress of stunning simplicity which revealed her shoulders and breasts, and would make a man want to touch her, as he suddenly wanted very badly to do.

The room was emptying rapidly now; there was no more people between them, no one to hide behind. She was standing silently, listening to the conversation which was now entirely between Lord Letwood and Robert Halstead. She seemed to him to have the look of someone who has listened to such conversations many times; he thought that she had schooled herself to look interested and not to interrupt, but she had escaped the conversation and her thoughts pursued their own course. They were staring at each other, and the glass had frozen just a little below her chin. He knew he should turn away, he should not let her recognise him, as she struggled to do. But he couldn't turn away. There were some things in life, he told himself, that no man can give up.

Then Halstead touched her arm, and took the glass from her. Obediently she walked beside him to the door. Rooted, Canfield still watched her, and it seemed to him that her head gave a quick, nervous half-turn, and her eyes sought him again. But he could have been mistaken; it could have been an automatic movement as her hand came up to flick back from her face that marvellously coloured hair.

But he told himself that he was not mistaken; he let himself feel nothing but the great gladness that she had looked again.

Lord Letwood had put her in the front of his box because she had the kind of face that drew many glances, and he was a man who enjoyed that. She spent the last act searching the darkened auditorium, the boxes that faced her, the orchestra seats below, for another sight of the man she had seen in the bar. She told herself that she could not have forgotten the name that went with that face, the hooking black eyebrows, the shock of black hair, the humorous world-weary crinkles at the corners of his eyes. She could not have forgotten where and how she had met him. She had to remember; she had to remember and find him.

At supper at the Savoy Grill Lord Letwood thought that Robert Halstead's fiancée was even more beautiful than at first sight, and it was a pity that she was a little stupid. She didn't pay very much attention to him.

IV

All winter the reports from André yielded nothing. Over the château in St. Martin there hung a curtain of inaction. Elizabeth O'Mara Spence did not venture beyond her own gates, not even into the valley; nothing of hers was published, the Spence press made no reports of future plans. All André reported was that she took solitary walks on the terrace of the château. By following a difficult and little-used ski trail André had found a vantage point from which the terrace of St. Martin could be overlooked and watched with the aid of powerful field-glasses. That was the closest he ever got to it.

André was growing restless now; he had attached himself to the daughter of a man who had worked in the château since the end of the war—she was one of a clan who made up a quarter of the village. From her all he learned was that life in the château had altered drastically since Devlin had disappeared, that the staff were confused and unhappy but that none of them thought of deserting Madame Devlin. All this did not take André nearer to the château itself or to Elizabeth O'Mara; and the girl, unhappily, had begun to take him seriously.

"Is this doing any good?" Canfield said to Willsden. "It could all be the longest string of coincidence, and you're wasting a man there all this time."

"Wait," Willsden said. "It has to mean something. Give

it time to develop, and we shall see . . ." Willsden seemed to Canfield supremely suited to bear the frustrations of his job. He searched now among the papers on his desk. "We shall want you to go to Berlin next week, Josh. You can do an article on the Wall while you're there."

"Not another one, surely!" Canfield objected. "Every journalist in the world has done his piece on the Wall."

"All the more reason for you to be among them. It doesn't do in this job to be different," Willsden answered unsympathetically. "We shall want you to contact Daniel . . ."

V

About the time the spring thaws were due in the Rhône valley, the time when the rumble of avalanches could be heard in the mountains above St. Martin—and long after the sooty crocus had bloomed in Sally's garden, and had given place to sooty daffodils blooming above the winter-hardened ivy—the first real news came. When he first read the report Canfield felt the tingle of excitement that was purely professional, the knowledge that a long-range guess held a particle of truth. Then his excitement gave way to depression almost at once as he realised that this piece of truth seemed to bind Devlin tighter into the net which Canfield would have him escape.

A stranger had been seen now twice at St. Martin—the first report of his presence had sent André to his vantage point, and to a long wait until he was rewarded by the sight of the stranger on the terrace. He had returned next day with photographic equipment—it was not always possible to arrange his hours off duty to coincide with the daylight needed to see the château. Cloud and snow flurries had obscured his vision; then he learned that the stranger had left St. Martin. He sent a description to Berne. The next week a friend had arrived to spend a late-winter holiday with André, staying at cut-rates at André's hotel. They greeted each other affectionately, and talked of the old days. They had never seen each other before.

And after that André's friend was always on the long cross-country ski hikes which André took. He cheerfully admitted that he wasn't much on skis, but he was a marvellous photographer. He made countless pictures of Sion and St. Martin; on clear days, with telescopic lenses, he got impressive pictures of the major peaks without the discomfort of having to climb too close to them; he made pictures of the proprietor of the hotel and his family, and pictures of André's girl-friend and *her* family; he openly sighed for a chance to photograph the château, but everyone said it was impossible. Even in the old days, before Madame shut herself up there, she had never permitted outsiders to examine or photograph the art treasures; only the Spence newspaper had ever done that. But his patience was rewarded when the girl's father said casually in a tavern one night that the man who had been Madame's guest some weeks ago had come back, and he had another man with him. Guests to the château were rare enough these days to be commented on. So André's friend made the trek painfully each day to the vantage point above the château, burdened with his cameras, which by now were taken as a part of him. When he returned to Berne he had pictures of the visitors to St. Martin walking on the famous terrace.

In London they studied the pictures very carefully and began a search through the files. The two pictures of Elizabeth O'Mara Spence, taken during her solitary promenades on the terrace, showed a startling change to those who knew her face. She was wrapped in dark furs, not mink but sable, one of their authorities said. The hair, which had once been blonde, and had been kept so by the hairdressers, now appeared to be white. The harsh, brilliant light of the Valais was cruel to her face, revealing the deep lines around the mouth, the darkness of the skin under the eyes. The face, always finely modelled, if not considered actually beautiful, was ravaged and gaunt.

Canfield hardly needed to learn the identity of one of the visitors to St. Martin to know one fact. Elizabeth O'Mara Spence was seriously ill.

The identity of the man was a confirmation. He was the

doctor attached to the Russian Embassy in Berne. The identity of the second man gave more trouble. It took them some time to find out that he was an Italian doctor from Milan, who had once run for election as a communist candidate.

"Shouldn't we let the Swiss know?" Canfield asked Willsden.

"No point in it, yet. They will merely point out that it's a free and netural country. The fewer people know, the less chance of tipping them off that *we* know."

"What about the C.I.A.?"

Willsden drew in his breath nervously. "If we go to the Americans with this we'll be stirring up things in very high places. Making accusations we'll have to prove. We'll have to tread very softly there. She's not in a position at the moment to do anyone harm. And every woman has the right to her own doctor." Canfield knew the last thing Willsden wanted to do was turn over the whole matter to the C.I.A. and lose control of it; it was one of the reasons, he thought, that mistakes and errors and even disasters occurred in this work. One ally, guarding its secrets jealously, would refuse to turn the information over to another; the other, sometimes, having received the information, failed to act on it. The other side had the advantage of being a dictatorship, with centralised control. It was an advantage, Canfield thought, that they could afford to do without.

He said to Willsden as he left the office that day, "You'd better start looking around for someone else to do these errands for you."

"You're not thinking of leaving us, Josh?"

"Not thinking. I *am* going."

"Well, of course we shall miss you." Willsden smiled; he didn't believe anyone ever left them.

It cost quite a lot of money and some time before they could find a way into the confidential records of the sanatorium where Elizabeth O'Mara Spence had been resting when the news came that Devlin had disappeared. A chill came on Canfield so intense that he actually shivered as he read the report, although the spring day in London was warm. Time was running out for all of them. Elizabeth O'Mara Spence had undergone an operation at the sanatorium in the pleasant valley outside Zurich. She was suffering from a cancer; the report indicated that her doctors did not expect the time of remission to be very long.

VI

The next piece of information for the Devlin dossier came and was laid beside all the others—unrelated, still waiting to be fitted into its place in the pattern. It was the way it came that troubled Canfield; it was a grubby, shabby thing to have done, and it made him no better than the man who peddled his information to the highest bidder. Willsden would have said that the end justified the means, but Canfield didn't elaborate on how he had got the information.

The chance to get it had come through his friends, the Ridleys. Part of his shame was the realisation that when the opportunity had come, he hadn't toyed with nice feelings about using his friends' house as a gathering place for information. Once he had scented the quarry, and the value of the quarry, he hadn't thought once about Molly and Philip Ridley, or the cause of their hospitality. The fact that the hunt had been easy, and the quarry had not given him much of a run, only made the distaste he felt for himself greater. What shocked him most was that when the opportunity had come, he'd acted like a professional. He had always insisted that he wasn't a professional, but Willsden's smile, when he had said he would do no more work for them, had suggested that he knew better.

Molly Ridley had invited him for dinner at Arlington Street. The spring evening was light and fragrant as he had walked there, but his thoughts had been inevitably driven back to the last dinner he had had there with the Ridleys, the night in the autumn that the news about Devlin had broken. He thought of the girl Molly had had for him that night, and he guessed that to-night's invitation was because she had found another girl for him. He wished that there was a way, without hurting her feelings, to tell her that he would rather look for his own girls.

This one was dark-haired, attractive, with the clean, groomed look that certain American women wear like another dress. She worked at the American Embassy, and had been in London eight months. He found her amusing and gay, and she seemed to be trying to please him, which wasn't the accepted view of American women. He was ready to take back that opinion; she was pleasing him very much. He was enjoying himself until she mentioned that in Washington she had worked for Senator Tom O'Mara for four years before deciding to take this job with the State Department. London was a plum for a beginner, and she wouldn't have been assigned here if the Senator hadn't had his position as Chairman of the Foreign Relations Committee. She didn't say he had used influence; she just said she had had a lot of experience that State found useful in this job. She added, rather wistfully, that she had wanted the experience of a foreign capital for a year or so.

After that he tried to prod her to talk about the O'Maras, even to flatter her. He found that Senator O'Mara had lost a good secretary; she wouldn't be flattered or prodded into talking more than generalities. But she was human, and London was lonely; when, after they had said good night to the Ridleys, he had suggested walking round to have a drink at the Embassy, she had been pleased. He wished she hadn't been so nice; it would have been easier to do what he was going to do.

He ordered large brandies, and during the first one he didn't try to get her to talk about herself. He talked, as she wanted him to do, about himself, the self that was for public consumption, the man who worked for Croft Newspapers. He even talked about the two biographies; she was interested in a special way, because they had both been political biographies. She had wanted to go on talking about writing, but he insisted they dance. She was a good dancer; he held her very closely and she admitted what he had suspected—that London was lonely, and she saw too many other Americans. By the time the third brandy was set before them she was ready to talk about Washington without having to be prodded or flattered.

"I miss the Senate, you know," she said. "It was like belonging to a rather special family. It had its own jokes . . . you know. And it's a darned important family, too." She twisted the glass between her fingers, looking down into the liquid; it was very dark where they sat, and her voice was low against the music. He found himself straining to hear it. "I specially miss working for Tom O'Mara. That man is just the greatest—oh, don't get me wrong. *Everyone* loves Tom O'Mara. You'd never think he came from a family like that. He's just so simple and nice—and one of the best brains in Washington. He never forgets when people do him favours—you know, even if you *are* paid to work for him, he never forgets that you worked late or worked week-ends. I was on the point of asking him the other day if I couldn't come back—but I decided I'd give London a try a little longer . . ."

Canfield dropped his gaze to his own drink then; he didn't even want to try to read her expression when she had said that. It was already plain that her opinion of London had brightened in the last couple of hours.

"You saw the Senator?" he said, and hoped it sounded casual.

"He was in London—just for one night. You know, he took the trouble to call me and ask me around to the Grosvenor for a drink. 'Any time you want to come back, Pat,' he said, 'it's all yours.' I damn' nearly broke down and said yes right then. But I have to stay with State a year . . ."

He cut in, fearful she would leave the subject. "What was he doing?—investigating his true and loyal ally, Her Majesty's Government?"

"Here?—no! He was on his way back from Vietnam. He came by way of Europe to see his sister, Elizabeth O'Mara."

"Oh, yes—one forgets she's his sister."

"She forgets. He doesn't. They've never been particularly close as a family—they *seem* close because their careers are always in the news, but they're not intimate close—you know what I mean? But still there's no need at all to behave the way she does towards them. None of the family can understand it. They don't know what they've done—she's suddenly cut them off as if they didn't exist. Doesn't answer letters, won't talk on the phone. She's always been an independent bitch, but it's gone way beyond that now."

"But he'd just seen her, you said."

"That's the point—he didn't! He'd just arrived from Geneva when I saw him, and he was so upset I guess he just couldn't help talking about it. And then—he trusts me. He'd been to that castle place of hers, and she'd shut the door in his face."

"Why on earth . . . ?"

"Who knows? The O'Maras don't. Whitney Spence doesn't. She won't talk to him either. Everything had been going along all right for years until Lawrence Devlin was killed last fall—she was married to Lawrence Devlin, you know. Well, the youngest brother, John, came over to represent the family—stay with her, you know. He got as far as Geneva, and there was a message saying that she was too ill to see anyone, and not to come any farther. Well, John got mad at that, and said to hell with it, and got on a plane and came home. Tom O'Mara and the Under-Secretary—that's the other brother—were all tied up with work at that time, and couldn't get away. This is the first chance the Senator has had, and he didn't tell her he was coming. Just showed up, and got handed his hat. Didn't even see her. He got out of there pretty quickly, and hoped like hell no one noticed what he did when he got off the plane in Geneva. It's one of those stories the newspapers love to . . ." She clapped her hand over her mouth. "My God, Tom O'Mara should never speak to me again! I've been talking like an idiot. And forgetting you're a newspaper man."

He tried to look offended. "I'm a political correspondent, not a gossip columnist."

She was contrite, and he smoothed over her feelings by talking about the O'Maras as if they had an exaggerated place in the world on international politics, which she was ready to believe.

She said finally, "I guess I've had too much to drink, Josh. Try to forget what I've said, will you? Tom O'Mara's such a great guy, and I guess I was almost as upset as he was about that bitch." She added, "It all began when Lawrence Devlin was killed. At least they think it began then. They think the shock may have sent her off her rocker a bit. They're wondering how they can get a doctor in there without causing too much of a fuss. That family always collects so much publicity . . . And they're sensitive to publicity."

The talk went on, and eventually she left alone the subject of the O'Maras. Canfield let her talk herself out, thinking that this was the least he could do in return for what she had unwittingly given to him. She drank another brandy as she talked, and he listened with patience because she needed a listener. He took her to her flat off Marylebone High Street, and kissed her good night, and then found that she clung to him in a kind of desperation.

"Josh?"

"Yes, Pat?"

"You're going to stay with me, Josh? For to-night? It gets so lonely in this damn' place. Sometimes I wake up . . ."

And he had stayed. He was finding it wasn't easy to make payment for what you had stolen.

FOUR

It lay on Willsden's desk—it had lain, probably, all winter on a stall in the Shor Bazaar in Kabul. The wonder of it was that in a country of camels, it had not long ago been sold to make some necessary repair to a piece of harness. Canfield didn't know anything about camel harness, but he guessed that this had been too thin and there had been too little of it. It lay there, innocent, and at the same time powerfully disturbing—a case for a camera, with hasty letters painted on its scarred leather—VLIN.

Canfield took it in his hands again, swinging it to see the way the strap rubbed the case itself. It was obvious that the friction had removed two letters. It would have been typical of Devlin, he believed, that he should not have had the initials stamped in gold but would have lettered his name himself, in these jerky capitals.

They had been lucky in the junior official of the British Embassy who had found it—he had been quick and discreet and persistent. Although the stall-keeper denied all knowledge of where it had come from, except that he had bought it "long ago" from a man he didn't know, the young third secretary had kept at him, and had come back to display the money that would be the stall-keeper's for the refreshment of his memory. The stall-keeper admitted that he had heard something of a plane of a foreigner that had gone off from Mazar and had not returned; he had heard of it and did not greatly care. Foreigners were of little interest except as possible enemies, and life was hard, in any case. Fortune, good and ill, was the gift of Allah. The stranger had been an unbeliever, and who should care what had become of him? The third secretary had waited, patiently and politely, through all the discourses and digressions, and had been made to swear by his own infidel god that the name of the stall-keeper would never cross his lips. The wreck of an aircraft had been discovered by a small caravan heading for the Amu Darya; it had been north of the river. A cousin of a friend had been with the caravan. The wreckage of the plane had been partly burned; there had been no trace of the foreigner. Had there been a camera in the case? He did not know; the Muslim religion forbade the making of images; cameras were of no interest. All that had come to him was the scrap of leather that they both saw, and remember that the Amu Darya was far away, and it had all happened a long time ago, before the winter.

They did not discuss the fact that north of the Amu Darya was the Soviet Union. The third secretary doubted that the stall-keeper knew or cared. A quarter of the people of Afghanistan were nomadic, and over the centuries they had developed a nomad's contempt for politically established borders; if this was illegal migration, who knew or cared about that either?

Canfield turned the leather case between his hands feeling a faint despair. Who knew, either, how much was truth? Had Devlin merely taken a swing north from Mazar-i-Sharif for a last look at the splendid ruins of Balkh before turning to Kabul and strayed across the border? But one did not cross the Oxus without knowing it. Had the plane climbed too high among the mountain ranges and suffered engine failure from lack of oxygen?—had Devlin succumbed to that? Had he experienced the over-confidence that lack of oxygen brings on, and run out of fuel? He had been an expert pilot, but he was also fifty-seven years old. The plane had gone down—had Devlin been conscious then?—a heart attack, a seizure? Had he simply, in the great, intoxicating wilderness of that country, simply not noticed or cared that he was violating the Soviet border? Had the plane been shot down, or had it been expected? Had Devlin been connected with the murder of Fergus in Beirut and feared that they knew more of him than in fact they did? Had he used this border as his escape route? Had Devlin lived beyond the crash?

Canfield leaned back in his chair. There was hardly need to speak the question, but he did, for the sake of hearing it come out.

"Where is he? Alive or dead, where is he?"

II

It went to the top level, and the decision came down. There were other negotiations going forward at the moment of extreme delicacy, and they could not risk upsetting them by making charges that were supported by slight evidence. They must find another way to learn what had become of Devlin and what was the link with Elizabeth O'Mara Spence.

Canfield shrugged when Willsden told him. "What else?" The direct confrontation hardly existed in this business; it wasn't very often a Powers-Colonel Abel exchange took place. Each knew the purposes of the other side, which was the gathering of information, the shaping of propaganda ploys, the estimation of the other's weaknesses and strengths. But they could get on with the business only so long as they all pretended that nothing of the kind went on. So that an agent was never admitted to be an agent, and a military attaché established in a foreign capital was that only, and nothing more. It upset the balance if each side continually made public charges against the other side, unless the time were right and it served the ultimate purpose.

"In this case," Willsden said, "it wouldn't be the right move. At the moment I hope they don't know that we know anything is amiss. If Devlin's alive they have some reason for keeping it quiet. He may have defected, or he may be there by accident. Whatever it is, our only hope to get close to the truth is Elizabeth O'Mara Spence."

The point of Canfield's pencil bit into the blotter and snapped off.

"And the closest we can get to Elizabeth O'Mara Spence at this moment is Sally Devlin."

III

They made their plans, plans which had to involve Sally Devlin, which had to use Sally Devlin without her knowledge, but before the plan was tried, Willsden insisted that one other attempt should be made to reach Elizabeth O'Mara Spence, and reach into St. Martin through a trusted source.

"I would rather not use the daughter," Willsden said. "Even without telling her what's going on there's always a danger in bringing someone like that close to the operation. If Devlin was *their* man it's extremely risky using his daughter."

"We've nothing against her," Canfield said shortly.

"We've only just begun to check her," Willsden answered. "In the meantime we'll see what Jackson Hayward can do for us. If he succeeds we won't have to use the daughter at all." He pointed his pipe stem at Canfield. "I'm going to have you go and see him, Josh, and explain what he has to do. We'll prepare the way, of course. He'll know he can trust you."

"And can we trust *him*?" Canfield asked, hoping Willsden got the point of the sarcasm.

"We've checked him as well as time permits. But he's all right. He was with Naval Intelligence during the war."

"And that makes him all right?"

"Don't get snarky, Josh. After all, if we have to put the second plan to work, you'll be a so-called Hayward author, won't you? By the way, we'll have to arrange with your other publishers not to make a fuss about it."

"That'll be a new twist," Canfield said as he got up. "I've heard of publishers giving their lives for their country, but not their authors."

IV

Being trained in intelligence, Jackson Hayward did, without too much protest, what they asked him to do. He was not surprised when most of his questions were not answered, because he understood that part of it too. He did not, however, like helping an investigation of Devlin, and he said so.

"We are hoping—*I* am hoping, Mr. Hayward—to *disprove* a suspicion about Devlin."

With that point in mind, Jackson Hayward agreed to what they wanted. Even without that argument, Canfield thought unhappily he would probably, finally, have agreed. Patriotism could begin to seem a dirty word when you used it to force decent men into what they considered to be indecent acts. And Jackson Hayward was definitely of the opinion that spying on a friend was an indecent act. That was another area where the other side had the advantage; they were rarely moved by such considerations.

So Jackson Hayward made a trip to Zurich with Henry Townsend of Tyne and Townsend, ostensibly to bargain about the price of printing a huge art encyclopedia. While he was there he telephoned St. Martin and asked if he could come down to discuss a matter of business with Mrs. Devlin. The reply was the same as any other caller to the château had received since October; Madame Devlin was not available and business matters should be communicated to her solicitors.

Happily, now, Jackson Hayward returned to London and reported the non-success of his trip, believing that he had performed his duty and he was free. Then they told him the second plan, or as much of it as was necessary for him to know.

They had it well in hand by this time, and so almost immediately Croft's most prestigious monthly, *Opinion*, published the article Canfield had written about Devlin. It began with a reminiscence of the morning of their meeting on the hillside in Connemara and developed into a tenderly handled tracing of Devlin's development from the man af action who translated action into novels to the writer to whom the man of action had become secondary. Hayward sent copies of it over to Sally at Tyne and Townsend by messenger, and to Elizabeth O'Mara Spence at St. Martin. From Sally there was a note of acknowledgment expressing her pleasure in the article. From St. Martin the acknowledgment of its receipt was signed by Hans Raedler, secretary to Elizabeth O'Mara Spence. It offered no comment.

V

They had watched Sally Devlin, and the watching revealed nothing. She led the kind of life that thousands of other young women in London led, there was nothing in the pattern of her living that the world could not have known about, except possibly the fact that it was often very late when Robert Halstead emerged from the door in the wall and drove off in the Aston Martin. She met no one she should not have met, nor made contacts with people who might not normally have played a part in her life. The agents assigned to the job rather enjoyed it; sometimes, to check on the people with whom she and Robert Halstead had dined, they ate at the same restaurants; that assignment was very popular. Halstead, Canfield learned, was something of a table-hopper, and he liked good wines. There were no men in Sally Devlin's life except Halstead, and the evenings she did not see him, she stayed at home. She also stayed up very late. Canfield could have told them that himself. They had not had long to do the check, but they had gone back to her schooldays, had listed every society or club she had ever joined; it seemed that Sally Devlin was not much of a joiner. They listed whatever they had found about her associates at Oxford, where she had skimmed through with a Third in History, and the number of times she had left the country to join her father. Since her father's marriage she had been abroad only twice, both innocuous-seeming visits to Ireland. Her mail was routine and dull. She was, in these aspects, a perfectly ordinary girl.

And then, at the end of the check, purely as a routine they had had an agent watch the studio when Sally Devlin was at the office. They had not expected any results, and were electrified when a man who had parked a van in front of the studio had entered and had been there almost two hours. The van had been marked with the name of a general contractor in Acton whom they found did not exist; the licence plate was false. Two days later the van returned, and the same man entered the studio. This time their photographers in their own van took his picture. Canfield thought, although the light had made it difficult to be sure about the man he had seen back in October, that it was the same one who had been with Alexi Kogan at Devlin's flat.

So they had entered the studio themselves, and found the shelves and cabinets crammed with books and papers, and they knew there was not time to complete a check.

"They're looking for something—something of hers, or Devlin's," Willsden said. "Twice they've been there, that we know of. All this stuff she has there seems to relate to Devlin in one way or another, or to be his own writing. Our boys can't make head nor tail of it. It needs someone who knows Devlin's work very well, Josh. An expert may just spot something that wouldn't be obvious to our regular men . . ."

He had protested, but the protests, like Hayward's, had been useless.

VI

It got grubbier, Canfield thought, and it got meaner. He stood in Sally Devlin's studio for the first time and remembered how all winter he had wanted to come here, and now he would have given a great deal not only to be out of the place, but never to have crossed the threshold. In himself he experienced all the sense of outrage at privacy violated that Sally Devlin herself would have felt—he knew he was being very unprofessional in this, but he couldn't help it. He was here, uninvited and unwanted, illegally and secretly; her poor ineffective locks hadn't kept him out, no more than they had kept out the man who had come in the contractor's van.

A movement in the room behind him reminded him that he was wasting time. The man with him, Price, the one who had actually opened the door since Canfield had never been trained in such skills, was trying tactfully to remind him that there was work to do, and they didn't have all day. They would not speak unless they were absolutely compelled to; they could not be sure that a listening device had not been planted somewhere in the studio.

Canfield tightened the thin kid gloves on his hands, and took, at random, the first envelope.

He had known at once that he would find nothing—or if he did it would be by the purest chance. It would have taken days—even for a superficial examination it would have taken days; it would have needed weeks for a more thorough search. They hadn't got weeks. Remembering the ravaged face of Elizabeth O'Mara Spence above the silky dark furs. Canfield knew that they would have to start in motion the slow turns of their machinery of guile very soon or the woman on the terrace might slip away from them, taking with her the truth about Devlin.

So for almost three hours he looked only half-heartedly into the envelopes he selected, not even wanting to read the writing he knew must be Devlin's. He felt a kind of soreness about him at the thought that he would have given a great deal for the right to look with permission at what he held in his hand; a biographer's material was here, a whole rich mine of it, and he was creeping in to snatch and paw at it, a thief who must take the dross with the gold.

Price had already advanced to his side, pointing at the dial of his watch when suddenly the walkie-talkie set he carried erupted into its harsh crackle. "Subject arrived in taxi. Paying off driver."

With a jerk of his head Price indicated the stairs to the gallery; he was acustomed to move quickly. He took the envelope Canfield had been working through, thrust the papers back into it, and put it back in its place.

There was no place for them to go except to the gallery. The only exit lay down the path to the gate in the wall, the way that was now blocked. Canfield pulled himself up the stairs three at a time, experiencing the mistrust and uneasiness of being run into a corner. There was no way out. As they flung themselves down on the floor of the gallery out of line of sight of anyone on the lower level, they heard the gate slam with a kind of cheerful force, and the tap of her heels on the brick wall. Price motioned to Canfield to draw his attention to the long clothes cupboard built against the back wall of the gallery with some of the sliding doors left open. Eventually they would have to retreat there, and trust that this would be one of the nights Robert Halstead would take her to one of his discreet and expensive little restaurants.

It was a shock, as she fitted her key to the lock, to hear her talking to someone—the watcher in the car outside had not warned them that she was not alone. Canfield raised his head to watch as the door was opened; a big grey and white cat preceded her. It must have sensed their presence because it went no farther than the middle of the room below, then stood stock still, tail raised, staring towards the gallery, its great golden eyes hostile. But she walked ahead of him, not noticing where he looked, still talking to him. They saw her fling her coat and a dress-box on the sofa—she had been shopping and that, probably, was the reason she had come home early. She passed from their sight below the gallery, and they heard the slam of the refrigerator door. The cat heard it also; he ran towards the kitchen. Price had started working his way back towards the wardrobe with great delicacy because the floor-boards were old and dry. Despite Price's frantic motions, Canfield stayed where he was. He could hear her walking about below. Then suddenly there was music—a record-player, not the radio. With a shock of pleasure Canfield listened to the gentle, disciplined rhythm of the Vivaldi concerto. She hummed a stretch of the melody, rather untunefully, as she cut the string on the dress-box. He watched her take the dress from the tissue, and shake it lovingly, hold it up against her. Clutching the dress she traced a few figures of a minuet-like step in time to the music, her final turn bringing her facing the gallery. He thought she couldn't help seeing him, but her eyes didn't go to this level. She seemed happy, and strangely innocent dancing with the new dress, a piece of unself-conscious femininity that was a delight to him. Again she sang, the tunelessness of her voice oddly touching. He thought that beside Devlin, he and the girl below also shared this love of Vivaldi. And then, following quickly on that pleasure, was the cold truth that he had no right that she had given him to share this, that he came as an intruder, to pry and probe her life.

They heard her voice again—either talking to herself or the cat; they heard the rattle of the lid of the kettle as the steam pressed against it. After a few minutes there was no further sound except the Vivaldi. Despite Price's headshaking, Canfield risked one more look over the gallery. Again it was madness to prolong that one look, but he did; it was something he had imagined too often in these last months, and here it was, in truth. The studio was flooded with the glow of the evening sun; she sat on the sofa among the rumpled cushions, the dress spread over the back. Her head was turned away from him, so that only the colour of her hair was her particular identity. A cup of tea was on the low table beside her, but she was leaning back and the smoke from her cigarette curled up among the golden dust motes.

She seemed not to be lonely, as she had seemed that day in Devlin's flat; and she seemed not to be vulnerable, as she had seemed vulnerable to the press of Halstead's ambition that night in Covent Garden. In the serenity of that moment she appeared to Canfield to have matured in these months, as if she had emerged from the sadness of this winter with some new edge of spirit that had not been present before. It occurred to him that, despite the little dance with the new dress, perhaps he had seen the last of the child who had skipped about on the mountain, somewhat precocious, demanding of Devlin's attention and love, disturbing the quiet of that sunrise fourteen years ago. There was a kind of excitement, a pleasurable anticipation in wondering about the woman who had emerged, the woman sitting smoking, listening to the Vivaldi, one hand lying on the gently heaving belly of the grey and white cat.

Before the record ended, Price signalled that it was time to take their places behind the row of dresses and coats. Canfield had to admit that Price possessed the sense of timing of the professional; they had barely positioned themselves in the wardrobe, with the hangers drawn together, when the record clicked to a halt. Canfield felt a kind of sickness of distaste in his stomach; before the studio door had opened they had had two choices—they could stand their ground and identify themselves and be forced to tell her everything, or they could hide. They had chosen the way of their function in life, and they had hidden. Now they must stay with the consequences.

The view from between the hangers was extremely limited, and the sliding doors, though open, restricted it farther. But the sounds were clear enough. Now that the record was finished she was in a hurry, and her hurry, Canfield thought, would probably mask a sense of their presence; she was not the sort of girl who went seeking for what should not be there. She went into the bathroom and they could hear the bath water running; she passed back and forth in front of their line of vision. Bureau drawers were opened and hurriedly slammed. The scent of bath salts reached them. Canfield knew that from this hour on he was going to possess a particular knowledge of this woman that only belonged, rightly, to a lover or a husband. She was going to go through the ritual of bathing and dressing almost before his eyes; suddenly he didn't want that kind of knowledge yet. There would be things revealed in those actions that it might be better for a man never to know; there would be vanities and smallnesses that no man should have to know until he was too far in for them to matter very much. He knew that this next half-hour could be the death of everything he felt about her. He asked himself if the job demanded even this intimate knowledge, and he knew it did not; he was using the job as a reason for knowing what should be none of his concern; he was becoming what he feared to become. He felt a kind of sadness because, in other circumstances, if he had ever had a chance to know Sally Devlin in the ordinary way, she might have offered him the kind of knowledge that was about to come to him by stealth.

He glanced over towards Price. The other man sensed his gaze, and moved his head slightly. One eyelid, dimly seen, came down in a broad and lascivious wink. Canfield felt it might have been a help to punch him in the nose, and at the same time knew it would have done no good at all. There came the pad of her bare feet on the carpet, and then the noisy splashing in the bath. The warm steam rolled out from the bathroom and began to cloud the mirror above the dressing-table of which Canfield had a slanted view; the scent of the bath essence seemed to grow stronger, and its message more sensuous.

Canfield learned several things; she had a noisy, exuberant enjoyment of her bath, and she made it quickly, without the indulgence of relaxing back into the embrace of the warm water. She took fresh underclothes from the skin out, but what she had taken off was left where it fell. She did not linger before the mirror when her work on her face was done; he thought she was professional, like a model, without a model's narcissistic reverence for her own image. Enough vanity to be healthy, but not too much.

If she was untidy, she also was accustomed to dressing in a hurry. She slipped her feet into shoes that waited at one of the open sections of the wardrobe while she dabbed on perfume; Canfield noted that it matched the scent of the bath essence, and he liked it. She filled a handbag, and searched for a minute for matching gloves in a jumbled bureau drawer. She had already telephoned for a cab before she reached swiftly into the wardrobe to get a coat; her hand fell on it automatically. Canfield couldn't help it; he craned to get a view of her swift dash down the stairs, coat on her arm, wearing black underwear, and he pushed out from between the dresses to watch, with a new wonder and delight, the moment when she picked up the new dress, and zipped herself into it. There was time only for a quick and inadequate look into the small convex mirror above the mantel. They could hear the cab outside. She planted a kiss between the ears of the cat, and once again they heard the light tap of her heels on the brick walk.

Price whispered, as they emerged fully from the wardrobe, "Now *that's* what I call a bit of skirt." Canfield answered with what, even to his own ears, sounded like a growl. As they moved cautiously down the stairs, Canfield avoided meeting the cat's stare. It bolted before them, using the flap in the door, but even so, Canfield had felt its knowing eyes fixed on him, and he experienced the shame of guilt.

FIVE

Mary was preparing to go out to lunch, and she was nearest the phone when it rang. "For you," she said to Sally, handing it over. "It's Mr. Hayward." She sat down at her desk again and prepared quite openly to listen to the conversation.

"Sal?"

"Yes, Mr. Hayward," Sally said.

"What about coming across for a drink this evening when you've packed up the typewriter?"

Sally hesitated. "I'd like to . . ."

"What's the matter?—you seeing Halstead?"

"Yes."

"Well—tell him you'll be a bit late. There's someone I'd

like you to meet. Shall we say about six then?" He gave her no opportunity to say anything else. "Right, then. I'll expect you." He hung up.

"What did he want?" Mary said.

"Nothing much—to come over for a drink—to meet someone."

"Who?"

"He didn't say."

"Nothing much?—I call that a lot. You know something, Sally—you're spoiled. You meet so many people—and you don't have any idea what it's like to be well—like me. If someone like Jackson Hayward asked me to come and have a drink to meet someone I'd die . . . And you're going to marry Robert Halstead . . . you'll go on meeting interesting people for the rest of your life."

Sally swung in her chair, her hands poised over the typewriter keys, not looking at Mary. "I am spoiled—I agree. I'm even spoiled enough to wish that just for once there might be someone who wanted to meet me just for myself."

Mary picked up her handbag again. "That's asking for too much. The world works on names—and you have a name. It's an inherited name, but it's a name, and you should count yourself lucky."

"I'll remember to, some day," Sally answered shortly, and began banging the keys.

II

The Hayward offices had emptied with a speed prompted by the fine spring evening; when Sally arrived there was no one at the receptionist's desk, the switchboard had its night lines plugged in. She hesitated at the foot of the stairs, and a young woman came down, on her way out. She nodded familiarly at Sally. "Mr. Hayward's around somewhere, Miss Devlin—he asked for you to go right up to his office."

"Thank you." She remembered Hayward's habit of prowling the offices just as everyone was leaving, trapping one or other of his directors at their desks to discuss that which couldn't be decided at any other time. It was the time, he said, when he got most of his work done. The offices were very quiet as Sally slowly climbed the stairs, as if the girl she had seen had been the last to go. It was an old and beautiful building—one of four terrace houses that served as offices—with a curving staircase that led upwards to a dome which gave now an eerie half light to the lower floors. It was thickly carpeted, but the creaking of the old wood of the staircase marked her passage in the deep quiet.

The man who waited in Hayward's office must also have heard the protesting wood. He was turned expectantly towards the door, and was half on his feet as she entered. She stopped there, hand still on the knob.

"Mr. Hayward was expect . . ."

He was coming towards her. "Yes, I know. He'll be here in a minute. You're Miss Devlin. My name's Josh Canfield."

"How do you do, Mr. . . . Josh—Joshua Canfield? The Joshua Canfield who did the article in *Opinion* on my father?"

He nodded. "Yes."

"It was a good article. I liked it. I liked it very much indeed, Mr. Canfield." But as she said it she wasn't really thinking about the article; she had to say something—what she wanted to say was that she was glad she had finally found him, but it seemed too soon for that.

He smiled. "I'm glad. You know, a journalist is always conscious of making his living off other people's experiences. Sort of trading on people like Lawrence Devlin. They do the tough work, and we simply report on and criticise their achievement. Most of the time miserably conscious that we can't do ourselves what they have done . . ." He broke off. "But look, the last thing Jackson Hayward said was to see that you got a drink, because they work you very hard over at Tyne and Townsend—and I haven't done a thing about it." Hayward's office had been furnished almost as a sitting-room, with the antiques he loved; the bottles and glasses and ice bucket were set out on an Italian refectory table. Canfield gestured towards them. "What will you have?"

"Scotch and water," she said absently. As he turned to pour it she said, "But you're not just a journalist, Mr. Canfield."

She thought he stiffened a little, and the motion of pouring was halted. "I'm not?" he said, still facing away from her.

"After that article I looked you up. You've written two biographies—one of Pitt, and one of Selwyn Griffith. I got the one on Selwyn Griffith. You know—my father very much admired Griffith. He thought he was, politically, one of the bravest men of this century."

He handed her the glass. "Is this all right?—It's just as I said, Miss Devlin. Biography is a superior form of journalism. Trading on other men's glory."

"You do yourself an injustice, Mr. Canfield. The Griffith book was brilliant. It made me understand why my father admired him so much. It taught me to recognise an act of political courage . . ." They had seated themselves in facing armchairs in the curving window of the office. The sunlight of the late spring day still lingered. She leaned towards him, cupping the glass with both hands. "I'm glad I've found you, Mr. Canfield. You've been worrying me . . ."

The hooking black eyebrows drew together. "Worrying you? Not for fourteen years, surely? That's a long time for a small girl to remember . . ."

She dismissed the idea, waving the glass at him. "Not *that*—oh, I remember, I think, one morning going up a hill with my father and meeting someone. But he talked to everyone—or everyone talked to him. I don't remember *you* particularly from that long ago. It's been much more recently, hasn't it, Mr. Canfield?"

He didn't seem to want to answer. "Has it?"

"You don't remember? I don't believe that. At Covent Garden—a few weeks ago? We spent ten minutes looking at each other, and trying to make up our minds where we had seen each other before. That's it, isn't it?"

"That's it."

She laughed in a kind of triumph. "I knew I'd find you

again. But where—before that? We know each other, don't we?"

"Yes—we know each other."

She suddenly challenged him. "I know—it was at the flat. It wasn't fourteen years ago. It was at the flat! You were there with Inspector Lester the day they found it broken into. What were you doing there? You're not a policeman too, are you?"

"No, I'm not a policeman."

"I'm getting angry, Mr. Canfield. How many more questions do I have to ask?"

He sighed and leaned back in the chair. The laugh lines around his eyes were tolerant and experienced, she thought; he would be surprised by very little, and yet the hooking black brows were insatiably curious. There was humour in his face, and knowledge that experience hadn't turned bitter. She couldn't remember having looked at any man's face so closely before, and she suddenly knew that she was looking at him in the light of what she had learned of herself—and of Devlin too—this past winter. And wildly, joyously, she wanted, she needed, to know the rest of it.

"Well, you've caught me, haven't you. I was hoping you wouldn't remember exactly where—or how. Of course I remember Covent Garden, and the day in your father's flat." She was warmed by the smile that crossed his face, the laugh wrinkles turned upwards as if in celebration of a memory that was good. "I'm not likely to forget. But my being there that day was very unofficial—Lester's a friend of mine and I was with him when the news came about the flat being broken into. I asked if I could come. He had to trust my discretion. I didn't want to bring anything down on his head, but I badly wanted to go with him." He pointed at her, and his face became serious again. "You're thinking that it was a journalist's curiosity, and I had no business being there. It's true I had no business there. I can only plead that every man has his heroes, and some even survive the age of disillusionment. Devlin survived for me. If you need an apology, then I give it, most humbly."

"That's all right," she said. "I'm not going to report Inspector Lester—and I'm not angry with you. I loved Devlin too."

They smiled at each other, unself-consciously. She was made sharply aware of the great pleasure it was to have him smile at her. There was a response growing in her, a kind of recognition of something that has been imagined, wished for, but never before experienced; it was the first recognition, startling, even shocking, of something that had so far been missed in every other relationship. Something had begun for her, and she wasn't sure what to call it. She felt oddly familiar with this man, as if she had known him a long time, and yet he excited her. She was glad that this winter had been lived through, and was past, and its learning done, that she was the new creature she had become and that he knew her.

"Then everything's all right, Mr. Canfield."

She stared at him boldly, and he returned the stare. She was joyously glad that he didn't pretend that this was an ordinary social meeting, and make ordinary conversation. If he hadn't been aware that something had happened for her, then it never could have happened. If he hadn't acknowledged it, it would have been an act of cowardice.

"Then everything's all right, Josh."

"Yes," he said. "Yes—I'm glad it's all right."

They were speeding along a road and all the landmarks of convention were flying by at an unrecognisable speed. The wrinkles of experience and pain and laughter around the eyes told her that he hadn't time for all the gambits and the ploys. He had played them and knew them to be tiresome and childish.

"You don't look much like that little girl in Connemara."

He didn't tell her what he thought she looked like now, which most other men would have done. He was giving her his opinion because it had importance for them both, because they had time to make up for. "You've changed in other ways, too," he went on. "You were much surer of yourself then—even though you were still a kid. I wanted to try to help you that afternoon in the flat—you seemed so alone . . .

lost. And that time at Covent Garden I thought the same thing, even though you were easily the most beautiful woman in the place. It was remarkable because beautiful women don't often look lost. It's been a hard winter, hasn't it?"

"How do you know?"

"*I* know."

Astonishingly it did seem as if he knew. In a kind of panic she felt the prick of tears behind her eyes, the catch in the throat that made words nearly impossible. She was tempted almost beyond resisting to tell him what these months since Devlin's disappearance had been like, the sense of aloneness, which he already knew, the suspicion, the half fears, the mounting burden of the papers, the guilt she felt about still holding on to them. She wanted to tell him because in these few minutes he had reached in and touched the truth of her, come closer to the heart of her than anyone had ever come. For a moment she stopped and tried to hold on to herself, saw for an instant the way ahead with Robert, the predictable way, sure and probably safe, the signposts there already; but she had taken, unexpectedly, a turning with this man in these last few minutes—or was about to take, a way unpredictable and full of chance, perhaps danger. Something rare could lie along the way, if she had the courtage to travel it. But stop a moment, pull back. The way back there was known, sure; this man had not yet offered to take her with him. Who was Josh Canfield?

"Is there some way I can help you?" he was saying, softly, insistently.

"Not now," she said slowly. "In time . . ."

In time?—what time, she had to ask herself. Her time was Robert's time, at Robert's bidding. She ached with the need to talk and to tell, but they would have to find their time, if ever.

They were sitting, staring at each other, silent, when Jackson Hayward entered.

III

It seemed odd to Hayward, the way they sat there. He felt

sure they hadn't spoken a word to each other for some minutes before he had entered, and yet it had not been an awkward silence. It was rather he himself who felt awkward, as if he were superfluous. After he had greeted Sally, he turned to pour himself a drink. As he fussed with the ice cubes he stole a backward glance to her, wondering why he thought she looked different. Of course this last winter had changed her; she had stopped being a girl; but she had worn a look of strain and preoccupation which he hadn't liked, and which, it seemed, Robert Halstead's presence in her life did not lift or counteract. He wished he felt happier about Robert Halstead, but that had to be Sally's choice, and she seemed to have made it. He turned back with his glass in his hand, and she was looking still at Josh Canfield; there was a faint flush in her cheeks, a delicious, rather sensuous half-smile curving her lips. For the first time in months he felt that she was awakened and stirred, that something had broken through her obedient acceptance of life. Sometimes one saw that in girls who were about to be married, this kind of starry radiance; but in that case why was she using her smile on Canfield? Hayward sat down heavily on the sofa between the two chairs, hoping that whatever it was he sensed in Sally's attitude wasn't going to complicate his problem.

"Sal, I wanted you to meet Josh—you remember his article, of course?—the one in *Opinion* I sent you?"

She nodded. "We've been talking about it. I thought it was very fine, as I said. I've been disappointed though, because I didn't remember Mr. Canfield from that morning he described." She was playing now, teasing. Hayward began to feel that something was getting wildly out of hand. Canfield hadn't prepared him for any of this, but Canfield wasn't doing any more than returning Sally's smile with the kind of mute encouragement that Hayward felt wasn't called for. "He wouldn't tell me," Sally added, "if he thought I'd made any improvement in the time since then."

Hayward opened his mouth, but Canfield was there first. "I didn't have the nerve to say to Miss Devlin what obviously should be said. After all, she might just think I was buttering her up, mightn't she, Mr. Hayward, in view of what you have to tell her? I had to avoid the smell of flattery . . ."

Hayward was lost; he didn't know what was going on. So he took his plunge into the first thing he had to say.

"Sal, what would you say if I told you that I've asked Josh to write a biography of Dev?"

The news didn't even seem to surprise her. "If it's so, then I'm very glad."

"You're taking it very calmly," Hayward said.

"I don't think I'm calm. Just pleased. After you sent the piece about my father in *Opinion*, I read Mr. Canfield's biography of Griffith. You remember Devlin was a passionate admirer of Griffith?"

"Then you approve?" Hayward took a big gulp of his whisky. It was going too well, and too quickly he had been brought to the hard part of the interview.

"Of course I approve. It's very good of you to consult me about it, Mr. Hayward—but you must have known I'd say yes. Mr. Canfield's a good writer, and you're Devlin's friend. I think you would have taken great care with your choice of biographer. I'm content." She swished the ice in her glass and seemed to stop to listen to the tinkling sound. Again that odd smile was on her lips, and something else was there, Hayward thought. She looked—was it relieved? Something was going too fast for him. He had expected more discussion.

"We'll see, of course," he said, "that the book on Dev reaches a very much bigger market than the Griffith biography. At the time you brought that out, Josh, Griffith was in a political limbo. I think the fact that he's had a sort of resurrection in people's estimation could be due a lot to the meaning of that book filtering through at last. The public is always years behind books like that. Well, that won't happen with Dev. He was always news. He's one of the last popular heroes we'll ever have. Extraordinary man, Dev . . . He managed to straddle the era of the war—it's hard to be an authentic hero to the people who fought and lived through the war, and still be a hero to the kids who march in the ban-the-bomb processions. To them, he's the Peace Prize man. I think you've got everything going for you on this one, Josh. A great subject and a big market."

"When will you begin, Mr. Canfield? There are a few papers I have that might be helpful . . ." She caught the motion of agitation that Hayward made, and turned to him, her smile widening. "Oh, just a few odds and ends. Mr. Canfield could come and look them over . . ."

He nodded, mollified. "Well, Sal, Josh should begin right away. But the biography is just part of a bigger thing I have in mind . . ."

"Yes . . . ?"

Well, he had come to it now. He stiffened himself by going back to the table and pouring another drink. Sally and Canfield didn't appear to have touched their drinks. Hayward returned to the sofa and sat down heavily.

"It is time, Sal," he said, "to do something about Dev."

"Do something?" She frowned. "What is there to be done? What can anyone do?"

"What I mean . . ." Hayward leaned back against the pile of cushions and the cigar smoke clouded the air blue about his head. "What I mean is to do something big in Dev's name. Something that he'll be remembered by in another sense than his books. It was such a shock to us when he went like that—I mean, if he'd died in bed like most men we might have started to think along these lines long ago. One usually does—memorials, and all that kind of thing." Hayward's pudgy hand, holding the cigar, sketched in the air before him a vague and expansive largeness. "But there it was last autumn—didn't know if he was alive or dead. Always a chance, you know, that he would turn up. It wouldn't have been the first time for old Dev. But here it is, spring, and there's no news, and . . ." His tone softened; he looked directly at the girl. "I'm sorry, Sal—but there isn't likely to be any news now, is there?"

She shook her head. "No—not likely."

"Well, it's time to see that he gets a fitting memorial. Something decent."

There was embarrassment in her tone when she spoke.

"I hope you don't . . . Well, it's not going to be some kind of monument, is it?—a memorial tablet?"

Hayward snorted, and looked pained. "I would never do a thing like that to old Dev. He just wasn't the sort of man to be memorialised by words scratched on a tablet of stone."

"Then what?"

"That depends. I was thinking in terms of something that would have continuing value—a foundation—something to help writers, perhaps, or students. Dev was a traveller, and it would seem fitting to me that we should try, in his name, to let some other people gain the kind of insights he got from travelling. Not just a simple student exchange—after all, all the wisdom in the world doesn't belong to the kids. It's often married men, with families to support, who should be getting out and seeing new things and listening to new ideas. And mostly they're the ones who can't afford it. Quite often they need grants when they're actually writing just to stay alive. It's the kind of thing that American universities and foundations are good at, and which we don't try very often in this country. I'd like to see it begun, and with Devlin's name on it." He was watching her face closely, the smoke clouding densely in the still air. "Now, Hayward's would be willing to go quite a way in financial aid—I don't want to pretend that we haven't made quite a nice pile over the years from Dev's books. But what a publisher could contribute to anything like that would be a drop in the bucket to what it really needs if it's to do any noticeable good. How far we can go and how big this can be doesn't really depend on me."

"On what, then?"

"On Elizabeth. And on yourself."

She had stiffened at the sound of the other woman's name. He watched her take up her glass, like a defensive screen. "Me? I don't see how."

"I think you will, Sal. I think you will. First we have to get Elizabeth's co-operation. And naturally I'm looking to her for most of the money. But don't you see"—he pointed the cigar at her—"don't you see that merely setting it up with

Elizabeth's money would make it very narrowly based. It would simply be the memorial of a very rich woman to her husband. That's rather too easy, and it doesn't have very great appeal to the imagination. I want as many people as possible to share in this—I want small contributions from the people who've admired Dev's books. A pound here, and a pound there—gives it a broad base, with a lot of people identifying with the outcome—the kind of writing that's produced because of it. As much as money, this foundation would need publicity. If we could get the Spence newspapers and magazines to fling the net for us—that could happen if Elizabeth would pave the way for us. I've always understood that Whitney Spence was very proud to have commissioned and been the first publisher of *Letters from South Africa*. In a way, I think he looks on the Peace Prize almost as his own."

She made no comment. Hayward wished she had because it might have made his task easier. He saw that from time to time she looked at Canfield, but Hayward was getting no help from him. He pushed on.

"Sal—I have the feeling that if we don't do this in a big way, we might just as well go ahead and carve those words on a stone tablet in some church, and be finished with it."

"I see." She sat for a time, her underlip slightly sucked in, turning and turning the glass between her hands. Then suddenly she stopped. "No—I don't see. I don't see where any of this depends on me. It's Elizabeth's help you want, isn't it?" She looked from one man to the other. "You know very well that I don't have any influence there."

Hayward rolled the cigar agitatedly in his fingers; "I've tried to do this without you, Sal—except that I would have wanted your approval of any final plans, of course. I've really tried not to involve you with Elizabeth. I know it's been sticky between you. But since Dev disappeared Elizabeth's acting very strangely."

"Strangely?" She was on the defensive, he thought; she didn't want to be told about Elizabeth.

"She doesn't see anyone, Sal. She stays shut up at St. Martin all by herself. I tried to see her, you know—no, you didn't know. I was in Zurich and I telephoned her. I wanted to come there and lay this whole plan before her. She didn't even talk to me on the phone—some secretary or other just said that all her affairs were being attended to by her lawyers, and that I should write to them. I tried writing—but you know what lawyers are. They probably thought I was after something for myself. Any rate, there's been precisely no response at all. I'm stymied."

Sally motioned with her glass. "Mr. Hayward, I'd like to help. You know that. But I simply don't see how."

He took a long breath. "Sal, I have my heart set on doing something like this for Dev. I don't want to take silence as an answer from Elizabeth. That isn't good enough. If I have to, I'll try to go it alone with this project, but it would be nothing to what she could make it. You see, I feel that nothing is getting through to Elizabeth at this moment. She has to be shocked into awareness of it. Letters won't do that, or telephone calls. I have to be able to *talk* to her. That means going to St. Martin. If she won't let me in, I've got to force my way in."

"How will you do that?"

"With your help, I hope. I want to announce a memorial service for Dev—get some really big names coming to it. As much publicity as it will bear—oh, I know it sounds cynical, but old Dev would have had a good laugh out of it, all his enemies turning up to get their names in the paper. I want to announce it as the kick-off to the foundation idea, and make the announcement of Josh's biography at the same time. All the releases would carry the idea that the success of the foundation would depend on help from Elizabeth, and that the biography would need her co-operation in providing whatever she had in the way of papers, and in her own accounts of the years they had together. It's going to be loaded against her refusal. It's going to be presented as a *fait accompli*. It's a trick, but it's all I have to play. I'm going to announce that the three of us are going to St. Martin to discuss the whole plan——"

"No!" The word broke from Sally. "No, wait a minute! *I* to go to St. Martin . . . ?"

"Yes, you, Sal."

"No, not me."

"Why not?"

"Because——" Her glass went down on the side-table, clattering against the ash-tray. The ash-tray slid off and turned upside down on the carpet.

"You know very well, why not." She stooped and gathered together the cigarette butts. Hayward could see her hand shaking. "I've never met Elizabeth O'Mara. She hasn't wanted to meet me. There was a time when we could have been brought together, but I think the time is long past. There's nothing I can do for you, Mr. Hayward."

"I *need* you, Sal. I need to be able to say that you are going to St. Martin. I couldn't get in there myself. Josh certainly can't. You're my trump card. Elizabeth's a woman who's worked in and for the Press all her life. She knows, better than most people, what a refusal would look like if I publicise it. Oh, yes, it's using a kind of pressure that I'd rather not use, but I have to do something. She's more stubborn or more reckless—or further gone—than I imagine if she ignores the kind of publicity I hope the announcement will get. I want to make her afraid that she'll be left out. If I know Elizabeth, she'll want control, once she knows it will go on with or without her. I'm counting on you to be just the pressure we need to get us to St. Martin and get her to sit down and talk this through. She'll know very well what the Press will make of a door publicly slammed in the face of Devlin's daughter."

"But privately she's done it all along. She had her chance. She's never wanted to see me. She wouldn't see *you*, although you've been at St. Martin before. If there's an overture it should come from her first."

"Sal, think again," he said quietly. "You can afford to be more generous than that. You've got a great deal more in your life now than Elizabeth has."

"Rubbish! She's Elizabeth O'Mara Spence, isn't she? She's famous and she's rich!"

"She's a lonely, sick woman."

" Sick?"

Hayward's glance slid over to Canfield; almost imperceptibly the other nodded.

" She's dying, Sal."

She sucked in her breath audibly. " Dying?"

" Of cancer. I can't tell you how I learned it, because doctors are not supposed to give that kind of information. But sometimes it's necessary purely for humane reasons . . ."

" Dying." Now it was no question, but an acceptance.

" So you see why I must press it. There isn't time to wait around for her to come out of her shock and grief over Dev. This is, of course, the reason why she's withdrawn, why no one gets to her. We don't have time to wait a year."

Her face wore a brooding, distracted expression, and he hated to see it that way; she had begun to twist the glass again, around and around.

He spoke again, softly. " I'm thinking of you now, Sal. Can you afford not to go? This is the only chance you've got, and you don't have much time."

She turned towards him, her expression questioning, the brows drawn together.

" At your age, Sal, one does a lot of growing and changing in five years. You've got a chance now to go back to the beginning with Elizabeth. You can put it right, if you want to. Put aside whatever Elizabeth has or has not done. It's you who can make the change now." He waved his hand. " I'm not talking about the foundation now. Forget it for a moment. Just think of you and Elizabeth—and Dev. You've got a chance to go back. Not many people can ever do that. Use it. It can't hurt to take the first step. It may hurt very much for the rest of your life not to take it. Sally, you're not the young girl you were when Dev married Elizabeth. You've changed. Perhaps she has too. Try it . . . *try it*!"

Suddenly she looked at Canfield. " And what do you say?"

" Are you sure you want to hear what I think?"

She gave a half laugh that was a little wild. " You're here, aren't you? You're part of this. And before you're finished with Devlin you'll know all about us—Elizabeth and me. And you'll have to come close to telling the truth, or it's going to be a bad book. Yes, you're in it—so what do you say?"

"You don't need to be told. You know what you have to do. Only it's better now that Devlin's dead. You aren't doing it for him. You do it for yourself. Because you must."

He rose and went over to her; her face was tilted upwards to his. As he stood there, next to her chair, Hayward felt the thin flicker of tension and involvement that leapt between them like electricity. At that moment he did not exist for them.

"This woman is alone—dying. There is a gesture you can make—an act you can perform—if you choose to do it. She may reject it, but that doesn't flaw the gesture itself."

Suddenly Hayward knew that this had nothing to do with the plan. Canfield had spoken as a man who cared deeply what became of this woman; it was a plea for her personal salvation.

They seemed to Hayward to wait a long time, their gazes locked on each other. Then slowly Sally nodded. The tension between them collapsed. Canfield returned to his chair.

"You'll make the arrangements, then?" Sally said to Hayward. "You'll tell me what I have to do."

He nodded.

IV

Sally wished that Robert had not wanted her to go; she wished he had made strenuous objections, had pointed out that she should be here to begin preparations for their wedding. But he made no objections; she knew that he looked to a contact for the future with the O'Maras. He liked the idea of the Devlin Foundation, but she sensed that he liked even more the publicity that would surround it.

"I just wonder if Hayward is the right man to handle it," he said. "He's all right as a publisher, but he seems a bit of a bumbler to me."

"He was my father's best friend."

He smiled indulgently at her. "That's rather beside the point, isn't it?"

She was left with the feeling that if the Devlin Foundation was established, Robert would somehow manage to become one of the trustees. There was no doubt he would do an efficient job.

"By the way," Robert added, "I've arranged for you to go along to Hartnell. They understand the problem about your being away, and they can take measurements and make a dress form and get started on some clothes while you're gone. It will just need a few fittings when you come back. They will do the wedding dress, of course."

"I don't much care for Hartnell clothes. They're not my type."

Again he smiled at her. "You'll look wonderful. You always do. It's so much simpler this way, isn't it? Saves you a lot of fuss, and you can stay longer at St. Martin. Oh, and leave me the list for the invitations, will you? Miss Ritchards and the girls can start working on them."

"I don't have a list. I've never been married before."

"Well, make a list." He was trying to be patient, but she could see him mentally ticking off the items he had intended to speak to her about. He reached the next one.

"And I've spoken to Simmonds about the cat. He's prepared to take care of it. He will come in a taxi and pick it up the day before you go."

"*If* we go. Elizabeth hasn't asked us yet."

Robert didn't reply; he believed in the pressure of the Press, and he didn't think that Elizabeth would hold out against it. Sally had not told him that Elizabeth was dying. Somehow she hadn't been able to make herself tell him that.

Josh Canfield had not been neglected, either. "He's been a correspondent for Croft's for quite a while. I made enquiries. They think quite highly of him, I understand. Then there was a book on Selwyn Griffith. Of course Griffith was an impossible man, but apparently Canfield did a good job with the material. Of course, this time it will be different—he has a good subject. It would have been a help, though, if Hayward had picked someone a bit better known. Oh, well, I'm sure he'll be all right. And it will be only the first of quite a lot of biographies on your father, I imagine . . ."

She wished he had cared what kind of a man Canfield was; she wished that he had sensed that he was threatened. She wished that he had kissed her very hard and said she was not to go; she wished that he had said she was not to stay more than three days; she wished he had insisted on coming too, even if it was to stay in the hotel at St. Martin. But he did none of these things.

She wished that Josh Canfield had telephoned. She wished that she could see him again before they left for St. Martin. If they did not go to St. Martin, she might be married before she saw him again.

V

It was done swiftly, what had to be done. Hayward announced that a memorial service for Lawrence Devlin would be held in St. Martin's-in-the-Fields in two weeks' time. Tied to the announcement was the information that he sought to establish a Lawrence Devlin Memorial Foundation, and expected to have the support of Elizabeth O'Mara Spence in the project. He had also commissioned the biography of Lawrence Devlin to be written by Joshua Canfield.

For Canfield this was the crucial time. He was in the open now. The strangers who had invaded the château of St. Martin now knew that he would be with Hayward and Sally Devlin when they presented themselves there on Elizabeth's doorstep. Public opinion would demand that they be admitted. This was the time then to enquire into the background of Joshua Canfield, and if they found anything there that alarmed them, it was possible that even public opinion would not open the door at St. Martin. It was not a lot of time for agents who have to work in a foreign country, with only the resources of an undercover intelligence organisation to work with; but it was time enough for a doubt or a suspicion to be raised. A great deal would depend on how much they had taken note of his trips abroad, and how carefully they might have checked his contacts there. It would depend on how deeply they went into his finances, on how long it took them to discover that he went regularly to a place that they probably knew was a centre of counter-intelligence, despite the trade name it masqueraded under. It would depend on how many seemingly innocent questions they could ask of his friends. It was possible to find out everything there was to know about Josh Canfield, given enough time, enough money, enough men. But in all the annals of Josh Canfield's business, the best cover story was the one that had the heart of truth in it. He was Josh Canfield and he could go on being Josh Canfield, and the obviousness of that truth might be so blinding that they would not immediately seek to the darker places beyond it.

Appropriately it rained the morning that London's literary world gathered at St. Martin's-in-the-Fields; most of the men wore a grave air, and the tan raincoat that becomes nearly the uniform of the Englishman. Canfield wore his, and thought that he merged very well with all the others. He chose a pew towards the back of the church—not so far back as to seem to want to hide, but far enough back for modesty. At this moment Lawrence Devlin's biographer was not very important. They had come to talk of Lawrence Devlin.

The usual hymns and psalms were not very appropriate to Devlin's attitudes, so they were kept short. Some of the literary figures said the expected, and a few unexpected things about him. But when Jackson Hayward spread his papers on the lectern, he said only a few sentences about his friend, Larry Devlin. At the request of Devlin's only child, Sarah, he would read a short quotation. He began on John Donne's familiar words.

"No man is an Island, intire of it selfe . . . any man's death diminishes me, because I am involved in Mankinde . . ."

Canfield did not believe that it had been Devlin's favourite passage; there was too much egotism in the man to have permitted him to love above all others the words that had been for ever earmarked by another and more famous writer. Canfield thought it had to have been Sally herself who wanted those words spoken, and he saw them as her justification, to herself, of going to St. Martin, of reaching out to Elizabeth in Devlin's name. Did she seem to say, to herself, that she would add on to herself, in this new relationship, whether it went well or ill, to compensate for the diminishing of the one with Devlin. Elizabeth now was dying, but a piece of her should stay alive in Sally. Was that what she was saying? Canfield hoped it was.

The last music, as they walked out, was the Bach D Major Toccata and Fugue, crashing, exultant, wildly triumphant; it was life with no hint of death in it.

Jackson Hayward and Sally stood near the main door to shake hands with everyone who filed past them; Robert Halstead stood a little behind Sally, wearing just the correct expression of solicitude and proprietorship. Canfield tried not to look at Halstead as he held out his hand to Sally. She was very beautiful, he thought, wearing black, the red hair and the white skin glowing in the sombreness of this rainy morning, and the umbrellas and the tan raincoats.

Afterwards on the steps Canfield was careful to nod and speak to as many literary editors of the newspapers as knew him, and would return his greeting. This had to be done for the benefit of those who were watching, who would note whether his position in the literary world was real, or was being invented by Jackson Hayward. He had to be marked now as genuine. But as he talked, and sometimes forced himself on one or two of the literary lions who didn't quite recognise him, but who would respond to flattery, Canfield wondered which of the tan-raincoated men among the crowd was there, not to honour the memory of Lawrence Devlin but simply to observe Josh Canfield.

And then, the long line of people having come to an end, Jackson Hayward walked down the steps to the waiting car. Sally and Robert Halstead followed him; Canfield knew their plans. They were going to the Savoy Grill to lunch. That, too, was appropriate. Canfield couldn't help his eyes following them. But so did the eyes of almost every other man on the steps.

The crowd drifted away; Canfield crossed Trafalgar Square, knowing that he probably was followed, and behaving like a man who had no reason to suspect such a thing. He thought of the scene he had just witnessed; of what had been said of Lawrence Devlin by the literary powers of London. Of that group, there had been only himself, and one or two others of the anonymous, tan-raincoated group who had either suspected, or known, that Devlin perhaps was not dead.

VI

Hayward bit down on his unlighted cigar and tossed the yellow telegram form across the desk to Canfield. " She's taken the bait," he said. " We're going to St. Martin."

Now that it was done, Hayward wanted some reassurance that what had been done through him was the right thing. " It's going to be all right, isn't it, Josh? I mean for Dev."

He got no comfort, only the coldness of the grey eyes looking at him steadily, without softening, without any attempt to bolster him up. He wished that just for once Josh Canfield would play the usual game of pretence, would give him his reassurance without scrupling too much with the truth; but suddenly the look in the eyes suggested to Hayward that Canfield was very tired, that he had played the game of pretence in deeper ways perhaps too often, and he was not capable of offering it now in things that mattered to him. Hayward knew now, beyond any doubt, that Devlin, and perhaps Devlin's daughter also, mattered very much to Canfield.

" That's what we're going to find out," was all that Canfield would say. The sparseness of the answer sent a chill through Hayward.

VII

Hayward put his head into Sally's office at lunch-time that day, a smile of relief flooding over his face as he saw that Mary Farrar's desk was empty. Sally was there, at the typewriter. He closed the door behind him carefully.

"We're going, Sal," he said. "A telegram's come from Elizabeth. Could you be ready day after to-morrow?"

"Yes," she said, and she knew what she had to do.

Before Mary returned from lunch she had taken Devlin's manuscript from the locked front drawer of the desk, and put it in an envelope to take back to the studio with her. That night she began to sort the clothes she would take with her to St. Martin. The last thing was to take out the small bag that Devlin had given her to carry in the cabin of planes when she travelled, and she packed in it the envelope she had brought from the office and the envelopes containing the first part of the Devlin manuscript that she had brought here to the studio back in October. It was heavy, and she thought that Hayward would have to pay for overweight; at the same time she knew that no one had ever been able to give Elizabeth O'Mara Spence anything like this.

PART II

ONE

The valley was white and dusty, the white swift river flowing between intermittent rows of poplars, the grey green of the young vines rising in stone-laid terraces from the grey stoney soil. After the softness of the scenery all along the lake from Geneva, they seemed to have come to a country where the bare bones of the land showed through. It was a broad, flat valley, and on each side of it rose the massive, inevitable barriers of the mountains. On their right, crowning a lateral valley of the Rhône, lay the Great St. Bernard Pass; straight ahead of them was Simplon and the passage to Italy. Their own journey was almost at an end.

It wouldn't be very far. It would only be minutes, Sally thought, before one of them spoke. She glanced around at Jackson Hayward in the back seat, but his head had fallen forward in a doze, as it had many times since they had left Geneva. His tweed suit was grey with ashes from the endless cigars; his face was crumpled with fatigue.

She was sorry that the journey was ending. It was not only that apprehension gripped her about what waited at St. Martin; the journey itself had given unexpected pleasure. In the plane she had sat next to Hayward, but after their arrival at Geneva Canfield had taken over subtly. It was he who found their hired car, and he who had taken the wheel. He was on the road to Lausanne and Montreux without hesitation, and he had taken a detour to the restaurant where they had eaten lunch, a small place on the shores of the lake where the imperious swans came demanding bread. There were no other tourists; the place and the menu were modest, and the food was superb. The sun beat down on them, and Hayward retreated under an umbrella.

"A political correspondent beats the path to Geneva so many times that he'd have to find some places away from it or he'd go either mad or broke—or both," Canfield had explained when she had asked about it. There was a simple enjoyment in the meal that she hadn't had for a long time, a pleasure of wine and sun and relaxation. There was no one to observe their presence there, no one to visit at another table, the waiter served them well but did not hover, and the bill was very small. She was remembering it, remembering warmly the sensation of ease, the lack of strain between the three of them, her own feeling that she did not have to extend herself, or live up to anyone or anything—it had been enough just to be, to enjoy, to savour, all of them had given themselves over to the mood of the hour and of the journey itself. She was remembering this, and wondering what Robert's presence might have done to it, how he would have altered the balance when the words she had been waiting for came from Josh, beside her.

"You can see it now. St. Martin."

She turned, weary herself and reluctant now to face what she must face. He had said the words quietly, as if not to make too much of them, but they sounded in her ears like the echoes of a thunderclap.

"St. Martin . . ." She repeated the name after him, slowly, like a child, and then also like a child she was suddenly and inexplicably afraid, and she wanted to draw nearer to him. She wiped her hands, which had begun to sweat, down the sides of her skirt. "I didn't think it would be so much of a fortress," she said finally.

It was a medieval fortification, a castle on a rock at the mouth of a narrow lateral valley that opened to the north. Its stones had been quarried from the rock itself, the grey rock, so that it was hard to tell where it had its beginning; its ramparts seemed to merge one back against the other, so that the side facing them appeared almost sheer. In profile it descended by jagged stages to the huddled clump of roofs of the village at its base. Its grey walls caught the light of the afternoon sun, slanting back in the direction from which they had come, softening the outlines somewhat, but doing nothing to make the pile more earthy or human. Apart from the green of the vines that embraced its walls in a few places, there was no colour except the grey stone. Sally could see nothing or no one move upon the ramparts. It could almost have been, she thought, that it was deserted; a ruin from which all life had long ago fled.

"He never talked of it as if it were a fortress," she finished lamely.

The last was a half truth. Devlin had never talked of St. Martin at all, because he knew very well that she hadn't wanted to hear about it. But now, with St. Martin and Elizabeth close upon her, Sally knew that the time had come to stop talking in half truths with Josh Canfield. That was what she had said to him back in Hayward's office about the book he would write. Five years ago the truth about Devlin had passed from her to the woman who lived here on this rock above the valley; it lay here at St. Martin. Together she and Josh Canfield and Elizabeth must reveal and declare it. In order to know Devlin they had first to know one another. It would not be an easy time for any of them at St. Martin.

Because she most needed it then, it seemed very natural to feel Josh's hand laid upon hers, the warm enveloping feel of a hard and masculine hand. Natural, and yet wonderful.

"Don't be afraid," he said.

She looked at him, keeping her voice to hardly more than a whisper so that Hayward would not wake and break this moment. "How did you know?"

"I knew."

"And you don't despise that?"

"I would be afraid for you if you weren't afraid—a little." He spoke quickly, not wanting her to break in. "Sally—promise me something?"

"What is it?"

"Just promise. Trust me a little, can't you?"

She had just been thinking that there could be no more half truths, and that meant more than just the absence of lies; it required trust. "Yes, Josh—what will I promise?"

"While we're at St. Martin don't forget about me, will you? Look—I'm here. I'm available for you to talk to. Forget that you don't know me. You know me a hell of a sight better than you know Elizabeth O'Mara Spence. I'm your friend, Sally—whether you realise it or not at this moment. She may not be your friend—not in the beginning—perhaps never. Just remember I'm here, and that I don't despise fear. And I don't think doubts ever made a coward of anyone."

"Thanks, Josh."

"Remember, will you?"

"I'll remember—and thanks."

Her hand was released, but the impression of the touch was still there. She looked back towards St. Martin, and already they were so close that the first outlying houses of the village were past, and she had to crane forward and look upwards to see the château, rising on the rock above them. The road narrowed abruptly, and the houses crowded in. They drove now on ancient paving stones, arriving abruptly in the tiny main square of the village. Opposite the Hôtel de Ville was the single café in sight. The day's work was over and the first of the evening crowd had established itself at the yellow tables. There were a number who heard the question when Josh stopped the car and leaned out to ask the waiter standing by the kerb.

"*Le château, s'il vous plait?*"

"*Le château?—St. Martin?*" The man gave a long hard look at the occupants of the car, and they could see the surprise and curiosity in his face. "*A la gauche, Monsieur—à la gauche.*" And his hand, matching the words, indicated the curving, narrow street that opened off the square to the left. He pointed left and upwards, and displayed his careful English. "Up the hill, sir—all the way. As far as the automobile will go."

The words were heard by everyone at the tables, and the gestures were unmistakable. It seemed that every head in the square turned, and every eye was on the car as it made the turn to the left, and began the ascent.

Jackson Hayward had woken. "I could have told you, dear boy—up the hill, as far as you can go."

It was very steep, and the cobbles had the patina of the centuries. There was an air of expectancy on the three of them that momentarily dispelled the fatigue. Jackson Hayward was attempting to brush away the ashes; Sally peered at her reflection in the tiny mirror of her compact, suddenly too much aware of the elegance of the woman whose photos she had seen; she looked dusty and hot; the suit which had been right for London was far too warm for this Valaisian valley. Elizabeth would consider her unkempt. Only Canfield looked right, she thought. She had noticed on the journey from London that he displayed the subtle characteristics of the experienced traveller the way that Devlin always had—the clothes that wore easily and did not crush, the single suitcase, the lack of fuss in the routine of travel. Standing beside him at the check-in desk at London Airport she had felt cluttered and overdone. She stared at the tiny reflection unhappily.

"You look great." He said it very softly, leaning sideways towards her, and not taking his eyes away from the twists of this upward pushing street with the houses so close that the afternoon sun was lost somewhere above them. He was smiling as he said it. The pleasure and the reassurance warmed her, sustained her up to the moment that he suddenly threw on the brake as they rounded a bend and were abruptly faced with the studded wood of the two great doors set in a stone archway.

"As far as we can go," Josh said, echoing Hayward. "And closed."

Hayward struggled to lean forward against the incline of the car. "Bloody inhospitable, if you ask me."

"There's a bell-pull," Josh said. "Think it works?"

Hayward clutched the back of the seat and leaned in between their two heads. "Elizabeth is an American. Everything works, dear boy. The plumbing best of all . . ."

"I'll get it," Sally said, as Josh started to open the door on his side. She was out of the car before him, suddenly compelled to carry through the role she had always played with Elizabeth. She had come to St. Martin, finally and at last; Devlin was dead, and a small part of a common past was all these women shared; they could have no common future. Sally stood now where she had always stood with Elizabeth. She stretched up and rang for admission to Elizabeth's house.

II

The gate opened as it later seemed to Sally that everything else did at St. Martin—reluctantly. First she heard the steps on the paving stones on the other side, and while she waited she was aware of the faces that appeared briefly in the windows of the houses that lined the street right up to the grey walls of the château. Finally a small door within the gate itself opened. A manservant in a striped apron stood there.

"*Bon soir.*" She gave their names, and it seemed necessary to add that Madame was expecting them. He nodded, and left the door ajar while he used the telephone to the house. After a shouted conversation, he hung up. He said something to Sally in an accent so thick she couldn't understand him. Then the small door was closed in her face.

She stood there for a moment, stunned, and then with a shrug, turned to walk back to the open door of the car. "I don't know what's going on," she said to Josh and Hayward, and tried to make her tone flippant. But Hayward was already pointing back to the gate. "There—told you everything works."

She looked back. Both sides of the gate were opening at once, with beautiful silence and precision. The man in the striped apron was standing by a small panel near the telephone, one finger pressed on a button that operated the gate; with the other hand he waved them on. Sally climbed in beside Josh again.

"I must be very backward—I rather expected them to open on creaking hinges."

"This, child, is Switzerland," Hayward said, at the same

time as they passed airily saluting the manservant, who didn't return the gesture. "Everything works in Switzerland—and in the home of an American in Switzerland, totally unexpected things work in very unexpected ways. Like that gate business. Don't remember that from the times I came before—when Dev was here. Seem to think that the gate was always open then, though."

Beyond the gatehouse and the wall was open space—thick green grass with the grey cobbled road twisting through it, always upwards, spiralling round the curve of the hill. As the car gained height, they could see over the wall, which was now below them, to the roofs of the village. Then a final curve of the road took them to the back of the last up-thrusting hump of the rock, out of sight of the village, and they had finally come as far as they could go. Josh parked on a broad, paved, completely empty space under the sheerly rising walls of the château. The deep oilstains on the cobblestones told them that at one time, many cars had stood in a row here.

"What do we do now?" Sally said.

"Wait—just wait," Hayward answered, struggling to squeeze his bulk out of the tiny car. "They'll come for you. Or they used to, in the old days—ah, here they are now. At least *that* hasn't changed."

They followed his waving arm, and looked towards a gateway set at right-angles to the wall. It was as though they looked up a narrow street of a small, medieval hill town. It rose in a long flight of broad, shallow steps, wrapping itself about the rock and the château, lined on both sides by rows of stone, slate-roofed houses. Those on the outer side formed an extra, protruding rampart to the castle; the inner one had its back walls cut into the rock itself; the street was a tiny, satellite village clinging to the mother rock of the château. Three small children played on the stair-street, as Sally instantly named it, their bright plastic toys oddly incongruous amid the hand-crafted perfection of carved doorways and deep mullions. But Hayward was directing their attention to the three men coming down the stairs towards them, all three wearing the same striped apron as the man at the gate.

"You can leave them the luggage," Hayward said, "and save your breath for the climb."

The men came forward, bowing slightly, offering their greetings in slow English to Hayward, whom they seemed to know, looking curiously at Sally. Josh opened the trunk for them. Sally heard Hayward's muttered grumble. "Dev used always to be down here himself—didn't leave you to traipse about like a tourist . . ." Then they heard the clatter of running feet on the stairs above them, and they turned and looked up.

He was not as young as his movements, Sally thought as he came close; he moved like an athlete in training, but there was a sprinkling of grey in his dark hair. He was neatly handsome; his skin was dead white, as if he spent little time in the Valaisian sunshine; although he was freshly shaven his beard showed darkly on the white skin. He wore a grey suit, somewhat old-fashioned in cut, and a dark, plain tie. There was a look of total greyness about the man which could have been mainly the colour of his eyes. His lips shaped into an automatic smile.

"Forgive me for not being down when you arrived. I am Hans Raedler, Madame Devlin's secretary. I am to greet you on behalf of Madame." He bowed slightly as he spoke, but his eyes appraised them rather than greeted them. He looked at Sally. "You, of course, are Miss Devlin. Welcome to St. Martin."

Sally inclined her head. She listened to Hayward introduce Josh. She tried to place Raedler's accent; it was very slight. Swiss-German, perhaps; it was the preciseness of his speech more than anything that made it foreign.

The three porters with the baggage had gone ahead of them. Raedler had gestured towards the stairs.

"Shall we go up, Miss Devlin?" He began an almost professionally slick chatter about the weather, the flight, the drive. As Sally listened and made a routine response, she was struck by the resemblance Raedler's manner bore to an assistant manager of a fashionable hotel, making his eternal patter as he showed guests to their rooms. He sounded as if he performed this task forty times a day. She saw, with amusement, that Hayward was having none of it. Despite the climb and his overweight, he had passed them on the stairs and was already nearing another arched gateway at the top. Sally was glad, though, that Josh had stayed beside her. She didn't want to be left with Raedler's professional coldness.

Something strange had happened to the stairway itself, though. Outside of Raedler's stream of talk, a silence had fallen on it. She wondered what had happened to the children who had played here moments before, why the doors that had stood open to the afternoon sun were now all closed tight. She glanced at the windows of the little houses as they passed, expecting to see the white curtains lifted by the hands of the curious; but nothing moved. She was gripped by an air of unreality in the whole place, as if these stone houses should prove to be painted canvas, as if the flowers in the window-boxes would turn out to be plastic, like the bright, vanished toys. But the children had been real, and it was more than the gesture of the well-trained servant families who whisk the untidiness of children out of sight of the guests which had caused them to disappear. It was like the silence itself, suggesting that life had fled, as she had thought when she had first seen St. Martin from the distance. One thing, though, had escaped. A red rubber ball lay forgotten against a stone flower tub. Sally bent and picked it up. Holding it in her hand, she turned from one side of the street to the other, expecting, hoping, that one of those studded doors would open and a child or a mother come to claim it. But no one did. Yet she was sure that the gesture had been seen. A little saddened she laid the ball back beside the tub. Raedler and Josh had stopped to wait for her.

"Do not trouble yourself, Miss Devlin. They will find it."

The coldness of the words struck her, but she looked past Raedler to Josh and met understanding of her reaction in his eyes. They moved on, but even Raedler's flow of talk had died.

Hayward had puffed his way to the top as if determined that Raedler should not assume the honours of the entrance. He stood, hands on hips, breathing deeply. "It's always worth the climb when you get to the top," he said as they drew near. He spread his arms proprietorially, motioning them through the gateway. The terrace of St. Martin, which had known fame of a kind long before the names of the people who had walked here in the last two decades had brought it into the world's headlines, spread before them.

"Welcome to St. Martin, Sally," Hayward said, ignoring what Raedler had said earlier. He took her firmly under the elbow and marched her across the flagstone paving.

It was a view that caused the eye to look upward rather than at the valley below. On each side of the river, beyond its flat, flood-scarred meadows, the mountains barred the way, the farther peaks, snow-capped, shading opalescent colours in the sun. The light was dazzling, almost harsh, translucent, dry light. The terrace itself was a kind of rocky promontory jutting free of the château itself, so that a person standing there could see the circle of the mountains complete and unbroken. An etched copper plate, set in the stone of the parapet, reproduced the profile of the peaks, and named them. Sally bent to look at it, but Josh came behind her and caught her lightly by the shoulders, turning her slowly.

"I don't know them all, but over there, south-west, is Mount Blanc. Almost straight down here to the south is La Dent Blanche—over there, beyond that, if you could see it, would be the Matterhorn and Monte Rosa. This range on the north are the Bernese Alps. We will go up to Montana and let you see everything better. But the valleys to the south over here are my favourites. We must go to Evolène and Arolla . . ."

"Monsieur knows the valley well, then?" The question seemed to Sally to have some emphasis, to be more than the polite chatter about the journey and the weather.

"Journalists usually move around," Josh said casually.

Raedler's dark brows signalled polite scepticism. "Are there stories to write of the happenings in such places as Evolène? One understood that Monsieur was a political correspondent."

"Perhaps that's why I've developed such a taste for the

remote and unspoiled. The mess politicians make in such places as Geneva almost forces one into the wilderness."

"Quite so," Raedler said, but his tone conveyed the impression that he regarded Josh as flippant. He squared his shoulders and Sally thought that he would have liked to snap his fingers to get them all back under his direction. He fixed his gaze on the one he thought most vulnerable, on her.

"I'm sure Miss Devlin would like to refresh herself after the journey. If you will permit me . . . I will show you to your rooms. Madame will be present at dinner. This way, please." He gestured towards another arched and iron-studded door, one half of which stood open. For an instant's hesitation, which perhaps only Hans Raedler discerned, Sally's feet seemed rooted. The grey eyes were on her coolly. "He knows I don't want to go in," she thought. "He knows—and he's glad of it."

She made herself move, and she passed before them through the doorway into the Great Hall of St. Martin. Something was amiss in this house, she thought. Much more than Elizabeth being ill, much more than Devlin's disappearance, something was amiss. When the door closed behind them and the shaft of light from the west was cut off, it felt to her as if the way of escape had gone with it.

TWO

Sally wondered if it wasn't a little too perfect; it would have cost, she thought, an immense amount of money. She knew little about medieval art and artifacts, but her senses told her that everything in this staircase hall was genuine, that a great deal of it was right in its period, and that the auction rooms of Europe must have been combed by a horde of buyers to have produced this show.

The massive stone stairway jutted into the hall and rose half its height before splitting into the classic Y to ascend to the second level; here a gallery of wonderfully sculptured stone surrounded the whole hall, passages opening from it to reach into the rest of the house.

Although Hans Raedler preceded them up the stairs, it was Hayward who had taken unto himself the duties of guide.

"It will be, of course," he said, "recognised as one of the great private museums of Europe if Elizabeth ever permits it to be viewed or photographed. But she always said that she worked for too many years on the restoration, and when it was finished she felt like living in it, not just showing it to swarms of art experts to have them pick it to pieces. I've told her there was a great book in it—something for Tyne and Townsend, wouldn't you think, Sal?—but I could never get her to agree."

He paused on the final broad landing to survey the hall below him; Raedler was forced to turn, half-way up the next flight, and to wait. Hayward spread his arms in the same proprietorial gesture he had used on the terrace.

"I think it looks best from here—especially in the afternoon when the light is hitting those high west windows . . ."

The three of them lined up along the stone balustrade. "I think Mrs. Spence must have a splendid sense of humour," Josh said. "Imagine what it must have been like saying no to the suits of armour that the dealers must have wanted to foist on her."

Hayward shot Josh a quick look, as if he suspected him of being amused. "I doubt," he said shortly, "that Elizabeth has had very much that she didn't want foisted on her in her life. Not Elizabeth."

"She sounds a formidable lady," Josh replied. "I'm terrified—aren't you, Sally?"

Deliberately, Sally thought, he had said it loudly enough so that Raedler and anyone else who was listening could have heard. Immediately it broke the grip of her sense of isolation; it shouted aloud to everyone that there was something too theatrical in this whole setting, this atmosphere of silence and reserve. One was either awed or amused, and Josh was telling them that he was amused. She smiled faintly, and was rewarded by an answering smile from Josh. The waiting figure on the stairs stirred with a certain restiveness.

"I shall be happy, Miss Devlin, to take you on a tour of the house whenever you wish it. You have only to ask . . . And, now, may I show you to your rooms?"

Sally looked up at him, the smile fixed on her face to cover her fury at the arrogance of the man.

"Certainly, Monsieur Raedler . . . I should love to see the entire house. But it seems a pity, doesn't it, not to enjoy each part as it presents itself. Tours are for tourists, surely?"

Slowly she turned her back on him and faced down into the hall again. Beside her she heard Hayward's mutter. "Bloody cheek . . ."

Raedler might have been meant to hear that too. But Sally had put away the impingement of Raedler as she stood and tried to think that this was where Devlin had lived.

It was Elizabeth's house, but it never could have been Devlin's. It was magnificent, and formal, and even the colour of the tapestries and the patina of the wooden tables and benches and high-backed chairs could not take away its essential coldness. Sally wondered how her father, who had loved the sense of openness and light above everything else, could have lived with the narrow slits that served as windows in the thickness of the walls. There was no dampness, and yet there was the impression of dampness, because the sun could never shine fully and strongly into the vast spaces of this chamber. In the growing dimness, the sun slipped lower, Sally caught the gleam of the jewelled chalice that stood in its glass case to the right of one of the two huge stone fireplaces. It was matched on the other wall by the primitive beauty of a crucifixion triptych painted on wood, its startling primary colours suddenly illuminated, as the light waned, by a spot-light concealed under the staircase. Hayward saw her gaze upon it.

"Fra Filippo Lippi," he said. "One of the great prizes of Elizabeth's collection. The tapestries are Gobelin. The entrance to the chapel is beyond the screen there. The choir stalls are fourteenth century, from Spain. No one knows how old the foundations of the house are—the present building was begun in the twelfth century and finished some time in the fifteenth . . . And then—oh, well, you'll see it all. . . ." Hayward sounded tired, as if he had run out of words and even of the desire to say any more.

Sally took a last look at it. It was a stage-setting, marvellous and faintly preposterous. She wondered if her father had been close enough to the woman he had married to risk a joke about it.

They followed Raedler along a passage which branched off the gallery. There was a velvet-soft carpet of royal blue underfoot that deadened the sound of their steps; it seemed odd to Sally that four people could move with what was almost an absence of sound. Again her thoughts were forced back to her father; he had been a man of silent places; but of places where the silence was natural. How had he felt about the quiet trapped within these walls? Her thoughts were cut off by Raedler stopping abruptly before a door, and opening it with what almost amounted to a flourish. "As if he were the hotel manager . . ." Sally thought.

". . . which Madame Devlin's guests use as a sitting-room," Raedler was saying. "This has its own terrace, you see. One of the battlements really . . . of course, the salons downstairs are always at your disposal."

"Yes, yes," Hayward answered testily. He was getting tired of the tour and the explanation. "I've been here before, you know."

Raedler shot him a look and for a moment Sally thought the façade of the hotel manager would crack. But he merely nodded, and accepted the rebuke. "Of course . . . Your room, Mr. Hayward, is next door, here, and Mr. Canfield's is this one on the other side." Raedler crossed each room to open the door to the private bathroom beyond. Checking the soap and towels, Sally thought maliciously. She could not get the image of the hotel manager out of her mind. The luggage had arrived before them, and somehow each piece had been placed in the right room. Where, she wondered, in these days did Elizabeth find servants to do such things, and she had to think again of her father who had lived with all these luxuries for five years and had probably never noticed their presence, as he would neither have noticed their absence; it was one of the ironies of that marriage that a rich woman was almost totally wasted on Devlin.

"A little farther for you to go, Miss Devlin," Raedler said, trying a smile on her that completely failed. "Your room is just above this, up these stairs here . . ." He gestured for her to move on.

"Just a moment!"

Canfield's voice made them turn. "There is something wrong with the arrangements, Mr. Canfield?" Raedler's tone dared him to find something wrong.

"Wouldn't it be more pleasant for Miss Devlin to have my room? I mean—here, near the sitting-room and not stuck away somewhere by herself?" The mildness of Canfield's expression was not meant to deceive anyone. "You know—fewer stairs and more company for her."

Again Raedler tried his smile. "I assure you Miss Devlin will be most comfortable. We have prepared the State Apartment for her—it has the view to both sides of the valley. It was originally . . ." He looked quickly towards Hayward, waiting to see if the other would tell him that they already knew this piece of history. "Originally, it was the living quarters of the bishops of St. Martin, whose seat this was. It was Madame's special wish that Miss Devlin should have it."

"In that case," Sally began, "I'm sure . . ."

Canfield broke in. "Just give the word, Sally, and we'll swop. If you're not happy up there, you've only to say . . ."

"Thank you, Josh. I'm sure I shall be——" She paused, "very comfortable."

"Very good," Raedler said briskly. "And now, Miss Devlin . . ." He turned and preceded her along the passage. Glancing back, Sally saw Josh give a shrug, and spread his hands in a gesture of helplessness. But she knew then, quite surely, that Josh Canfield was not helpless at all.

The staircase was narrow and curving, and enclosed between two solid walls without windows; it was lighted by electric sconces. Sally struggled to throw off the silence that threatened to close in again, fought not to be intimidated by Raedler.

"I would have supposed that the bishop would have had a more accessible approach to his apartments. These stairs seem so narrow—I thought most of the business was done in one's bedroom in those days."

"Quite so," Raedler answered quickly, as if his statements were called into doubt. "I was not here, of course, when Madame was carrying out the restoration, but I understand that the principal approach was an outside staircase with antechambers which started about where the parking space is now. Much of it had crumbled, and it was thought impractical to attempt to reconstruct it." He did not wait for her comment. They had reached a landing where the way was barred by double doors elaborately painted and gilded. Raedler flung them open.

"I understand this used to be Madame's own bedroom."

Sally walked in slowly. The room was a great oval at the east end of the building, with five long windows reached by two steps up from the main level; each window was itself an alcove, with stone benches built into the thickness of the walls. The peculiar, intense light of the Valais had dimmed, but there was still enough of it to flood the room. The middle window gave a view down the valley, the mass of the mountains receding and diminishing until the point where they met at the end towards Simplon. From the side windows there was nothing to see but the close slopes of the mountains at right and left, dotted with farmhouses and the patches of vineyards and lush, sloping meadows. Sally stepped up into one of the alcoves and below now, about half a mile away, was the grey-white foam of the river, the poplars marking its banks. In the distance were the roofs and spires and the great church of Valère at Sion. Directly below was a sheer drop to the greyish white slopes of the vineyards terraced right up to the rock of the castle. On this side there were no outer fortifications; the drop itself was the castle's protection.

"Why did Mrs. Spence move from here?" Sally kept her face away from Raedler as she spoke, not wanting him to know the great distaste she felt for the place. She didn't want to use Elizabeth's room, or to sleep in the bed that had been hers. She wished now that she had done as Josh had suggested. It was almost on her tongue to say that she would change, and then she knew she couldn't. Elizabeth would know why she had changed.

Raedler smiled the smile that she had grown to distrust, and seemed to enjoy the trap that she had worked her way into.

" I never questioned Madame on that, Miss Devlin. But surely——" His gesture indicated the space about him. " This is magnificent, is it not?—but the room that served for Madame alone was possibly not suitable for the accommodation of two such people as Madame and her husband. Madame now occupies the suite of rooms that she shared with your father."

Sally swallowed dryly. " I see."

She stepped down to the room again, her face composed now. She even managed a smile that tried as hard as Raedler's own. " It was most kind of Madame to let me have this room." And then she gestured about her. " It seems somewhat wasted on me, though, since I have no work to do here."

A great canopied bed stood between two fireplaces. Mid-way between the three windows that formed the curve of the oval was a long oak table, with three high-backed carved chairs drawn up about it. She pointed at it. " Surely Josh should have had the benefit of all this working space—and the view. Aren't writers supposed to work best with a view."

Raedler looked at her coldly, and she felt foolish for having tried to be flippant. " I really couldn't say about writers, Miss Devlin. Madame is the only writer I have ever known. But I would have thought your knowledge of your father would have given you an insight . . ."

" Yes, yes," Sally cut him short. " We all know that writers don't give a damn about a view. Most of them prefer a blank wall. But Josh would like this room . . ."

" You know Mr. Canfield well, Miss Devlin?"

She swung around. " Why do you say that?"

"You call him—that name I have not heard before—Josh? Joshua is his name, is it not? A strange name . . ."

"Joshua is a good, English, nonconformist name," she said quickly, hotly, not sure that that was correct. But Raedler had, somehow, to be kept in place.

"Well," he said, "it is pleasant for you both to be here together since you are old friends."

She closed her lips on the denial; instead she looked about the spaces of the room, the magnificence of the bed-hangings, embroidered with a crest and motto that was beginning to appear familiar to her, the silken splendour of the carpets. Along the back wall of the room were two enormous ceramic stoves, tiled with the ancient arms of Savoy; the bishops, she thought, had believed in keeping themselves warm. Small steps on each side led to a platform on the stoves themselves where servants had slept. They were curious, rather ungainly relics; the whole château would now be centrally heated. Her eyes moved on to the great carved table and the chairs, to the intricately wrought sconces, all belonging, surely, in a museum. The whole apartment was wonderful and impressive, and seemed infinitely lonely, as impersonal as the mountain view it framed. It cut her off, forced her into a splendid isolation. And somehow Josh had guessed that this was the way it would be. She looked at the man standing before her with the beginnings of hatred. For some reason he or Elizabeth wanted her to be alone, and she was determined to make one bid to destroy, at least figuratively, the separation they had built about her.

"Yes, it's always pleasant to be with old friends. I've known Josh—why it must be fourteen years since I first met Josh."

"Ah, so . . . Well, I hope you will enjoy your visit, Miss Devlin. Now, I see your luggage has been delivered. I will send the maid to unpack for you."

"That will not be necessary. I am quite accustomed to taking care of myself."

"You must not deny us the pleasure of serving you, Miss Devlin. It is rural here, but St. Martin is not rustic. Most ladies enjoy the pleasure of dressing up. I will send the maid. Her name is Marie."

Then he bowed and retreated, and she was left staring at the painted doors. She wished she had not been so clearly reminded of Robert.

II

Hayward leaned back in the big armchair, closed his eyes, and let the whisky and the sense of comfort lapping about him soothe his irritability. Very soon, he thought, St. Martin would seem to him almost as it had always been, or had been in the five years that Dev had lived here, and he, Hayward, had always been a welcome and pampered guest. It was the strangeness of being here without Dev, without Elizabeth to welcome him personally that had so disconcerted and upset him. God, how he missed Dev—Dev would have been here now, perched on the end of the desk there, glass in hand, talking. Talking in that non-stop, sometimes maddening fashion he had had, but spellbinding still, breaking sometimes into that wild shouted laughter that was somehow softened by grace and wit. With Dev the place would never have been so quiet as this. Hayward didn't like the quiet. That upset him too. He didn't remember St. Martin being like this. Surely, even allowing for Dev's absence, the place was unnaturally quiet, as if somehow everyone had packed up and gone, as if the life had left the house. Well, Dev was dead, and Elizabeth was dying. The life had indeed gone, and it was the end of St. Martin as he remembered it.

Hayward sighed and opened his eyes. Nothing was changed in the room, nothing physical. He had had this room before and all the small luxuries were just as before. There were still the stacks of towels in the bathroom, the rum-scented soap, and cologne that Elizabeth imported from the Virgin Islands; there was still the twelve-year-old Scotch and the flowers on the bureau, the assortment of writing-paper in the desk drawers, embossed with the crest of St. Martin, the open type-writer—Elizabeth's guests were the kind who could never be very far from a typewriter and the telephone. The telephone still had its elaborate internal communication system—the buttons that could be pressed to connect the different parts of the house. He glanced at it now on the table beside him, running his eyes down the list of names—Mrs. Devlin's bedroom, Mrs. Devlin's bathroom. Mr. Devlin's bedroom . . . They hadn't changed that yet. He started a little at the sight of his own name beside one of the buttons, freshly typed. Mr. Hayward . . . that was a new touch. In the old days the rooms had been numbered. Here was Josh's name . . . Mr. Canfield. And here was Sally . . . Miss Devlin. Perhaps this was Raedler's idea of making them welcome. Just like the efficient German mentality. Well, he supposed he meant well. Hayward thought of Sally upstairs, missing the conviviality of the sitting-room that Josh and he shared, missing the Scotch as well, probably. He thought of pressing her button and speaking to her, cheer her up a little. She had seemed strained and tired at the end of the journey. Who wouldn't have been strained, coming to St. Martin for the first time under these circumstances. Sally was a good kid, though. Sally could take lots more than one thought. Sally was Dev's daughter, wasn't she? God, how he missed Dev. The place was terrible without Dev . . .

He wouldn't phone Sally. He was tired, too.

A small sound in the room brought Hayward out of his doze; he struggled for a second to recall the name of the man who stood there.

"Lancome!"

The old man bowed. "I came to see that Monsieur was comfortable, and had everything he desired."

"Well, of course—of course. Everything is perfect, as always. I'm glad to see you again, Lancome. Very glad." He meant it; the face of Elizabeth's butler was a familiar and welcome sight. He had missed seeing him in the hall, and wondered what other duties besides the one of escorting Elizabeth's guests to their rooms Raedler had taken over. But there had been no other guests that Hayward knew of since Raedler's appearance, so that old customs were not merely changed, but vanished.

"Monsieur Hayward is most welcome at St. Martin. We are all happy to have him here—him and Monsieur Devlin's daughter."

"I am afraid we are all going to give you a lot of extra work, Lancome."

"It has always been a pleasure to serve Madame's guests, Monsieur. In the present case, where Madame has been alone for so long, the whole household is not only willing to serve, but anxious. May I pour Monsieur another whisky?"

Hayward didn't, at the moment, want another drink, but he sensed Lancome's almost desperate need to do something for him. "That would be delightful," he said. Lancome left the door to the sitting-room open as he went to get it. He watched as the old man made a little ceremony of the whisky and soda. One of the things that had impressed Hayward about Elizabeth was the fact that she kept her servants so long. He remembered some of what Dev had told him of Lancome's history. The old man had been born in St. Martin and had gone into the hotel business as a boy. He had served Elizabeth many times at the Ritz in Paris, and after the war, after her divorce from Whitney Spence, he had taken over the running of her household. It was Lancome who had directed her attention to the ruined château of the bishops of St. Martin, and had urged its purchase. Through the restoration and Elizabeth's residence here he had become a source of patronage to his village. Hayward thought that Raedler's usurpation of powers must have been particularly hard for the old man to bear.

"Thank you, Lancome—ah, excellent. And how is Madame Devlin? We will see her, I hope, at dinner?"

"One hopes, Monsieur, but who knows? Sometimes Madame stays within her apartments for days and even a week at a time, and no one of the household sees her."

"Then who serves her?"

" A woman—someone who calls herself a personal maid. Marie has been excluded. Marie has been with Madame nearly twenty years."

" Who is this woman? Where did she come from?" Hayward heard his voice rising, and couldn't help it. There was more at St. Martin than Josh Canfield had prepared him for.

" She came almost at once after Madame returned from the rest cure at Zurich. She is a nurse, Monsieur—not a maid. Beyond that——" Lancome shrugged. " No one knows."

Hayward was startled to see, in the eyes of the old man, the brightness of tears; the impersonal mask of the well-trained servant was shattered. He knew that Lancome had come to his room, not to enquire about his welfare, but because he had had to find someone to whom he could talk.

" Monsieur," Lancome said hoarsely, " we have been waiting here at St. Martin. We have been waiting for someone to come. Suddenly, when Monsieur Devlin goes into that place where he died, we are cut off. No one comes. No one is permitted to come. Not us, who love Madame, and serve her, are able to approach. Monsieur, is this normal grief? We make allowances, but we think not. There is something here we do not understand, but what can we do?"

Beset with agitation, Hayward rose and paced between the desk and the window. He didn't know how to handle this. He wanted to call Josh, but he was afraid of stopping the flow of Lancome's talk.

" But surely you could ask her?" he burst out, beginning to feel irritated by being beyond his depth. " You are more Madame's friend than her servant."

" I once believed that, Monsieur. But no longer. How can I? I have few words with Madame these days."

" Then why on earth didn't you call someone else in? Her brothers—Mr. Spence—even myself?"

" You think I had not proposed that? Once, when I was alone with Madame briefly, I said to her that her brothers should come, as she was not well. I did not exactly know how to say it—if she wished, I said, I would carry a message myself to America to Madame's brothers." Hayward could see that Lancome actually trembled at the thought of America. "I never witnessed such a reaction, Monsieur. Madame became deranged—absolutely forbade me to have contact with any of her family or associates. She said—I hope I remember the words correctly—she said it would have mortal results if I did. I did not understand, but I obeyed. One usually obeys Madame." He added, "So we have waited, all the ones who love Madame and have served her, for some help from outside. Someone to give us directions. At last you have come—you and Monsieur Devlin's daughter."

Hayward said, "And what do you expect us to do?"

Lancome shrugged. "Who knows? But we wait. We are at your service."

Hayward leaned against the desk, feeling the weight of what Lancome had thrust upon him. He watched as the other man made an unnecessary fuss about little objects in the room, straightening the blotter on the desk, looking to see that the waste basket was empty. Then he abruptly faced Hayward again.

"The worst thing—the thing that most troubles me. It is so——" He gestured with his hands. "So bizarre that I have not known what to think about it—what to do."

"Well, what is it?"

"The day that Madame returns from the rest cure. We do not know then that Monsieur Devlin has crashed in his little plane. We do not know to expect this Raedler. But there he is, with Madame, and immediately the charge of the household is given to him. And Madame herself—terrible! She looks desperately ill, and undone! Near frenzy. In the confusion of the unexpected return, for we are not notified, there is a little time alone with her. This is before this Raedler arranges matters so that no one shall be alone with her again. She turns to me—I am, as you say, her friend. She turns to me—a desperate woman, Monsieur. She takes both my hands in hers. 'We have lost him,' she said. 'We have lost him.' And then she said no more.

"But it is the next day, Monsieur, before the news comes

that Monsieur Devlin is missing. Late next day come the telephone calls from all over the world. The Press. Madame's brothers. She says nothing, and refuses to speak. But she already knew, Monsieur. She already knew."

III

Canfield had gone to the telephone almost at once, and the sight of the three names there, freshly typed and invitingly ready, made him pause. It suggested two things to him; the first was that Raedler had prepared them, and had placed Sally in a far-off room in order to promote the use of the internal telephone so that their conversations could be recorded. A trained agent would never use such a telephone, but an innocent man would; he would have to remember that he was an innocent man. The second thought was that the freshly typed names had no significance at all except as an act of courtesy to Elizabeth's guests, that there was no motive save that of offering an added convenience to what was already lavished on those in this house. This would mean that all of them in London had been wrong about St. Martin—that there was no more here than the desolation of the illness of the mistress and the loss of Devlin. This would also mean that the agent from Geneva had been wrong that day at the beginning of the winter, and that Hans Raedler was merely Hans Raedler, and not the Zotov the man remembered. It would mean that his, Canfield's, seeing the Russians outside of Devlin's flat that night in October had been coincidence; that a long chance had taken Devlin across the Soviet border, that a long chance had brought back to them his camera case and the information that his body had not been in the wreckage. It was a long chance that had led them to Devlin in the first place—the meeting between him and the murdered Fergus in the bar of the St. George in Beirut.

Canfield looked down at his name again, and thought that there were just too many long chances; on the face of it, it appeared that he was not suspected, and yet the foolish thing would be to let himself believe that, and to act on it. He could think of a number of men who had never reported back to London because they had let themselves think that way. It was possible that Fergus had been among that number.

He spent the next fifteen minutes searching the room and bathroom, wondering where, if at all, the tiny microphone heads were placed. He didn't find any, but he couldn't be certain they were not there. He suddenly knew fully the inadequacy of his training to be in a position like this; to places like this they sent the field experts, the men who could scent danger, who had an inner ear for trouble, who had developed the sixth sense for handling it. But the experts hadn't been able to penetrate the château of St. Martin, so they had risked sending him. And now he could think of other skilful amateurs who had never come back to London because skilful amateurs weren't enough in a world where only the real professional can give himself the chance to survive. The thought struck him freshly that it could have been in their minds back in London that, because he already had announced his intention of getting out, they were risking him because they reckoned him expendable. All of them were expendable, of course, but those they would use no more were doubly so.

The sweat broke on his palms. He was thinking of Sally Devlin as she had sat next to him in the car that day, the way she had turned her face to him, a seeking, almost pleading look that had asked something of him. The remembrance of that look was painful. He wanted to give to her whatever it was she sought—whatever and whenever. He wanted very much now to survive; he wanted not to be expendable. He wanted to have the chance to do something with the time that lay beyond St. Martin.

He unpacked and had a bath, and when he was dressed he went to the telephone. He would use it with the kind of innocence they expected of him. He would do what any other man would have done, but doing it because he wanted it, not because doing the expected thing was part of the defence of those who played this game.

He lifted the receiver and pressed the button beside her name.

She took a long time to answer, her voice faint and wary.

He wondered if she had expected Elizabeth O'Mara Spence to be on the other end.

"Yes?"

"I'm bringing you a drink. Scotch and water—right?"

"Josh?—it's you? Yes—yes, please."

IV

The maid, Marie, had come and Sally had sent her away. The squat, pleasant-faced little woman had seemed disappointed, and Sally had hated the churlishness of her action; but she had to maintain some independence from Raedler, but mostly she needed to be able to unpack her bag in privacy. If the contents of those heavy envelopes—Hayward had grumbled about the weight of that small bag—were to be given to Elizabeth, they would be given in her own time.

So she had unpacked for herself, and now her clothes hung forlornly in the enormous closet of the dressing-room; her two bags which had so crowded the trunk of the car, seemed shrunken as they sat side by side on the long padded luggage rack. The marble and mahogany bathroom swallowed her toilet articles; she spread her cosmetics as widely as she could, but they did nothing to diminish the spaces. It was hard, she was finding, to be untidy in rooms like these. The dressing- and bathrooms were marvels of efficiency, with allocated places for everything, so that there was no possibility for the clutter that would have made them human. Although nothing personal of Elizabeth O'Mara Spence remained in these rooms, whoever followed her in possession here would be affected by the intangible presence she left behind her. The woman who had planned and occupied these rooms had admired efficiency and order; she would impose it on whomever came after her.

Sally bathed quickly, and put on a bare-armed black sheath dress, but decided against any of the pieces of costume jewellery she had brought with her; if Elizabeth wore jewels, they would be real ones. She looked at herself critically in the triple mirror, and knew that because she was almost thirty years younger, there would be no real contest, and this particular victory would be easy and flat. What was strange was that the man for whose attention they might have been competing was dead, and would never see them together. But when she splashed on perfume with a gesture that she had never been able to make frugal, it was suddenly Josh Canfield she was thinking of, not her father.

When she was ready she took the envelopes and went back into the salon. The drawers and compartments of the dressing-room seemed too obvious a place to leave them, and yet she was troubled by the thought that she must leave them somewhere, and by the thought that Raedler seemed to move at will through this house, and that it was possible that the pleasant-faced maid was the kind who would look at every item of a guest's luggage. She didn't want the existence of the manuscript reported to Elizabeth; she had nothing left now but the choosing of the time to give it.

Out in that vast apartment the light was leaving, finally, slipping from the valley, the darkness gathering in about the river and enclosing the slopes and vineyards. The lights of Sion had begun to appear, but up in the narrow valleys that opened from this one, in the hamlets and isolated farmhouses they were more frugal; they would wait, she thought, until the true darkness came, and then the lights would shine only briefly; up there, in the high meadows where the cattle grazed, they would go to bed early and be up before the sun. She was caught, in spite of herself, by the splendour of the sight, the soft dusk down here in the valley, the last flush of light on the mountain-tops. She hesitated, and did not flick on the light switch which would have cut it all out. The great chamber was full of shadows. Treading softly, she stepped up into one of the window alcoves, breathing the light, dry air, the scent of dust on the vines now that the tide of spring had gone. She had not meant to fall captive to Elizabeth's valley, but she had; she stood now, as she knew her father must have stood, and listened to its noises and its quiets.

It was not the Switzerland of the picture postcards, it was not the country the foreigner expected, not the idyllic lakes and the tidy, flower-decked chalets, the streams, the softly wooded slopes that led to the higher mountains; this was harsher, a dry, almost savage landscape. There was nothing fashionable about this place, and that was what had surprised Sally most. She had thought to find Elizabeth surrounded by the conventional sights, the conventional comforts, the rather saccharine quality of the landscape where everything that meets the eye is perfect. From her first sight of the Rhône valley, from first revelation of the massive austerity of the place where Elizabeth had chosen to make her home, Sally had begun to understand that few of the conventional standards applied to this woman. She had grown more formidable, and, somehow, for all the contradictions of this place to what her father had sought in his own dwellings, more the kind of woman who might have interested and fascinated him.

She had been picturing Devlin in a cuckoo-clock setting, and she had found that Elizabeth was not a cuckoo-clock woman. Her father would have liked this valley.

Then the buzzer sounded in the room behind her, and she started and the packages nearly slipped from her hold.

After straining her eyes into the last of the light outside, the room by contrast was in nearly total darkness. She banged into a chair as she made her way to where she remembered a light switch. The whole apartment came to life richly, and the gathering night was closed out; but a quick glance round the room did not reveal the telephone. She followed the direction of its sound to a tall carved chest that seemed as if it must always have stood there. But the slight pressure of her hand caused the door to slide sideways revealing a telephone and a whole panel of buttons. The furnishings of the room would not permit the anachronism of the modern telephone, but of course Elizabeth O'Mara Spence could not have been without one.

She was almost afraid to pick it up. It would have been easier to face Elizabeth than to grapple with a disembodied voice on the phone.

"Yes," she said; she wished her voice hadn't sounded so uncertain.

"I'm bringing you a drink," Josh's voice said. "Scotch and water—right?"

"Josh?—it's you?" She felt herself relax into relief and pleasure. "Yes—yes, please."

When she hung up she knew she had to find a place for the manuscript very quickly, and her gaze roamed the great chamber, searching.

The whisky was in a tumbler. "I made it a large one," he said. "It's a long way down those stairs."

She took it and closed the door behind him. "I was almost on my way to find you. I was sure there was a drink cabinet concealed behind one or other of these medieval fixtures, but to tell you the truth I'm rather frightened to try them all. I don't know what kind of mechanical marvels are going to spring out at me, and I feel like a country girl. You know——" She spread her hand with a small giggle. "The toilet flushes by stepping on a button in the floor. The first time I did it by accident, and I nearly died of fright." She took a long drink of Scotch. "I think I really am rather frightened, Josh. I wish we could meet her and get it over with."

"We will—soon enough. She's ill, Sally—she probably doesn't have the strength for too much socialising. She'd probably rather be left in peace."

"And I would rather not have come. How long must we stay, Josh?"

"Who knows?—how long are we welcome?"

"We're not welcome at all."

"But we're here. That's what's important—that we're here. Important for Elizabeth—important for you, Sal." He was advancing into the chamber, staring about him. "Now come and show me the marvels of this place—she really *has* given you the state apartment, hasn't she."

"I wish I weren't here, though," she said, returning to the subject. "I wish I weren't here at St. Martin."

He spun around. "No, you don't. You don't wish that at all. You're not the kind of person who says no to any experience—no matter what."

"Is that what you think of me?" She walked close to him. "Is it what you think of *me*?—or is it because my father went out of his way to meet everything. He let everything happen to him that could happen—and you expect me to be the same?"

"Not the same—forget you're Devlin's daughter. You'll do what you have to do because you expect it of yourself. You're not Devlin's daughter—you're yourself."

She thought he would not ever know that he had said exactly the words no one had ever said before and which she had needed so badly. He would not know that she was grateful; people did not see thoughts or feelings; they could hear words, but words were only words, and actions were actions.

She put her arms up across his shoulders and stretched on her toes to kiss him. And as her lips met his, she had the shocking, sudden conviction that in some impossible fashion he had known what her feelings were. Their lips met as if he had been waiting for her. They still had their glasses in their hands, and yet their bodies were pressed very close. As if he had been waiting for this too. There was a kind of joyful recognition and sureness in the way they came together. When she drew her lips finally away from his, she said simply "How?" wondering how it had come into being so quickly.

He shook his head. "Don't ask. Never ask questions about things like that. Just kiss me."

And she did, and smiled beneath the kiss.

"What now?"

"You ask too many questions—you're still young, that's why. When you're older you'll learn not to ask so many questions. You'll just let it happen." He had taken the glass from her hand and set it down. Then he put his arms about her again, and she was drawn into him, and the embrace was wider and deeper and more urgent than anything she could remember.

"Josh . . . so much? Like this?"

"Shut up, Sally Devlin. Some day I may tell you for how long and how often I've waited for this." The pressure of his lips bent her head backwards.

Nothing more was said; there was only the movement and the pressure, until the sound of Raedler's voice.

"Excuse me, Miss Devlin."

They left each other's arms reluctantly. Canfield could feel the anger rise in him, but before he looked at Raedler he looked at Sally, wondering if he would see regret or embarrassment in her face. The anger was almost wiped out by the joy of seeing only the slow and prideful turn of her head towards Raedler, the natural, beautiful dignity of the movement that had no fear and no regret in it.

"What is it?" she said, as if Raedler were a minor, annoying interruption.

"Forgive me—I did knock, but there was no reply."

She inclined her head slightly towards Canfield, and her look at the secretary was cool. "Understandably—I was engaged."

Canfield took a malicious pleasure in the flicker of discomfiture that passed across the other man's face. "I do beg your pardon. When I had no reply I thought perhaps you had already gone down to the sitting-room, but that I should find out before I went down myself. I have come to conduct you downstairs to dinner. Madame was concerned that you might lose your way."

"As you can see I am well attended. But it was kind of Madame to be concerned. One moment."

And while she went to collect her handbag, and replace her lipstick, Canfield and Raedler faced each other. Now that Sally had gone, the tempering force was also gone. Canfield looked at the other with an anger that had grown more cautious, more cautious because he was reminded of where he was, and for what purpose. He was reminded of whom the man standing at the doorway was. Because of Sally he was suddenly vulnerable in a way that he had never been in any other task they had given him. Always before, he had been for himself, and his contacts had involved only professionals, people who also knew why they were there, and what they were about. He had never had to watch it from his side and from the side of the innocent and unknowing. And then he saw that Raedler's rigidness had relaxed; he was taking a cigarette from his case in the manner of a man who has, for the moment, ceased to watch.

"Miss Devlin says she has known you for a long time, Mr. Canfield. It must be rewarding to be given the task of writing Mr. Devlin's biography . . . Madame will be most interested in learning your plans for it."

Beyond the wild surge of pleasure in hearing that for some reason Sally had claimed a long friendship with him, Canfield was aware of one other thing, and the knowledge made him feel cold and shabby. The scene Raedler had just witnessed had caused him to lower his guard; Canfield's position as the biographer was accepted. The cover was working very well. What worried him was the thought that at some time Sally might come to question how well it had worked, and to question if what they had just shared had been part of it, manufactured and devised along with the rest of it. That was the greatest danger of the job; when you told so many lies, when could you believe even yourself.

"A great honour," he said to Raedler, and accepted a cigarette.

V

Sally felt a sharp sense of relief when Elizabeth, finally, did not appear at dinner. They had waited for ten minutes past the hour in the salon, sipping drinks and not saying much, before Raedler reappeared and ushered them towards the dining-room.

"Madame's apologies. She will join you for coffee." And then Raedler himself took the place at the end of the long table opposite the empty chair where Elizabeth would have sat. Glancing over, Sally saw Hayward's face working strangely, as if he didn't know whether to protest or to try. And then she realised that Raedler had taken Devlin's seat at this table.

"Mrs. Devlin has been ill for some time now," Hayward said. He tore at the bread on his plate, as if he were angry and had to find something to do with his hands. "I hope she's having proper medical attention. Shouldn't she be in Paris or Zurich . . . ?" He glared at Raedler accusingly, and then about the great room where they sat, with the two hooded fireplaces and its stone walls and floor as if he suspected the house of being medieval in its attitudes as well as its furnishings. "Home treatment is all very well, but I should have thought a hospital . . ."

Raedler motioned to Lancome to begin pouring the wine. "Madame's ailment is of the liver, I understand, Mr. Hayward—debilitating but not dangerous, so we are assured. Do try this wine, Miss Devlin. It is Fendant—of the region. A very young wine, but one grows fond of it. Perhaps I should have chosen something more splendid for your arrival, but I thought you would enjoy this of the château's own vineyards."

"Mrs. Devlin no longer selects her own wine?" Hayward's tone was almost a growl. He banged his soup spoon down in the plate.

Raedler raised his eyebrows just a trifle. "You forget that I did not know the household when you were here previously. Madame has left much to my direction since I came here. I understand since Mr. Devlin's death she has not cared to be troubled by details of the household."

"A piece of good fortune for Mrs. Devlin to know you—to know that you could take over such things as well as handle her affairs." Canfield watched Raedler's face very carefully as he threw out the half question, but he was not hopeful of much reaction. Raedler would not be where he was if he were not well prepared to meet it.

"On the contrary—it was my good fortune. I met Madame Devlin some years ago when I was one of the secretaries to Herr Helmut Ritter, the industrialist. We became acquainted when Madame stayed at his house. I learned that she was searching for a confidential secretary—it is most interesting to work for those whose interests are so varied . . ."

"Ritter died, didn't he?" Hayward said. He accepted a second helping of the white asparagus.

"Ah, so—yes. Two years ago. Since then I have found nothing that really pleased me. Some jobs are very dull. I was very happy to accept Madame's offer."

He would pass on the information to Willsden, Canfield thought, and they would have it checked. Probably a Hans Raedler had worked for Helmut Ritter. After Raedler, as

Zotov, had disappeared from Australia it was entirely possible that he had been worked into such a position as Ritter's secretary, or one of them. He would have been excellently placed to give information to his masters on the old armament baron's affairs. As in his own case, the closer the cover to the truth, the better the operation. He gave up his attempt at probing; it was an elementary exercise, and Raedler had long ago graduated from that class. He nodded absently, as if he were bored with Raedler's jobs, and smiled across the table at Sally. Behind her shoulder he noticed again the motto chiselled into the stone mantel of the fireplace.

"*Veritas Praevalebit*," he read, motioning towards it. "I see it all over the house. Is it . . . ?"

Hayward cut him short. Not even glancing back at the carved letters he said quickly, as if to forestall Raedler, "Truth will out, dear boy—or something like that. The motto of the bishops of St. Martin. Jolly good thing for a churchman to keep in mind, I should say, particularly when you were salting away as much as those old rascals habitually did. Excellent bit of trout . . . and this Bordeaux is a decided improvement over the Fendant. Elizabeth never believed in being provincial." He bestowed a smile on Raedler that was pure acid.

And Sally, looking down, recognised again what she had been seeing many times since she had entered this house. The motto was delicately conveyed in gold on the plain white plate. It had appeared discreetly on the painted doors to the bishop's apartments, mingled with the embroidered flowers and birds on the bed-cover. It was, as she had first thought of the house, slightly theatrical. But now she did not feel like laughing at it.

VI

While they had been at dinner someone had lighted the piles of wood that lay stacked in the two hearths in the salon—even though the night was still warm. The great room seemed dim, shadowed; only the sconces on the fireplace wall burned. The glow from the fire flickered among the shadowed places, ran into the darkness and out again, sought out the richness of the colours of the tapestries, the watery sheen of fine, pale carpets. Slender hounds of ancient silver decorated the fire-dogs, hounds like the whippets in the two Jan Van Eyck paintings that hung each side of the entrance doors, like the thin, eager white hounds of the tapestries. Sally remembered Devlin saying, of great houses where he had stayed, houses like this one, "Trouble is, you can never find a comfortable chair in a museum." But Elizabeth had done better than that. The stiff carved high-backed chairs of the period stood along the walls; before the fireplaces were the long sofas, deep sofas for tall men, all of them covered alike in a mole-coloured velvet that did not draw the eye, so that you were not distracted from what you should look at in this room, the Van Eycks, the Memling, the three tapestries that were known as The Graces. It had been done skilfully and to a purpose; Sally was reminded that the people who had used this room had not been the kind who often had the time to linger idly before the fires. Somewhere about them, concealed, would be the ever-present telephones.

Between the two fireplaces a long table had been set with the coffee service and the liqueur bottles and glasses. Raedler went to it at once, as if it were not the practice for the butler, Lancome, to serve in this room after dinner.

"You will take coffee, Miss Devlin?"

"Thank you—black."

Hayward had almost elbowed Raedler aside at the table. "Let me give you some of this, my dear. Elizabeth has a wonderful cellar—an enviable cellar. Some of this brandy is priceless now—or at least not the kind of price that one cares to pay."

"If it would interest Miss Devlin, it would be a simple matter to arrange for her to see the wine cellars. They were constructed from the old dungeons, I understand," Raedler said, standing before Sally with her coffee.

Hayward shrugged. "No need to bother, Raedler. I know my way. I'll just get the keys from Lancome some time when Sally and Josh feel like seeing them."

Raedler half bowed. "Certainly, Mr. Hayward. Just let me know—it is I who now keep the keys."

Hayward didn't answer; he turned away and roughly splashed brandy into a glass. "Here, Josh—I didn't ask you what you wanted. I couldn't let you miss the chance to taste brandy like this." Then he thrust his hand in his pocket, gripping his own glass tightly in the other, and turned his back on Raedler's offer of coffee. "Never touch it at night," he muttered. Then he went to stand before one of the fires, his head bent in uncharacteristic moodiness.

Sally was left alone at the table with Raedler. With a fluttering sense of panic, she looked about for Josh, but he had wandered towards the end of the room, his face turned upwards to the tapestries. She wished he would come back, and her mouth opened to call him, and then closed again; she didn't need him beside her—he was there in the room with her, and that was all she needed. She turned back to face Raedler.

"You have much to do here," she said.

"I enjoy my work."

She shrugged, suddenly knowing that he didn't like the half question, knowing somehow that Raedler never answered questions if he could avoid them. She pressed him teasingly. "Where does one find a paragon like you, Monsieur? You have charge of everything—and as one can see, nothing is neglected!"

He gave his peculiar half bow. "I am happy if you are pleased. As for the rest——" He shrugged. "It is my job. And as to how one finds such a person . . ." He permitted himself the faintest smile. "All that is needed is money."

The reply had a kind of sneering vulgarity that she hated. For the first time she felt that she wanted to rise in defence of Elizabeth. "The rich surely cannot help being rich," she said. "And you, Monsieur, seem to know how to find the rich." She held out her cup to him, smiling with a false sweetness. "If you would be so kind, Monsieur . . ."

And she was as bad as he, she thought, to have met vulgarity with vulgarity, to treat him like a servant. She was beginning to loathe Raedler, but she had now discovered, because of Josh, that she no longer feared him. She could only wonder that Elizabeth's need of his efficiency could overlook the man himself. Perhaps Elizabeth did not care. And where was Elizabeth herself?—did she mean to leave them for ever in the hands of this man. She wondered how long she, any of them, could stand around, knocking on Elizabeth's door, waiting to be admitted. There was a kind of arrogance in this behaviour that matched Raedler's own. Perhaps she was right —Elizabeth simply did not care what Raedler was; either that, or they were two of a kind.

She accepted her cup from Raedler without looking at him again, and turned and went to join Josh.

She found him standing before a tall wooden press, whose carved doors were open, the interior lighted, and sealed with glass. He was bent forward so that his forehead almost touched the glass; the page of the open manuscript book he was studying was of astonishing vividness and colour, jewel tones on ancient parchment. She gave a little gasp as she saw it.

"Oh, lord! How beautiful!"

"Isn't it?" He turned and smiled at her pleasure, and put the cigarette he had been putting to his own lips into hers. She used the excuse to reach up and hold his wrist while he held the lighter towards her.

"So are you," he said.

Then behind them was Hayward. "Marvellous thing, isn't it," he said, nodding towards the manuscript. "The *Belles Heures* of the Duc de Berry. I was here in this room once when the director of the richest museum in the world offered Elizabeth a positively appalling amount of money for that. I don't believe he was ever asked here again." He gave a heavy sigh. "One forgets how much there is here." He put the brandy glass to his lips and sipped delicately. "How much there used to be . . ." He swung slowly on his heel, and his gesture indicated the whole room.

"Great things have happened in this room. Elizabeth was such a hostess . . . But of course it wasn't money that did that —you don't get the kind of people Elizabeth had here just because you can afford to invite them. It was Elizabeth who drew them, and, of course, Dev after they were married. She knew everyone—and everyone who came to this house might expect the sort of company that you only read about in the newspapers. I sometimes . . ." a sly smile of false modesty came to his face, "wondered how a lowly British publisher ever came to be mixed up here with Foreign Secretaries and Senators and even some Prime Ministers from those new nations that Africa is always sprouting these days. But Dev wanted me here . . . he was my friend, and Elizabeth became my friend because of him." Hayward was searching for a cigar, and Canfield's lighter came out again. The flame flickered close to Hayward's face, and Canfield saw that the red-veined eyes had glazed a little, narrowed, as if he were truly seeing other days, other nights in this room.

"They trusted Elizabeth, you know. They knew she would never write about what they asked should be kept under cover—but of course that paid off, because when they had a story for publication, she would have it before anyone else. I've known this house used secretly as a meeting-place when Geneva or London would be too public. A man could hide from the Press for a day or two here, and thrash things out. Dev once told me that some of the very early discussions for the Common Market started here—that was before *his* time, of course. They've had their tragedies, too. Bouchard was here when the call came that sent him off to the Congo. You remember what happened to him . . . And de Bec left here two days before he was assassinated in Algeria."

There was the sound of regret, some sadness, in Hayward's voice as he surveyed the room, sipping at his brandy. Sally could almost see it as he remembered it, as Dev had known it—the smoke rising from the cigarettes, the goblets of this old, rare cognac set down on the oak benches that served as tables to the sofas, and the hands of the speakers, some of them black hands, gesturing in the air as they made a point. Famous men, and some who had been great men, had gathered here, but they had gone now; they had gone when Dev had gone. It had all come to a stop. Sally sensed that this room had not been used for months past; she suddenly knew, though, that it had been Elizabeth who had ordered the fires lighted to welcome back the ghosts. It was a gesture of more grace than Raedler could command.

So she let her gaze wander back and forth across the room again, sharpened now, beginning to understand that life had flowed here, and laughter, even among the august guests; that at times it could have seemed not a museum, but a home. Hayward felt it this way, and Sally knew that if she could have believed that love had ever dwelt here, she could have felt it this way too. And then her eyes found a part of what she sought, the beginning of proof. Beyond the lighted press of the *Belles Heures*, at the farthest end of the room, she was suddenly aware of the portrait of her father. In the midst of all the splendour of Elizabeth's medieval collection it was wildly incongruous, almost shocking. It had been hung there with a recklessness of someone who did not care that it ruined the perfection of this room, someone determined to give Lawrence Devlin his place along with the greatest names that this room had ever contained. It was either an act of love or of flaunting possessiveness.

And Sally had seen it because it had suddenly come to life; someone had pressed a switch and light had been thrown on it abruptly. On the darkness of that farthest wall it was the only thing that could be seen clearly—the way a monument is lighted, Sally thought, the way a shrine is tended.

The woman's voice came then as a throaty whisper. "We had our moments here, didn't we, Jackson? I'm glad you remember the good ones. Welcome back to St. Martin."

"Elizabeth!"

She was seated on the stone bench that lined a darkened window alcove. The only illumination came from the light thrown on the portrait. Sally could see just the outline of a thin woman wearing a white gown that reached to the tips of her slippers and covered her arms to the wrists, a loose gown, girdled at the waist, resembling, Sally thought, a luxurious habit for a nun. They had all turned sharply at the words, all except Raedler, who had probably been aware of Elizabeth all along. Now as they looked, Elizabeth reached out a slender long hand and took up the brandy goblet from the bench beside her, took it up defensively, like a weapon.

Hayward hurried towards her. "My dear Elizabeth! I hadn't a notion you were there. How *are* you?" She gave him her free hand briefly, and he bowed over it.

"Well enough, Jackson—well enough." He would have kept her hand longer, but she withdrew it. "Did you dine well? You must forgive my absence. Food doesn't give me much pleasure these days, and I don't care to sit and watch other people eat. I hope Raedler gave you something you liked to drink with it—we have grown very rustic here of late."

"Everything was just as always, my dear," Hayward lied. "Except that we missed you."

"Ah, well . . ." The hand was waved dismissingly. "It was a long journey you made for such dull company as I am these days. But you always were kind."

Hayward snorted. "Kindness?—not at all! I have been ready to come at any time you needed me. I would have come, as you know, directly we had the news of Dev . . ."

"No use," the tired, throaty voice grew sharper. "No use then. It was done . . . you couldn't have changed anything. I am better left to myself."

"I find that hard to believe, Elizabeth. There were so many people who would have liked to be able to come and offer their help at that time. I believe it could have been a support to you just to know that they were there."

"No!" The glass moved up, and she drank with a rapid, jerking movement. "No—I want none of that kind. They gathered for the sensation, not to help. All they want is to be able to tell everyone how Elizabeth is taking it. 'She's taking it very badly,' was all they would have said. I needed none of that. I had enough to bear without bearing it for my friends too."

Instinctively Hayward stepped back. "My dear Elizabeth!—I'm shocked! I'm shocked that you should think so little of those who loved Dev—who loved you both."

Suddenly her hand shot out again; she caught his coat

sleeve. "No—don't go. Don't *you* go, Jackson. Of course you must be right. I've grown such a savage here alone. I've no one to remind me that I'm still alive."

Jackson's expression of hurt disapproval melted at once; he was visibly moved. "My dear, you mustn't say such things. If you only knew how many of your friends would think it a privilege to . . ."

"No use!" Again she stopped him with a gesture. "There's only one person who's ever been able to convince me that living was worth the trouble that it is. There's only one Dev."

As she said this her hand fell away from Jackson's sleeve limply. She bent her head as if she were inhaling the brandy, but they all knew that it was a moment for recovery; her voice had broken as she had said the name. They waited, and at the table, Raedler busied himself with the coffee. Sally felt rather than saw him at her elbow.

"May I refill your cup, Miss Devlin?"

"What?" She could not take her eyes or her attention from Elizabeth. Crouching defensively on that bench, hiding from the light and from the people in the room, was not the creature she knew must have existed for her father, not the woman of money and power, not the woman of the newspaper by-lines and the press photos, not the international hostess. She saw a thin, ageing woman huddled there, huddled as if she were frightened, the white gown painfully revealing the boniness of her frame, the hair that had been blonde, and now was a dirty white, drawn back sharply and fumbled into some kind of knot behind her head. Standing, she would be tall, but that was the end of the resemblance to the photos. No picture of Elizabeth O'Mara Spence had ever looked like this.

"Some more cognac, Miss Devlin?"

"No," she said. She found herself placing her glass in Raedler's hand because Elizabeth had lifted her head and one long finger was beckoning with a gesture that had the remnants of authority left in it, a vestige of the imperious quality that Sally had always imagined Elizabeth O'Mara Spence to have possessed. But as she took her first step forward to answer the summons, the shock came. It was not to her that Elizabeth was beckoning, but to Canfield.

"This is the man, Jackson, that you say will write about Dev?" Canfield moved towards Elizabeth, and for a moment his body blocked Sally's view. "Can you do it, I wonder? Can you write about Lawrence Devlin as he ought to be written about?"

"I shall try, Mrs. Devlin." He said it firmly, with no hint of conciliation. Sally knew that he was telling her that he would do it whether she agreed to it or not. "Part of Lawrence Devlin belonged to everyone who ever read his work. I believe I have the right to try."

"It's too soon," was the answer he got. "Jackson, it's far too soon to begin telling about Dev."

"One has to make a start, Elizabeth," Hayward protested. "I tried to outline some of my hopes for the Foundation in my letter—and a biography should come about the time of the first awards of the fellowships, I think. There has to be something to explain what Dev stood for—what kind of a man he was." With a gesture he silenced the protest he saw was coming. "Good heavens, no one expects the definite biography at this stage. But we must make a beginning—after all, Dev belongs in the public domain. How would you feel, for instance, if some hack from Fleet Street should decide to throw together a couple of hundred pages about Dev just because he had managed to squeeze an advance out of some publisher? How would you feel if *that* were the first book on Dev to appear? It would break my heart if someone else beat me to that first book—Hayward's have published every book Dev ever wrote, and it's *we* who have the right to the first biography—a good biography, which is what Josh will give us."

"But it should have been mine! It was to have been ours! Dev and I were going to write . . ."

"My dear——" Hayward broke in strongly. "I think Sally would like to meet you. She also has come a long way."

Elizabeth's head turned in Sally's direction. "Yes . . ."

She faced Sally with her eyes wide, as if she was making herself look at what she would rather not see. Her fingers gathered up the folds of her gown, clenching.

" Elizabeth, this is Sally," Hayward said.

" Ah . . ." Elizabeth's breath was expelled in a long sound, almost a sigh. Her fingers reluctantly let go of her gown, and she raised her hand a little, and then did not seem to have the strength to complete her gesture. " So . . ." Sally was forced to bend and take the proffered hand; it felt cold and thin. Close to, Elizabeth's face was ravaged; the lines in it were dark furrows, the eyes, deep set, were sunken and underlined with grey shadows. The eyes themselves, heavily lashed, were beautiful, Sally thought—none of the photographs of Elizabeth had prepared her for the beauty of these ice-blue eyes. They appeared the only thing of life left to her; they were intense and burning, for all the coolness of their colour. It seemed to Sally that all the remaining strength of that gaunt body was being consumed to provide the force and intelligence and life of those eyes.

Finally Elizabeth spoke. " You do not look like Dev." The words had the sharpness of a blow to Sally. She let the thin hand drop.

" Some people thought there was a considerable likeness," she answered. She spoke with difficulty through the sense of shock and outrage at this woman.

" No—it is not there," Elizabeth insisted. Her tone was rising. " A superficial likeness, perhaps. But no true likeness. You agree, don't you, Jackson? You don't think she looks like Dev?"

Hayward thrust his hand in his pocket; for a moment his eyes half closed as if he were making an effort for control and patience. " Well—I don't know, Elizabeth. I've always thought there was a resemblance."

As if in desperation now, Elizabeth turned to Canfield, the stranger, demanding affirmation of what she must believe. " What do you think?"

She had come close to hysteria, he thought, and no one but she knew what hells of loneliness and isolation had been endured through this long winter past. Even her voice had seemed strange to Canfield, from the moment she had first spoken, as if she had almost given up using it, as if there had been no one to hear it. She had become something of a savage, as she had said, leaping across all the ordinary conventions of manners and custom to reach the one thing that still held meaning for her. Devlin was the only one thing of importance left in her life, and she had energy only for him. She held him to her jealously, and would not have any part of him taken from her, not whatever words a biographer might write, not even the inherited resemblance of child to father. She seemed curiously threatened by the thought that Sally's resemblance to Devlin somehow drained away a part of what was left to her. Canfield was stirred by a strong feeling of compassion for her; he knew it would have eased her torment if she could have been told that there was no one who really looked like Devlin. She would have been secure again in her belief in his uniqueness. But compassion was not part of the errand on which he had come to St. Martin. He had come to find the truth, and if brutality would unleash the truth, then that would be the weapon.

"The likeness is unmistakable," he said. "If Devlin had been a woman, he would have looked just as Sally looks."

"No!" The word was a shriek. "Dev is . . ." The shriek cracked and diminished to a sob. "Dev is my own—my love! There is no one like Dev! And when I see him . . ." She faltered, then like a tormented creature she turned on Raedler. "They *said* I could go . . ."

"Madame!" Raedler's tone was instantly silencing. He was beside her and had grasped her arm, almost roughly, Canfield saw.

"Madame is overwrought . . . fatigued. She should retire."

She didn't attempt to deny his helping her to her feet; she leaned blindly on the arm he gave her, her other hand spread across her face, her head bent into it. She sobbed now without control; they listened to the anguish of the sound, as the two moved slowly down the whole length of the room.

Through the sobs she kept reiterating her passion. Canfield caught the words, like an echo. "Dev is my own . . . Dev is . . ." Raedler jerked the door closed behind them, and they heard no more.

Canfield moved first. He went to the table and poured three fresh brandies, carrying them back to where Sally and Hayward still stood, staring towards the door where Elizabeth and Raedler had disappeared. Hayward accepted the glass from Canfield eagerly. "Extraordinary," he said. He gulped at the liquor, a thing that would normally have offended him. "A tragedy. I could never have believed it of a woman like Elizabeth. Of course it was partly our fault for leaving her here alone . . . we should have insisted. *I* should have insisted. But how were we to know it would take her like this? Who could have believed it of a woman like Elizabeth? She has never taken interference in her affairs in the past. How were we to know the time had come to insist on interfering . . . Ah, well." He heaved a great sigh, and drank half of the brandy.

Canfield pressed the glass into Sally's hand, sealing her unresponsive fingers about the stem. "Drink it," he said.

She obeyed him automatically, her eyes still staring, eyes that Elizabeth had denied were Devlin's own.

"I didn't believe it either," she said. "I didn't think it could be true. Do you think . . ." she asked the question of Canfield, not of Hayward. "Do you think that she really loved him?"

Canfield nodded. "Yes." But mentally he corrected the tense she had used. Elizabeth loves him. His senses tingled with what he had just heard, the shriek, the sob; "And when I see him . . . they said I could go . . ."

Devlin was alive, and Elizabeth knew it.

"Then what——" The light that flooded Sally's eyes was suddenly warm and strong, as if she had wakened from her shock. "*Who* is that man? What is he doing here? Why does she stay here alone with that man? The least we can do—Mr. Hayward, you and I must take her away——"

She choked on the last word because Canfield had abruptly placed his hand across her lips. He shook his head, and gestured Hayward to silence.

He leaned close to them, and spoke softly. "We'll finish our brandy on the terrace, shall we?" He jerked his head urgently towards the door, and then only very cautiously took his fingers from Sally's lips. She looked at him with wide, startled eyes, and without understanding, knew at once that he was to be obeyed.

"Yes," she said, playing a part to which Canfield impelled her for no reason of which she yet knew. "The fires are too warm in here. I've always heard that the Americans overheat their houses."

She did not wait for them but moved quickly down the room where Elizabeth had gone only moments before. The sharp staccato of her heels was the only sound. Canfield, watching the lovely spirited swing of the hips, the long legs, thought that she had acted instinctively as Devlin would have done, going forward with a kind of gallant gaiety into whatever waited for her. He had never hung back, and she did not either.

At the door she said, again improvising the role he demanded of her, "Is there a moon to-night? I would love to see the moon on the snow up there."

She had Devlin's kind of courage, he thought, and in the next few minutes, when he would have to tell her about Devlin, she would need all of it.

VII

There was no moon, but starlight washed on the high peaks where the snow lay, the clear air brought them close, sharpened them, so that they seemed just a hand's touch away. But under Sally's hand was the age-smoothed stone of the parapet; it was strange to feel the warmth of the day's sun still captured in it. She clung to it, and while the warmth remained in it, her own fingers grew cold as Canfield spoke, as he told them who Raedler was.

"Does this mean you think Dev's alive?" Hayward asked

the question first, his voice a hoarse, excited whisper. They had left the terrace in darkness, and they bunched together at the parapet, as if they drew support from one another.

"Elizabeth thinks he's alive," Canfield said flatly.

Sally spun around to face him, straining towards the pale blur of his face in the darkness.

"Do *you* think he's alive?" She had suddenly begun to shiver violently, her whole body shaking with an emotion that she couldn't control or keep hidden; she put her hand up to her jaw to try to hold it still. Josh slipped off his jacket, and she felt him arrange it about her shoulders and button it. But it did no good; the cold was inside her, the too sudden burst of hope and mixed with it fear of the grimness of Canfield's manner, the fear of Raedler, the fear because Elizabeth, believing him to be alive, was not permitted to reveal it.

"*Do* you?" she insisted.

"I don't know, Sal. I just don't know. We think——"

"We? Who is *we*? Who are *you*, Josh?"

He had dreaded to hear the anger and suspicion in her voice, and here it was. They had finally come to it. If the visit to St. Martin had told them nothing, she might never have had to know what it was he worked at behind the façade of Joshua Canfield, writer, or never needed to know in the context of her own father. The cover had now to be broken, voluntarily, because if they had needed her help to get in here, they would need it doubly to break through the barrier of hysteria and indifference with which Elizabeth had surrounded herself, the barrier of dominance. So she would have to be told—all of it. And he would have to risk everything that might come from this telling, her refusal to help, her retreat, the shattering of the precious communication that had grown between them. He thought of all the checking his people had done on Sally Devlin. She had checked out—an ordinary, sane, law-abiding girl, whose loyalties might be taken for granted. But what could be taken for granted where her attachment to Devlin was concerned? All that the checking could do was take the obvious things about her and add them up to a neat answer; what it could never take into account, not accurately, was the humanness, the love and the hate. These never showed in the records, and yet, if it came down to it, these were the reasons why each of them could be said to be here at St. Martin. Love went for himself and Sally and Hayward; Raedler might be on the side of hate, depending on which way you looked at it. And Elizabeth, was hers hate or love?

"Answer me!" Sally's voice cut into him.

He was making a mess of it, he thought. One of their regular men would have done better, would have found some way of reaching Elizabeth without involving Sally, or needing to tell her the real reason for the visit. The way he was handling it was unprofessional, messy; they always warned you that things got messy and dangerous once you let the human element get mixed into it. Translated that meant you could never care personally about the people who were in the business with you—you could certainly never fall in love with them.

Sally tugged furiously at his arm. "Answer me!"

He roused himself. "I'm trying to."

"Then try harder. Are you some kind of a policeman—I asked you that before. Do you remember when I asked you that?"

"I remember—and I told you the truth then. Partly the truth. I'm not a policeman. But they're not the only ones who are looking for the truth. That's all it is, really. That's what I tell myself I do when I'd rather not think about the rest of it." He was making a plea to her, a justification. And he knew at once that if he had come to this stage, he was finished. He was not going to be much use to them from now on. "Sometimes the truth is good—sometimes not. But we have to know it, otherwise we work in the dark. It's old-fashioned these days to talk about our country's enemies . . . but we haven't achieved our One World yet, and so we have to keep our eyes on those we're accustomed to calling our enemies. The habit of fear and suspicion is hard to shake—on both sides. And so we just go on gathering information . . ."

"Intelligence," she said. "You mean intelligence. *Intelligence.* I can understand that. I don't have to be told."

She was still angry, and she was still shaking. She turned on Hayward. "You too? Are you in this?"

"Only during the war, Sal. And about this business . . ." He shrugged. "I knew only a little more about it than you until this evening. Just," he added miserably, "that they needed to find out something about Dev."

"Then they——" This was said with a bitter jerk of her head towards Canfield, "didn't trust even you."

"That isn't the way it works, Sally," Canfield said. "We trust only those that we want—and only finally when we must. Even such people as Jackson Hayward."

"And what about Sally Devlin? Why are you finally trusting Sally Devlin? *Am* I being let in, or is it only because I've seen things here you can't explain away." A new thought struck her, and her voice rose, so that Hayward moved agitatedly to quiet her. "*That* was why you needed me to come to St. Martin—just to get to Elizabeth. What a stinking rotten way you work!"

"Yes," Canfield said. "All of that, Sally. These are the ways we work."

"God, I hate you!" In the faint light he could see her clenched fist half raised. "Why?" she said. "Why Dev? Why Elizabeth? What have they done?"

"Perhaps something is being done to them. There are two sides to it—remember I said we had to know the truth? Then listen to me, Sally. Listen carefully."

She subsided, and they drew closer together, a small circle by the parapet. Canfield longed to put his hand on her, to hold her, to steady the shivering which still gripped her. But he talked the words of suspicion, and she would have no part of him. He knew that he talked the words of an enemy as he began to recount the story of Devlin. He drew for them both the picture as it had steadily built up over the winter, his first sight of Kogan on the night that Devlin's disappearance became known, the ransacking of the flat, and the ominous appearance of Devlin's name in the report of Fergus's murder, the loss of the cypher. Nothing but odd coincidence until that recognition of Raedler as Zotov, and a realisation what his origins and connections were. When Canfield talked of the camera case, and the information whispered in the Kabul market-place that the wreck of Devlin's plane had been seen on the Soviet side of the river, it was Hayward who finally laid his hand on Sally's shoulder and tried to give her the comfort of that awkward contact.

"But he—his body was not there?"

"They say not."

"What does it prove?" she said fiercely. "You base all this on some garbled story told sixth-hand by some stall-keeper. What does he know—or care? I would bet someone paid him for that information. Why couldn't he have invented it all? If he was dead, why wouldn't the Russians say so? And if he's alive and he . . . and he defected, why wouldn't they tell the world? It would be quite a catch, wouldn't it, to have Lawrence Devlin go over. After all—he's no drunken homosexual like most of their other catches."

He took the taunt as she meant it. "Every bit of it could be coincidence—or fabrication. Except Raedler—he's real. And except for the fact that Elizabeth, for some reason, is convinced he's alive."

"So you are here to spy on her."

"Spy is a silly, useless word, Sally. There are very few spies in these times. There are people who collect information. Fergus carried information. But he was murdered for it. A collector or a carrier of information—and I don't know if Devlin was either of these things. I hope he wasn't."

"Spies are spies," she said. "I've been listening to you talk a lot of nonsense about who one's enemies are. But nothing changes the fact that spies are people who sell information—perhaps they sell other people. You have been poking about in my father's life, spying on him. You're here to spy on Elizabeth. I suppose you've been spying on me."

"Yes," he said, "and if we'd done it sooner we would have known just that much sooner that our so-called enemies had also been spying on you."

"On *me*!" She shrugged off Hayward's arm with a violent gesture of rejection. "What are you talking about?"

"At your flat. When we started to check you we found that they seem to go in and out—pretty much at will. We decided that it was without your knowledge, but we wondered that you hadn't discovered that yourself. People can usually tell when someone's been going through their things. Didn't you miss anything? We checked the police files, of course. There is no record of a complaint."

"No . . . there wouldn't be. I never made a complaint. There was never anything missing." Her tone had dropped; it was subdued, thoughtful. She was beginning to believe, Canfield thought. The doubt had begun and was working its ferment in her, as it had in him. She said, finally, "Why? Why were they searching? What were they looking for?"

"We don't know. But we think that whatever they were looking for in your studio, they had hoped they would find that time they broke into your father's flat."

"*That* was them? No! It wasn't! You're trying to tell me that they're common criminals who go about stealing things. You forget there were things stolen from the flat—the jade horse, the Chinese bowl. I would have supposed," she added, "that they had more to do than breaking into people's houses and stealing."

"It was made to look like house-breaking. We believe that they meant only to—go through the papers. We think that they were warned while they were actually in the flat that the news of Devlin's disappearance was already in the evening papers—they thought they might be discovered there, and they didn't have time to put back the papers as they had found them. So they made it look like a burglary by taking the pieces that were missing. In your studio they were more careful—but then they had all the time they needed. You never knew they were there. At least we believe," he said, "that you never knew they were there."

"I didn't," she answered slowly. "I never knew what they were searching for. Or why. What," she said again, "were they looking for?"

"We don't know. That's why we're here."

She looked up at him, and he knew from the rigid, pained set of her face that he had been wrong in thinking that she was beginning to believe. She had not crumbled, not yet. The doubt had begun, but it had not worked to its end; she still clung to what had been her life, and he was glad, because for him it would have been wrong if she had given up on Devlin so soon, so readily.

"No," she said. "That's not the final reason that you're here. You're here because you believe that Devlin has defected. Only your paid information gatherers haven't been able to tell you why. And now you want me to help you."

"Yes. I want you to help us."

He saw her fumble with the button of his jacket, and then she thrust it off her shoulders and it fell to the ground.

"What fools you are—you, Josh. Both of you. All of your kind of people. Lawrence Devlin is a great man. You were talking about it being old-fashioned to care about your country. It's old-fashioned—it's square—to talk about anyone being great. But I'm saying he was that. It's very simple. It's all you have to take into consideration. I know a lot of people said that Peace Prize was a political award. Maybe it was, in a sense. But I also know that he happened to believe all the things that he wrote that earned the Prize. That's what counted. If he's really gone behind the Iron Curtain he has his reasons. And they're good ones."

And then she was gone. They listened to her running steps on the terrace as the darkness received her. Then the brief flash of light as she opened and closed the door to the Great Hall.

"What do we do, Josh," Hayward said worriedly, humbly.

"I don't know. Let me think about it." But he wasn't thinking about it, or his inadequacy to handle it. Inside of him was a kind of shouting tumult of joy and pleasure because she had not at once bowed to the crack of officialdom, because she had kept on believing in Devlin.

THREE

The two men walked for a while on the small terrace outside the guest rooms before they finally parted for bed. By now Hayward had fully understood the need to avoid the microphones that could be hidden in the rooms; they had paced as they talked, so that their footsteps should mask their voices. This part of it Hayward understood and was familiar with; with the rest he had a kind of nervous need to take some action, any action.

"Can't we *tell* someone? The Swiss authorities?—splendid people."

"Where's the proof? Raedler is here by Mrs. Devlin's wish. Unless she makes the complaint, we're stuck."

"But good God—Dev may be alive! Are we to do nothing about it?"

"You heard what Sally said—if he went of his own will, then he had his reasons. If he went unwillingly, the Russians have yet to show their hand. We have to play their game to the end. If we announce to the world that Devlin may be there, and they want to deny it, they will simply dispose of him. No—Elizabeth Devlin is the key." He added slowly, with the beginning of despair, "And I don't know how to reach her."

He watched Hayward gloomily flick ashes over the low parapet. "You'll have to try," he went on, "since I've made such a mess of it with Sally. You'll have to try to get Elizabeth away from Raedler—talk about the Foundation, about the biography. It could be difficult. Raedler, I think will hardly let her out of his sight."

"Perhaps not as difficult as you think. We have some helpers in this house—helpers that Raedler can't count on." Then he related to Canfield what Lancome had told him about the staff, the quiet turmoil in the house since Elizabeth had arrived back from Zurich with Raedler, the antagonism towards him that only the devotion to Elizabeth kept from breaking into open revolt.

"The old ones will not desert her, you see. Lancome and a few others have been with her since she came here, almost twenty years ago. They hold the young ones in check. But all I have to do is tell Lancome that I must see Elizabeth alone. They will find a way. It will mean getting Raedler out of the way. The maid, whom Lancome says is really a nurse, will have to be shaken off. Though not even Raedler would be able to justify business conversations with the maid present . . . we'll see . . . we'll see. There must be a way."

Canfield searched Hayward's room in the same way he had searched his own. There was nothing he could see that indicated a microphone, but he wasn't an expert, and it was possible that Raedler was, or had used, an expert. He had a picture in his mind now of Raedler listening to the tape-recorded conversation between Lancome and Hayward. Hayward's own ignorance at that time had been his protection, but Raedler had been warned. He thought of Raedler listening to Lancome telling Hayward that Elizabeth had known, before the news arrived, that Devlin had vanished, and he cursed the excess of secrecy that had caused the blunder. If Hayward had been properly briefed before they left London, he would not have permitted Lancome to confide that information to a microphone. That was the way it worked sometimes too; secrecy created its own trap.

He didn't decline Hayward's suggestion of a last whisky and soda. It had begun to seem a very long time since they had boarded their aircraft in London that morning, and he thought they had probably had already too much to drink. But it had been that kind of day, that kind of evening. But finally Hayward let go the stub of his cigar, and drained his glass.

"To bed, dear boy—to-morrow there's work to do."

He made some suitable reply, and reflected sourly that since they had come in from the terrace, they had been talking for the benefit of a possible tape-recorder. And then he went back to his room, which greeted him, in spite of its muted luxury, with savage bareness. He thought of the girl in that immense room upstairs, thought of her arms about him and her kiss on his mouth, warm and hard; he wondered if there was anything to be salvaged from the wreck he had made of what had promised to be.

In spite of the interminable length of the day, and the weariness that seemed to numb his limbs, he was still awake when the telephone buzzed beside him.

"Josh—it's Sally. I'm coming down."

And that, he thought, would be something for the tape-recorder.

II

She looked to him now as she had done the first time he had seen her in Devlin's flat, the same sharp cast to the face, the eyes somehow sunken but too fiercely bright, the air of harried grieving, of something near desperation. Two hours had done this to her, he thought: in two hours she had come to wear something that resembled the tormented look of that ill and possessed woman they had seen downstairs.

"I've got to face this, haven't I?"

She had come down with an unbuttoned robe thrown over her nightgown, her feet bare. They sat now, Sally wrapped in a blanket, on the floor of the terrace, with their backs against the parapet. She had understood very quickly why this had to be so. The vague menace that the house had seemed to hold for her had found a tangible reason. She feared it less because she understood its nature.

"I mean—I can go away, can't I? I can just say, 'To hell with all of you. Solve your own problems. Don't expect any help from me to condemn my own father.'"

He lighted a cigarette for her, and placed it between her lips. She took it and drew on it hungrily, almost without noticing. He wondered if Raedler was watching somewhere above them, watching the points of light in the darkness. And what if he was?—it would just be something to keep him awake.

"Yes," he answered. She would have to be led to say the words of surrender herself. He had said too much; she must hear no more persuasion from him.

"It will last a day or two—a week or two, perhaps. The feeling that I've stuck by him, and refused to have anything to do with your lot. But if I don't know the truth, how can I ever tell if I did the right thing? What's there for me but endless wondering, years of it, probably. For ever, Josh . . ." Within the blanket, she suddenly began to shake again. "I couldn't take for ever . . . wondering. If there's ever to be any peace for me—any sanity—when this whole thing is over, I'll have to know the truth, or as much of the truth as any of you will know, as much as *she* knows. I don't believe there was a part of him that he was able to keep hidden from me and from everyone else for all these years, but if there was, I want to know that too. I don't believe there was—I think he died in just the way I've always thought he died. But if he's alive, then he didn't go over *to* them—he fought his way into them because he thought he could make some change. He must have had a plan. It's the kind of thing Dev might have done. He *could* be alive—but if you find that out, I believe you're going to find out too that he was working on something that none of us understood. If he's alive, something has gone wrong with his plan—*if* he's alive. And if he's alive, then he has to be got out alive. I can't say no to that. I can't refuse to help when that's a possibility. I can't do that."

"You may not like what we find out, Sal."

"I'll have to risk it, won't I? You see, I just don't *believe* Dev was on their side. I have to back that belief. I have to lay my money on that one, Josh. If I walk away from you—if I refuse to help—leave here—it could pull the whole thing apart, couldn't it?"

"Very nearly. We haven't much hope here without you, Sal. Yes, it could pull that whole thing apart. Hayward might break through to her, but I doubt it. He's too much a gentleman, too much afraid of hurting her. When she begins to bleed, he won't probe. He keeps thinking of her with Dev—and he just can't do it. And myself—I have no chance at all. She's living on an emotional level—and in the past—where someone like myself, who has no link to that past, could never hope to reach her. She knows the truth, whatever it is, but someone will have to force their way in on her consciousness before she'll speak. If anyone can do it, it will be you, rather than Hayward."

She sat for a while in silence, her head tilted back against the stone. Her body was still now, no longer shaking. She crushed out the cigarette against the flagstones. He lighted another cigarette from the end of his own and handed it to her.

"Why?" she said, "and how?"

"Why?—because her whole life and being now is Devlin, you are Devlin's flesh. No, wait—don't shake your head like that—it still happens, you know. The pull of a close resemblance, of a blood tie as close as yours, is very strong. I think she can't hold out."

"She's held out for five years. What will change her now?"

"They were the years she had Devlin. She didn't need anyone else. The difference is that you're here before her eyes. You're reality now, you're right here, and she hasn't Devlin to interpose. I don't think she can hold out," he said again. "I *know* she can't hold out. You saw what happened this evening . . ."

"Yes, I saw. And that's why I don't see how I can help. She wanted nothing to do with me. She would have had me thrown out if she could. Instead, she did the only other thing—she ran away herself."

"Have you ever seen anyone fighting an almost irresistible temptation, Sal? They either give in, or they run. To-night, she ran. I think the moment is coming when she can't run. When the temptation will be too much. You are the most of Devlin that's left. She has his manuscripts, the things he was working on, but *you* are his child. She's human, like the rest of us—and in desperate trouble, Sal. People in trouble usually need to talk about it, to tell someone. She's a woman whose business it is to communicate. She's been bottled up here all through the winter. No one to talk to. I've a feeling the need to speak must be nearly overwhelming. If she chooses to, I think it will be to you, or you will cause it to happen."

She drew on the cigarette thoughtfully. "She almost did—once."

"Did what?"

"Speak—communicate. Whatever it is you call it."

"When?" He didn't mean his tone to be sharp, but he couldn't help it.

"Just the time when Dev disappeared. The second day after I had the news—about three o'clock in the morning. There was a telephone call put through in her name. But before we could speak, the call was cancelled."

He stopped looking at her, and let his body sag against the stone alongside hers as a wave of dismay and frustration hit him. He thought of the winter of waiting and watching—time gone, lost. "I wish we had known, Sal. I wish very much we had known about that. It meant that at one time she wanted to get in touch—possibly to tell you what we want to know now. If we had known about that call we would have been thinking about all this in a different way. I think we would have got you here much sooner."

Her voice answered him, small and far away, retreating. "And who was I supposed to tell? Who *was* there to tell?"

"You're right. There was no one to tell—no one to whom it would have meant anything. If we had only told *you*—well, we didn't . . ." He shrugged. "That's been the trouble with this whole thing. No communication. We've been running around in official circles, and no one would risk making a break-through. It's all been a bloody mess. Oh, hell, Sal—I've had enough of it. I never meant to get this far into their business. In the beginning it was nothing much more than patriotic errands I did for them. But it's a difficult business to break away from, unless you've reason to break."

"Do you have a reason to break now?"

"Perhaps," he said. "But I have to see this to the end. As far as I'm able. That's something else that's wrong with it. Sometimes you never know what the end finally turned out to be, because someone else, someone across the other side of the globe, finished it up for you. For a writer not to know the ending is a hell of a frustrating way to live."

"Will you be *able* to leave it?"

"Perhaps," he said again. "Now forget about my problems,

Sal. We'll solve them later, if ever. Our job here is to watch Elizabeth. You have to wait for your chance."

"How will I know? I'm not much used to this kind of thing."

"You'll know." He smiled faintly, and didn't know whether, in the darkness, she could see it. "You're not stupid."

"You hope," she said shortly. "You make me nervous, Josh. Supposing I mess it up?"

"You won't. At least you won't do any worse than we've done up to now. Remember what I said to you in the car—lord, was it only a few hours ago?—that I'm here. Lean on me, Sal. You're going to need it. You're watching another woman in disintegration. But don't try to be a heroine yourself. Lean on me, cry if you want to. Do anything. But just keep watching Elizabeth. I think you'll know the time when it comes."

"I did remember—that's why I came down. Even hating you when I found out what you were, I couldn't believe that you said that to me just in the hope of getting me to confide. If you were acting as an intelligence agent then, well . . ." She drew a long breath. "Well, then, I'm a bad judge and I'll have deserved whatever mistake I've made this time. But I haven't made a mistake, have I, Josh?"

"No mistake. I never meant anything more in my life." Reaching into the folds of the blanket his hand sought hers. "God, you're cold. Your hand's like ice. Here—hang on a moment."

He left her, and came back with another blanket, and the brandy bottle and glasses. She giggled faintly as he poured it, "It's sort of mad, isn't it? Sitting here . . . Not very sensible, at any rate."

"I have the feeling, Sal, that very often you don't want to be sensible. Which is fine with me. I've sometimes had the feeling, all this last winter, that part of you didn't fit very well with Robert Halstead."

She turned to him sharply. "You've been following me about!"

"No—not that way. Not for them. Not until towards the end, when they had to know what kind of a person you were. No—it was just the impression I had of you that first day in your father's flat. I couldn't fit it with Halstead. I watched you that night at the opera. You seemed to be drifting from his side all the time—as if you were floating loose."

"I remember that night—I kept looking at you and wondering why I couldn't put a name to your face. Because I kept telling myself that if I ever had known you I wouldn't forget who you were. I almost went to you that night. I had a sudden feeling then that I'd known you somewhere else and had somehow lost you. I didn't want to let you go again." He felt her hand, still cold, clutch his. "Do I have to let you go, Josh?"

"Not unless you want to. But there's your Robert. I can't stand around and wait until you have some time you can spare from him. And I don't want a behind the scenes affair either. I've had enough of that. I can't tell you what an undignified thing it is to stand outside a woman's flat, and wait, like a thief, as many times as I've done this last winter. I've wanted to kick his bloody Aston Martin—and that's a pretty stupid way for a grown man to feel. I hope I'm not getting drunk, Sal. I'm talking. I'm not supposed to talk. But now I want to more than I've ever done in my life before."

"Yes, talk. Quickly, Josh—talk! What is it—fourteen years we've got to make up?"

"Fourteen years," he answered. "Does Robert get the next fourteen, Sal? I have to know."

"No—whether you do or not, Robert won't. I lost Robert somewhere. Somewhere on the way here I lost him. And since I've been here I've come into possession of myself again. I suddenly know that I don't want my life ordered and moulded. I don't want to be told what to do, and how to do it. I don't want a Raedler in my life—tidy, clever, quick. I would lumber behind him, and I couldn't ever love him enough to be his buffoon. I amuse him now, but pretty soon he'd start being impatient with me—I'm clumsy, untidy, and my feelings get hurt easily. Robert wouldn't take time to understand how important it is to have hurt feelings mended by a little patience. It's quicker and easier to have Miss Ritchards telephone for some flowers. I'm a mess, Josh. Robert thinks I'm a charming mess now—but when I'm forty, he's going to find my being a mess an awful bore. I've thought I could change for him, but I can't. I don't even want to change."

"Change? Why on earth?"

"I don't know—or change to what. But Robert makes me feel as if I *should* change . . ."

Josh sat very still and watched her drawing on the cigarette and occasionally sipping the brandy, and he listened without interruption while she talked. He listened while she talked herself out of Robert Halstead. He listened while she drew the outlines of the dimensions of Halstead in her life, right back to the beginning, and then listened while other names came tumbling on his. He listened to the discovery of first love, and the loss of it, and the slow dawn of apprehension and disillusion. Through it all the name of Devlin came and went; Devlin also had listened to these stories. Canfield saw Sally grow from the child—almost as far back as the time he had seen her on the mountainside in Ireland, to the woman who had walked into Devlin's flat that day back in October.

"Of course when Dev married Elizabeth I was sort of on my own. But I was twenty-one then, and you expect to live your own life. He was always there to talk to, though. Funny . . . I never thought of him in connection with women. Fool, wasn't I? I haven't talked to anyone like this before. You listen awfully well, Josh."

"I seem to have been standing outside your door for a long time waiting to hear anything at all you cared to say to me. You think I'm an idiot?—well, I'm an idiot. Every man is at times, over certain things or people. It's better to know it."

"What else are you, Josh? I want to know everything you are."

"There's time, Sal. There's plenty of time for that."

"How do we know?" she demanded. "How do we know

what will happen? Suppose this turned out like the night in Covent Garden? You might just disappear. And I wouldn't have known you—only this small bit, and it's not enough."

"I'm not going to disappear." But he talked, knowing at once the feeling that he hadn't known for years, so long ago that it was almost forgotten, of complete release. They could not fully see each other's faces; to aid them was the kind of quick intimacy that can be reached in the darkness. He found it easier than he expected to talk about Linda, and about the marriage. "We expected too much from each other," he said. "I've grown more human since then—I don't know if she has, but it doesn't matter. Linda isn't in my life any more. What I don't deny is the part she was."

As he talked, he kept moving forwards and backwards in time from that morning on the mountain.

"Funny," she said. "I don't remember you then. I don't remember that morning more than any other morning. How is one to know?"

"One doesn't."

He told her what had happened after that morning, not disguising the role Devlin had played in whatever he had decided to do.

"I admit that I was looking for something that was not routine. After that morning I knew I just couldn't go back to teaching, even if I starved trying to do something else. At times I seemed to come pretty close to it, I remember. For a while back in those years I thought I was trying to be another Devlin. Then I found out it wasn't only impossible. I didn't even want it."

"I don't want it either."

"Are you sure of that?"

"There's only one Dev. That's what Elizabeth said. I loved him, too, but I'm not looking for another Dev. I want a man of my own—a man of my time, my choosing."

He did not answer to that. He did not want to take the moment further than it was; almost, he was afraid to, as if the gods of good fortune had been tempted enough. There was the feeling too, of greed, that he must hold back some, as if he had been starving and couldn't quite believe the promise of abundant food, and so must scrimp on his first good meal. For the time being, enough would be enough.

He turned to her, and was startled to find that he could see her face clearly now. Around them was the debris of their night; the litter of cigarette butts, the glasses, the half-emptied brandy decanter. Behind her head, the mountains were beginning to be outlined against a lightening sky.

He rose; his limbs felt stiff and the morning had grown chill. He held out his hand to help her.

"I'll take you upstairs," he said.

She almost tripped in the folds of the blanket. He steadied her, but let go his hold almost at once, not able to trust himself in even the briefest embrace, because in her dishevelment and weariness she seemed to him more desirable than he had ever seen her. She was beauty stripped down to an essential essence, without artifact, too tired for coquetry. Through the brandy and his own fatigue, he was agonisingly aware of her body through the careless robe.

She leaned against him as he led her back through his room. "I've stayed up all night talking before this," she said. "Any number of times. And it's never been to any purpose. Before to-night, it seems as if I've never talked in my life before."

He touched her lightly on the head, as one would pat a sleepy child. It was as much as he could let himself do.

"Open the curtains, Josh," she said when they had reached her room, and she had flung aside her robe and slid between the sheets. "That's the east there, isn't it? I want to see the sun come up along the valley."

He did as she asked him, drawing back the thick curtains from the window that faced towards Sion and the east. On the floor of the valley the twin mounds of the town were beginning to emerge. In the farms dotted all over the lower mountainsides the cocks had begun crowing. He clenched the fold of the curtains between his fingers, and wondered how he was to make that walk past the huge bed where she lay, past that to the door.

"Josh?"

He turned and looked at her. She was raised on one elbow, and the mass of her burnished hair had slipped forward across half her face, and lay silkenly on her bare shoulders. In the pale light her breasts seemed luminous and incredibly white. Her smile was serene.

"This will be our second sunrise," she said, as he went to her.

FOUR

The sun was fully risen, and there was even the beginning of some heat in it when Josh came back to the terrace outside his own room. He carried the glasses and decanter to the sitting-room, and returned for the blankets. They had lain in the sun, and as he gathered them up in his arms, the scent came to him, faint, almost vanished, of the perfume Sally wore. He remembered the first time he had smelled it, the day he had hidden with Price in her studio and had known that he had fallen in love with the young woman whose presence had haunted him through the winter. He stood in the sun, staring absently down at the terraces of vineyards below the sheer drop, wondering how a man like Josh Canfield could have fallen in love when he had long ago given up the idea that romantic and wayward things could happen to people like him and at his age. Now he was not in love; quite simply, he loved. "I love," he said to himself. "I love her," he added aloud, to hear how it sounded. It sounded good—the best thing he had ever heard himself say. He felt as if he had been readmitted to the world, integrated, alive to it in a way he had not been since the time he had been very young. There was a kind of hopefulness in him that belonged to that younger time. He leaned against the parapet, the blankets clutched in his arms like a talisman, and viewed the new world that he had acquired that morning. He found it wonderfully beautiful, intense, throbbing with a kind of life and spirit that pervaded all his senses; he breathed the air of his new world deeply, sucked it up. His vision seemed sharpened and given awareness; he did not look any longer, he saw—saw the sun on the ancient stone, the grey green of the vines, the dusty swing of the traditional black skirt of the Valaisian peasant-woman as she made her way along a path among the vines. The arrogant roosters had ceased their chorus; he heard the muted clinking of the cow-bells from the distant hillsides, and somewhere closer, the soft cries of doves. The insects were awaking to the scents of the spring day, of fruit trees and sweet new grass. There seemed to be a tumult of small and lovely sounds. He listened to it with ears sharpened and grateful. "I love her," he said again.

And then one more sound was added, something very close, persistent, rhythmical, something not belonging to the other sounds. He forced himself to block out everything else, and to listen only to that. Then he leaned far over the parapet and looked to see where the sound came from. By twisting sideways he could catch the blurred arc of a rope as it flashed through the air and hit the flagstones, producing the swish-and-tap, swish-and-tap sound that had intruded upon him.

It was Raedler there, on one of the château's jutting ramparts, clad in a grey track-suit, and the skipping rope rose and fell with the rhythm of long practice. His feet were held together; he jumped precisely, evenly, with an effortlessness that told Canfield that the man was in superb physical condition. It was a disturbing sight, the alert, watchful Raedler skipping easefully in the early morning sun. It all but destroyed the world that Canfield had tried to enter, dragging him back to the problems of the hour and the day, dragging him back into the shadow of the fear that lay on this house.

He turned and went back inside, and he ran the shower very cold, and stayed under it, gasping, for a long time, until the sweet languor of the sunrise was stripped from him, the night of no sleep forgotten, until he could face Raedler again.

II

When he was dressed he went, without knocking, into Hayward's bedroom. With the curtains closed, the room was dark;

from the bed came the sounds of the publisher's peaceful, deep-toned snore. Before he pulled back the curtains, Josh turned on the radio beside Hayward's bed, loudly, so that even the first sound of protest was masked, if not drowned, by the noise.

"Josh!—what on earth?' His tone subsided at once as he recognised Josh's warning gesture, and remembered how he must act. He struggled out of his sleep, and listened intently, as Josh, with the radio turned up high, whispered directions to him.

In fifteen minutes Hayward had completed the task of shaving, showering and dressing, with only one cut on his chin, and a string of a mild, muttered abuse. He was holding a paper tissue to his chin as they made their way towards the back stairs, Hayward straining his memory for the geography of this ancient house where stairs and passages led off deceptively to nowhere, or turned about on themselves. But they found their way at last to the back passages where the kitchen sounds told them that they were nearer to Lancome's pantry. It was empty; Hayward put his head inside the kitchen and motioned towards a young footman. The whole kitchen came abruptly to a halt as Hayward pulled the young man outside the swing-doors and told him to find Lancome at once. If Lancome happened to be in the presence of Monsieur Raedler he was to say that the chef required the presence of M. Lancome in the kitchen immediately. The beginning of amusement lit the young man's face as he listened and nodded, and Canfield knew that it was not only the old ones who were with them against Raedler.

Lancome arrived within a few minutes, breathing heavily, as if he had been hurrying. He was puzzled but agreeable when Canfield motioned that they should withdraw to the private bathroom that belonged to the butler's suite, and turn on all the taps fully. They kept their voices low and the water roared above them as Canfield explained what he wanted. Lancome listened carefully, and then a slow smile began on his wintry lips.

"It can be arranged?" Canfield asked.

" I am certain of it, Monsieur."

" And discreetly?"

" With the utmost discretion."

" And beyond this first step—the man in the town?—it can be fixed with him? He will co-operate?"

" This is a small town, Monsieur. We are all more or less related, and this house has given much employment and much patronage in the past. If Monsieur Raedler should be in touch with this man's superior . . ." Lancome shrugged. " I cannot answer for that. But for *this* man, here in St. Martin. Yes—for him I can answer."

And then he led them quickly down into the cellars of the house to the place where Canfield hoped he could show him what he wanted done. They walked along stone passages where no daylight ever reached, passed massive iron-studded doors; down here, not even the efficiency of Elizabeth's heating system and the glare of the many lights could quite drive out the sense of age and damp. They had come down to the living rock foundations of St. Martin.

Lancome paused as he searched for his key, and again the strange smile touched his face.

" Other things have begun to change, Messieurs," he said. " And Madame herself has started them. You will see—you will see when you go to the dining-room where Monsieur Raedler waits."

And then he swung back the door and stepped aside to let them enter.

III

Canfield and Hayward made their way back to their rooms by the same route they had come, and then emerged again, as if it was for the first time. For Raedler's benefit, Hayward made conversation as they came down the stairs and crossed the Great Hall to the dining-room.

" One thing I've always liked about staying here is that you get a decent breakfast—none of that Continental rubbish about some coffee and a miserable croissant or two. Elizabeth always put up the kind of breakfasts one used to get on hunting days in country houses before the war in England. Never see anything like it these days. She did it to please Dev, of course. And he could see that it pleased her to do it, and I don't think he ever let on that before they were married he never ate any breakfast at all. Odd what people will do to please someone, isn't it?—well, here we are," he added as he opened the door.

The room was empty except for Raedler. There was no food on the sideboard, nor any places laid at the table. Hayward stopped short. "Oh, good morning—have we come to the wrong place?" he said to Raedler. "I always remember it being here."

"Good morning, Mr. Hayward—Mr. Canfield." Raedler's smile was as before, correctly polite, not too expansive, just the right shade of formality. He was carefully dressed, his hair was neat, but not offensively so, he looked as if he had slept well. He probably had, Canfield thought—in whatever little time he had had to sleep. Canfield was uncomfortably reminded of the efficient skipper on the terrace, the athlete who greeted the sun religiously with his exercises. The man was formidable.

"This morning," Raedler added, "there is a small change. Madame has decided to have breakfast served on the terrace. I have waited here to inform you . . . so if I may lead the way."

"Thanks," Hayward said. "I don't think we shall get lost between here and the terrace—shall we, Josh?"

Raedler gave his slight bow, and again his smile which this time seemed to stick somewhat. "In that case, may I accompany you? I have not yet, myself, breakfasted."

"By all means," Hayward said magnanimously. "Go ahead, Josh." He gestured, and then glanced back at Raedler. "I'm glad to hear Mrs. Devlin feels well enough to appear this morning. And out on the terrace, too—well, nothing better than the sun for someone who's feeling a bit off colour, wouldn't you say? Nothing better."

"I agree, of course," Raedler answered. "We are, naturally, delighted."

He was not delighted, Canfield knew. Elizabeth had given

an order and Raedler had not felt strong enough to countermand it. The position had begun to break, to crumble. A change, even this tiny change, had come; Canfield guessed that, of all things, it was change that Raedler was not equipped to deal with. He felt almost lighthearted as he stepped out into the sun.

Elizabeth greeted them with a determined attempt at animation. "Good morning. Good morning. I hope you both slept well. I thought you would enjoy breakfast out here. The sun . . . we get used to it here in this valley—hot and dry. But I always remember English people holidaying on the Continent and acting as if they would never see the sun again in their lives. I couldn't understand it until I'd lived a year or two in London."

"It is, of course," Hayward said, "the only reason why we ever think of leaving our blessed plot of earth. A little sun is all we ask to take back with us, and it's most kind of you, Elizabeth, to arrange a little more of it for us." He bent over her hand. "How charming you look this morning, my dear."

She had taken some trouble, Canfield thought; her clothes had been chosen with care, not thrown on with the indifference of a sick and distracted woman. She was wearing slim creamy pants and a suède jacket that exactly matched them. Her eyes were hidden behind dark glasses, and the large-brimmed hat, the kind that Garbo used to wear, shaded and screened her face. The shocking-pink blouse threw a kind of glow on to her skin, so that it was almost possible to believe that she was not ill at all, only rather tired.

"May I ask, Mrs. Devlin," Canfield said, "are your clothes by Pucci?"

"How clever of you—how can you tell?"

"Frankly, I can't. I'm told it's a name that all fashionable women revere, and I thought I couldn't go wrong. They are, in fact, extremely becoming."

He could not see her eyes, but her smile had the beginning of warmth. "For that, Mr. Canfield, you may pour me some coffee. No, no, Raedler—Mr. Canfield will do it. No, nothing to eat," she added, as he gestured towards the dishes set out on a side-table, and kept hot with spirit lamps. "I've already eaten—but do help yourself. You will find all the things an Englishman likes for breakfast. I learned them all from Dev—he was always such a wonderful breakfast eater."

Canfield returned to seat himself at the round table laid with a bright pink fringed cloth, and partly shaded by a striped umbrella; the crested white china of last night had given place to a blue and white pattern, the honey and jam pots sparkled in the sun. The scene had a certain intimacy and gaiety, a mark of a hostess who knew how to create the atmosphere she desired. It was what, yesterday, this place had totally lacked—a presence to hold it together, to give it life, to prevent it being a museum. It was a change that seemed to make Raedler uneasy.

The man now hovered behind Elizabeth. "Permit me to adjust the umbrella a little, Madame. I fear the sun will be too much for you."

"Nonsense!" Her head jerked round to him swiftly. Canfield could not see Elizabeth's face, but the reflection of her look appeared on Raedler's own, fleetingly, and swiftly erased, a look of challenge thrown out and accepted. "The sun will do me no harm. Now do sit down and have your breakfast. No—not there. Miss Devlin will sit there. You have sent word that we are out here?"

"I have dispatched Marie, Madame. I wonder, though, if Miss Devlin will care to come down. She may be tired and prefer to breakfast in her room." Raedler's glance moved sideways to Canfield as he spoke, and the other man knew that the glow of their cigarettes on the terrace had been watched. It was possible Raedler had even counted the butts; he was that kind of man. "The journey must have been tiring," Raedler added.

"Dev's daughter . . ." Elizabeth pronounced the words carefully, and then repeated them as if they were a new discovery. "Dev's daughter was practically born travelling. I should be surprised if she is too tired to come down."

The change, Canfield thought, had gone deeper than the

clothes and the gay table under the umbrella. Or perhaps the need was greater than even he had suspected. Sally had become "Dev's daughter." If they could stay long enough, the change could run beyond Raedler's control.

Raedler inclined his head slightly in answer, and then settled to his place opposite Elizabeth. Canfield noticed that his food was carefully moderate, the choice of a man who eats for energy, but never to gain a pound of weight. This morning, however, he had not even spread his half pat of butter before Lancome came striding across the terrace towards the group. Raedler's back stiffened, and he laid down his knife.

"What is it, Lancome?" It should have been Elizabeth who asked the question. Lancome ignored him.

"Madame—I regret. The electricity is off. Nothing works. I have telephoned the town, and everything is normal there. It is a problem of the château, Madame."

Elizabeth nodded her head, the big hat dipping. She said, casually, and Canfield noticed the slight malice in her tone. "A problem. How tiresome for you, Raedler."

Raedler rose. "I will go and get my keys."

"Yes, do that. We will be quite safe here." Raedler gave her one backward look as if not quite believing her mockery as he followed Lancome back to the house.

"I think, Mr. Canfield, that I will have something to eat after all. I'm afraid I was less than truthful when I said I had eaten. I simply wasn't hungry until now."

IV

The sound of the tapping came to Sally as she slept; she woke to it and was not sure, at first, that it was not still the dream, and the sound was the light rain of a dream. But consciousness came fully, and the sound persisted still. It became a waking sound. The room was flooded with the morning light, and she remembered that Josh had drawn back the curtains. They had had their sunrise together. She smiled and closed her eyes again, and wanted to hold the memory, and to shut out the obtrusiveness of the day. But the sound persisted, and impelled, and at last she turned and looked at the clock on the table beside her and saw that she had slept only a short time, and that Josh had barely gone.

She left her nightgown where it lay on the bed and pulled her robe about her. The light was harsh and strong when she leaned from one of the south windows to look down below; she blinked and squinted and it was some moments before she found the source of the sound, and made out Raedler's figure in the grey track-suit, on a small jutting terrace—more a rampart than a terrace—on a level half-way between her room and the guest-rooms below. His eyrie commanded a view of all of this south side of the château, and each level of its terraces, and by turning he could follow the line of the river until the mountains closed up at either end. The rope flashed in the sun with a powerful hypnotic rhythm, accompanied by the slap-slap on the flagstones. He would stop for breath soon, she thought, but he went on. It seemed part of the inhuman quality of Raedler that he did not stop for breath, and this, too, had a part of Robert in it. In a different fashion, Robert had not stopped for breath either. She thought of what Josh had told her about Raedler, who he was, what he was, and in the strong sun she shivered. She thought, too, of Elizabeth, who had borne this man alone for all these months. For whatever reason Elizabeth had done this, or had had to do it, it took courage of a kind to endure him and not to crumble completely; but she was near to it—time and illness were working on her, and suddenly the tapping of Raedler's rope seemed more like the cracking of an imperative whip, the sound ugly and brutal. He seemed so supremely in command there on his perch, overseeing the whole château, confidently facing the morning sun. Sally thought that he had probably seen her up here at the window, and she drew back. But she stayed in the alcove, sitting on the stone bench and letting the sun play on her. The sound went on—endlessly it seemed. Her eyelids drooped and closed.

The image of Robert was back again, but it seemed to have lost its power, its dominance. To-day—yes, to-day, since that was the day that Josh had set her free—she would write to Robert. She would write and tell him that it was over between them; she would tell him about Josh, but he would not understand. She would have to tell him in terms as strong as she could muster, or he would not believe that she was capable of making this kind of decision by herself. He would be angry, and for a time his pride would be hurt, and then he would begin to forget whatever it was in her that had drawn him, and he would remember only the parts that he had wanted to change; even, in time, he would be glad that he had not had to go through the effort of changing her, or more, that he had not had to suffer the penalties of failure with her. He would find a woman moulded more to his liking, and he would forget that it had ever hurt to love. She told herself these things out of a sense of guilt and compassion; wonderingly, she even knew that she pitied Robert—she pitied herself as she had been until now—because neither of them had known that kind of fearful joy that had come to her on this morning. But she would not write that to Robert. He could forgive her, in time, what she was doing to him now, tell himself that she had always been far too impulsive, console himself by reflecting that by going to Josh Canfield she had made a mess of her life, as he had always been afraid she would. He would think these things, and forgive her, and even be relieved that she was gone; but he would never forgive her her pity. So she would not be gentle in her letter, because there was no gentle way to say what she must say, and Robert would take gentleness as an insult. She began to compose the phrases of the letter in her mind, but the thought of Josh kept breaking in, and she could not deny him, could not deny the feeling of ease and trust that he had given to her, could not deny the warmth and the sweet fatigue that he had left with her.

"I hope I do not disturb M'selle."

She wakened with a jerk. The woman whom she had sent away the night before stood close to her, her head cocked enquiringly.

"Oh—no, I was awake. I just dozed . . . what time is it? Am I late for something?"

The woman smiled. It was a real smile, not Raedler's one. "No, no, M'selle. It is just that the electricity has failed, and no bells ring downstairs. I thought you might need something . . . and then Madame has given a message."

"A message . . . for me?"

"Madame breakfasts on the terrace this morning, M'selle—the big terrace."

"She has sent for me?" Sally jumped to her feet.

"Not *sent* for you, M'selle. It is just that Madame breakfasts on the terrace this morning with her guests. She has not done this for so long. . . ." Sally was startled to see, suddenly, tears stand out in the woman's eyes. "So gay . . . the parasol up. Madame picks her clothes herself. Suddenly so different, after all this time. She has been alone for so long . . . no one comes. She speaks to no one. Then you are here, and it is almost as it used to be."

"I suppose . . ." Sally said. "She must have been very lonely since my father went."

"Lonely! Ah . . ." The woman flung out her hands. "I have been with Madame for nearly twenty years. Everywhere with her—Paris, New York, London. She speaks to me always—what is happening, what is doing. Suddenly, no more. She speaks no more—except to herself sometimes when she forgets I am there. She goes silent. Until this morning. Then she is up, and tells me she will have breakfast with everyone on the terrace. I can't believe it. But she is there now."

"Then quickly." Sally started towards the bathroom. "I have to get down."

"I have the bath running, M'selle. If you will tell me what you will wear . . ."

"Anything will do," Sally called back to her. "What *I* wear to-day isn't important."

V

Elizabeth was tiring, Canfield thought. The effort was still being made, but it was becoming visible. She had started to eat with a show of enthusiasm, but it had evaporated, and now the knife and fork were set down, and she sipped her coffee—holding the cup between both hands, as if that also had become an effort.

But he saw her make the last and greatest effort, saw her gather together her resources as Sally came, half running, across the terrace. As he rose, his gaze moved quickly between Elizabeth and Sally. Sally was wearing very little make-up, and she should have looked tired, should have betrayed the long night. But she wore the badge of the night's ending still in a tender radiance, bearing it with pride. Canfield hoped his own smile wasn't possessive but there wasn't much he could do about it.

"I'm sorry—I'm late." She had looked first at Elizabeth, but her glance went to Canfield at once, a questioning glance, and he felt desperate that she still had to question, that he had left her with even the slightest doubt. So as she seated herself at the chair he held, he let himself hold her shoulders for just a second, and he didn't care that the gesture was possessive, or that both Elizabeth and Hayward saw it.

"No, not late," Elizabeth said. "But I'm happy that you came down. I hoped to catch a glimpse of you before they make me go off and rest. It is very tiresome, all this resting."

Suddenly she took off the dark glasses, a move that Canfield thought could have been to let her look at Sally more closely, or could have been the small mark of courtesy that allowed Sally to see her. The two women stared at each other across the table.

"I don't have to ask—you have had a good night," Elizabeth said. "This morning you look . . . blooming." She turned swiftly to Hayward. "Don't you think so, Jackson? Wouldn't Dev like to see her now—here."

The publisher looked bewildered, as if something was happening he had not caught up with. "Yes—of course. Yes, indeed he would. Yes, blooming." He looked closely at Sally. "The only time I realise that I'm not young is when I see someone who *is* young. Looks as fresh as a daisy after all that travelling yesterday . . . and last night . . . and everything . . ." he finished lamely.

"You'll have something to eat," Elizabeth said. "What would you like?"

Canfield had moved to the side-table and was lifting the lids of the dishes so that she could see to choose.

"Everything," Sally said. "I could eat everything there."

Elizabeth laughed. It was a strange sound; Canfield realised they had not heard her laugh before. But this came loud and natural. "You see, Jackson—*that's* what it means to be young! She will eat everything."

Sally coloured, and looked uncertainly at Elizabeth. "I must seem a pig. But it all looks so good . . . and I *am* hungry."

"Of course you're hungry," Elizabeth answered. "Yesterday was a very long day." The way she said it made Canfield wonder if she also had watched the cigarettes glowing in the darkness. If she had, she didn't mind. She was treating Sally with a strange gentleness, a kind of a brooding interest that wanted, just now, to pamper and coddle her.

"Mr. Canfield, please cut Sally just a slice of that smoked ham there. It's a Valaisian specialty—very strong tasting and tough. They live on it all winter up there in the mountain villages. Dev had it every morning for breakfast."

Canfield held out a strip to Sally on a fork. She took it between her fingers and bit into the curling, dark meat. "It takes some chewing," she said, "but it's good."

"You must take her," Elizabeth said to Canfield, "up to Evolène for lunch. They will give you that, and cheese and Fondant to eat. To-morrow you can take her to Crans-Montana, where it is fashionable, but for the first day she should see a high Alpine village, a real one. It's primitive up there—only the climbers go. It was the first place I took Dev. He didn't tell me, lovely man, until much later, that he'd already seen it. He let me show it to him, and I did, just like a newspaper woman—as if I were the only one ever to have found it. I remember . . ."

She put on her glasses again quickly. "Yes," she added. "You must take her to Evolène."

Then she leaned back in her chair as if she were very tired, and the thought of Evolène had stirred more memories than she could share now, or wanted to share. She lapsed into complete silence, and behind the glasses, Canfield thought that her eyes were focused on nothing—nothing but the far mountains. She seemed to have slipped away from them.

Canfield filled Sally's cup. "I'll take you to Evolène," he said. "That is, if you promise you won't tell me later you've already been there. If you have, never admit it. I want it to be the first time."

"I swear it's the first time, I have never been to Evolène. Are you coming, Mr. Hayward?"

He put down his cup. "Me?—I think not, Sal. Those roads—of course, it's admirable that the Swiss manage to get roads into those places at all. But no—I've been to one or two high Alpine villages, and it's not something I care to repeat. I was once in a car when we met one of those postal buses on a narrow bend. We were on the outside. They have the right of way, of course. No—I don't think I'll go."

Elizabeth's silence enforced a silence on them all, but it was, Canfield thought, a more companionable silence than he could have hoped for. Something of ease and trust was growing up between Elizabeth and the people about her. Sally had stopped casting her quick, wary glances at the older woman after every bite; she ate her food steadily and with enjoyment, and when her plate was empty, she automatically handed it to Canfield for another helping. He refilled everyone's coffee cup, and Elizabeth put in sugar and stirred and sipped almost without noticing what she did. Wordlessly he offered her a cigarette, and she took it and let him light it, only nodding absently in thanks. Nothing was said until Lancome's footsteps on the flagstones roused her.

"Lancome? What is happening about the electricity?"

"Who knows, Madame?" he said cheerfully. "Monsieur Raedler has been down in the electricity vault, but I think he does not know what is wrong. Monsieur sends for Maurice, who knows something of these things, and always puts in the fuses when they go, but to-day Maurice is off. He set out for Hérens at dawn—Maurice is a climber, you remember, Madame."

"So . . . ?"

"So, Madame, Monsieur Raedler is now on the telephone.

He has attempted to reach an electrician in Sion, but they are engaged in work at Montana. So he tries Sierre . . . if no one can come, he says he must try the firm in Zurich who made the installation. He has asked me for their name—I remember them very well, since it all took so long."

Elizabeth looked amused. "That seems very extreme, Lancome? It just may be a little fuse."

"That may be so, Madame—but when one looks at all the boxes and cables down there, it seems like a power station, and where is one to distinguish the particular fuse? Monsieur is very perturbed."

"No doubt," Elizabeth said. "However, we shall leave it to him. Being Raedler, he will find a solution."

"Extraordinary," Hayward said. "I just cannot think of being without electricity in Switzerland, of all places. But still, fuses are fuses . . . Never have understood them myself."

"Can we manage in the meantime, Lancome?" Elizabeth asked.

"Assuredly, Madame. I have ordered the perishable food to be taken down to the cellars. The candles I always have on hand. It may be necessary to start the men pumping water by hand but that can be done. Not hot water, I am sorry, but the weather is favourable. The old wood stoves we have still in the kitchens. But if it is only a little fuse . . ." He shrugged. "Such a fuss, Madame." He evidently enjoyed the display of his organisational talents. "It is no different from the old days before Madame made all the improvements. In those days, though, one knew what to expect. Now, a little fuse goes wrong, and the ménage no longer functions."

Elizabeth shrugged. "Do not trouble yourself, Lancome. That is for Monsieur Raedler. Just one thing . . . take the keys from Monsieur Raedler and bring up some of the Romanée-Conti. To-night, we must make a welcome dinner . . . yes, to-night I will be well enough to come to dinner. And now, Lancome . . . tilt the umbrella a little, if you please. Bring fresh coffee and clear the dishes. I will stay a little longer."

"Certainly, Madame." The old man adjusted the umbrella

so that its shade lay across Elizabeth; watching, Canfield saw the thin lips of the old man stretched in a secret grin of pleasure. He touched Sally's arm lightly.

"Finish your coffee," he said. "I have an urge to be up in the high mountains. You can have your next cup up there . . . if Mrs. Devlin will excuse us."

"Why did you leave?" Sally said. "This might have been our chance. She might have begun to talk . . . with Raedler out of the way."

"Not to the three of us," Josh answered. "We mustn't crowd her—or try to push. She's known Hayward longest . . . and accepts him. Let him have the first try. If it doesn't work with him, we'll have to invent some other way to get Raedler away from her."

"Then you . . . *You* blew the fuse?"

They halted at the top of the staircase that Sally had called "The Street" leading down to the parking space, the old stone steps lined with the small houses and the window-boxes of geraniums. To-day it seemed to swarm with the life that yesterday had deserted it; about five young children played a ball game with practised disregard of the uneven ground, two babies were in neighbouring playpens, a younger one slept in a pram, the doors to the cottages stood open to the sun, and the sounds of radios and voices reached them clearly. A woman sat in a doorway peeling beans; a dog saw them and started towards them.

"A fuse?—well, it needs more than one blown fuse to put a place like this into darkness. What I did was to show Lancome how to trip the transformer. It seemed to me that a house this size, and so recent a restoration, would have to have a big power supply. And there it was—down in one of the cellars—the most beautiful switchboard installation I've ever seen. Rows and rows of fuse boxes . . . immaculate, beautiful. Of course, it wouldn't have meant much if Raedler had happened to know much about these things. I figured he would have to have a weak spot *somewhere* . . ."

"How long will it take to fix?"

"No time at all—once the right man looks at it. The transformer will have to be reset, that's all. I'm hoping it will take a long time for Raedler to find the right man. Lancome already spirited away *his* man, so with a little luck Raedler will have a few hours of trouble, and Elizabeth will have a few hours of peace."

The dog had reached them, a happy-looking mongrel who raised his nose to Canfield's hand. Canfield squatted and fondled his ears. "Whose mutt are you?" he said.

"Josh—how do you know about things like transformers?"

He looked up at her. "I told you I was an unwilling landlord. Well, wages being what they are in London, I've been forced into becoming an amateur electrician, plumber and carpenter. I'm not much at any of these things, but I've learned enough to know when I'm being cheated by the so-called experts. I've given up paying for switchboxes that were never installed and gallons of paint that never got on the walls. Result is, all the local contractors know me, and won't work for me any more."

"I *knew* there had to be something wrong with you—you're a black-hearted landlord, that's what you are. Now stop making up to that dog . . . the ladies all the way down the stairs are waiting to eye you. I'm going to hang on to you very hard, and let them know what's what."

"They've come out to look at Dev's daughter . . . but if it will help to make you jealous I'll smile at all of them."

"Just save your smiles for me. That's all you have to do."

They started down; there were smiles from every doorway. "*Bon jour, M'selle . . . Monsieur. Bon jour . . .*"

One of the toddlers in the playpen gravely offered his rattle for inspection, and as Sally stopped to speak to him the mother came and smoothed out his blond hair proudly, and straightened his overalls, all the time talking rapidly. Most of it escaped Sally except the repetition of "Monsieur Devlin."

When they reached the car Sally said, "It was too quick for me. What did she say?"

"She said that Monsieur Devlin came and talked with the children almost every day he was here. They loved Devlin."

" They loved him? But yesterday they took in the children and closed the doors."

" Yesterday Raedler was with us."

VI

Sally had been mostly silent on the drive up to Evolène, and he had said nothing about the car that he kept in sight in the rear view mirror. There was no reason to believe yet that the two men who had sat looking at maps in the car in the square of St. Martin were anything but tourists, and no reason why they should not be headed to Evolène also. Once one had started on that upward spiral of the mountain road, there was no place to turn off. They passed through the small villages where the chalets of hand-hewn logs seemed to perch precariously on their pedestals of stone, looming over the narrow streets. The road pushed deep into the valley, passed by tunnel through the weird, wind-eroded shapes of white rock called the pyramids of Euseigne, crossed the spring torrent of the Borgne by narrow bridge. High up on the slopes they could see small clusters of houses, and sometimes whole villages reached only by winding, switchback tracks. The valley was not for tourists; the reality was the bare living scratched by the herds of goats and cattle from the thin soil of the slopes, with always, far above, the sight of the snows.

Sally said, in a small voice, " It seems so hard, doesn't it—the life here? The young girls look so old in those black long skirts and the black hats and boots—even their faces look old, as if they've been working from the time they could walk."

" It can't be easy to live with the idea that any winter you could lose your house and even your whole grazing land to an avalanche. They live on several levels—the population of whole villages migrate with their goods on their backs when it's time to move with the cattle to the high pastures. They follow the snow line as it recedes, almost. It's hard and it's primitive, and a girl wouldn't stay young very long, I'd think . . ."

Evolène greeted them with the noon bells of the Angelus.

The unpaved road, dusty, wound through the tight-packed houses, three storeys high, some of them, their balconies wearing the brave ribbons of summer, the potted plants, but all of them still, somehow, breathing the air of winter, their roofs of rough, hand-cut slabs of slate suggesting age and the weight of snow, crouching under the rock wall of the mountains that rose behind them. Rearing up behind this first barrier was the massive pinnacle of La Dent Blanche, and across the valley the jagged shapes of Les Dents de Veisivi; between them flowed the frozen torrents of the Ferpècle glacier. In the warm dust down in the village, the eyes and the mind were drawn irresistibly to the threatening whiteness above.

"I'd like that cup of coffee," Sally said faintly.

They had lunch at the Hotel Eden, where no one was expecting guests, but the *patron* produced the ham, cheese and Fondant that Elizabeth had predicted. The windows of the austere dining-room sloped to the river. After lunch they left the car there and walked down through grass that was dotted with the tiny, wondrous flowers of the high valleys. The river ran with the blue-white colour of the glacier. They sat down on Josh's coat, and he brought out his cigarettes. Sally took her first draw slowly, and then at once stubbed it out.

"I'm giving up cigarettes," she announced.

Josh looked at her with raised eyebrows. "Why?"

"All at once I think I don't need them any more." She smiled at him, and stretched out fully, half burying her face in the tweed that had taken on the smell of the grass and the soft earth. In a very little time she was asleep.

The two men were outside the post office when Josh and Sally walked back through the town. It had begun to cloud over, and in the sudden changes that come at that altitude the mountains had disappeared behind a curtain of mist in a few minutes, and looking up, the rock wall above the village seemed to end the universe. It grew cold, and the mist turned to soft rain. They went into the café for coffee; the modern

Italian Espresso machine wasn't working, so Josh ordered Remy Martin for them both.

" In case of sickness," he said to Sally.

He didn't tell her that the two men had gone into the café opposite theirs; he wondered if they had had any better luck with coffee. Nor did he say anything when the same car followed them down the valley—after all, there was only the one way out. The mist persisted, hanging whitely down below them, veiling the river, and sometimes obscuring the other side of the loop of a hairpin bend. He drove carefully, and didn't try to evade the following car. If they were Raedler's men, then they were well kept out of St. Martin; if they were tourists, there was no hurry for them either. If they were Raedler's men, they were recent arrivals, not able to penetrate the château legitimately, but simply there if they should be needed—as for to-day's chore. Well, in the game they played, Canfield thought, there were much worse ways of spending a day. Then he concentrated on his driving, and beside him Sally sat quietly, drowsily, and did not light a cigarette all the way down.

There had been no rain down in the main valley, reinforcing the feeling that they had descended from some other world.

" I'm glad we had this day . . . just you and me," Sally said, ". . . to be normal people again for a few hours. I feel as if I've just taken a deep breath."

In the square of St. Martin they saw Hayward sitting under one of the umbrellas at the café sipping Campari. When Josh and Sally joined him, and the two men from the car also took a table there, Josh was almost forced to believe that they were tourists. They were just too obtrusive to be anything else. And yet, with one café and one hotel in the town, where else could they go? Josh began to enjoy their difficulties.

" Well?" he said to Hayward when their order of Dubonnet had come.

Hayward shook his head, his large face gloomy. " No good, I'm afraid. We talked for an hour after you left, with Raedler popping up every few minutes to try to get Elizabeth inside and away from me. Then he had to keep going back to the telephone, and finally he had to drive into Sion. But that was after Elizabeth had gone, so he felt safe, I suppose."

"She didn't say anything?—anything about Devlin?"

"Nothing but Devlin—but nothing that we didn't know already. It wasn't something I relished doing, Josh. I mean —sitting there talking about the Foundation, and the good that could be done, and the best way to make the memorial really say something about Dev himself—and all the time the poor woman could barely keep control of herself. It wasn't just that talking about Dev was painful—I think she was in actual pain herself. It was almost like seeing her go to bits in front of my eyes. In the end I had to insist that she went to her room. And the way she looked at me . . ." He sighed. "I could almost have believed that she guessed I knew the truth about how ill she was. She took off those glasses, and her eyes looked quite desperate, as if she was begging me to do something, and yet couldn't say what it was. I tell you, it was pretty damnable."

"Damnable . . . yes. I wonder if they're giving her anything for the pain . . . if there is pain. She didn't seem drugged to me."

Sally said, "She's the kind who would hold out against drugs. I think she would bear pain, so as not to miss everything else." She added, softly, "I always thought that my father believed courage was the highest virtue."

FIVE

The château was decked in candles, and it wore their glow as a woman wears jewels; its beauty was real, of its own time. It had bloomed and come into its own; the richness of the great house was richer for being less clearly seen. This night it was a house to dress up to; it needed, Canfield thought, the gowns and the graces of women to complete it. Sally wore a topaz pendant on a dress of amber silk, the warm sherry hair combed simply to her shoulders. Elizabeth had responded to the mood of the evening with a gown of medieval splendour, a long, loose robe of garnet velvet, the slashed sleeves revealing a flash of satin, a single great ruby on her right hand. Canfield had seen, from the smile of pleasure on Hayward's face, that this was how he remembered Elizabeth, how he remembered St. Martin.

As they passed into the dining-room Sally hung back with Josh. "I have written to Robert," she said softly.

For an instant he let his hand rest on her arm, a caress, a gesture of thankfulness, a touch of love. Then they moved to their places.

There was a fire lighted in the dining-room to cast its own glow upon the aged patina of the long table, to bring the colour to the crystal, to light the silver candelabra so that they reflected the hues of the tapestries. And Elizabeth was seated in the chair that last night had remained empty; there was colour in her cheeks—perhaps false colour, but the gesture had been made, and it, too, was in the spirit of the evening; she ate as if she actually could taste her food.

"Simon has surpassed himself," she said to Lancome. "The lack of electricity in the kitchen does not trouble him?"

"Simon is happy that Madame has guests for him to prepare food for. The lack of electricity—it is nothing to Simon. I think, Madame, he enjoys the change."

"You see, Raedler," Elizabeth said. "All your efforts are unappreciated. Here you have been telephoning and driving about all day in search of electricians, and here they say they do not mind that we go without. If it were not for the extra work it gives to everyone, I should rather like it to stay this way myself. It is," she added, and gave a mock sigh, "so much kinder, this light, to the older ones." And then she looked down the table to Sally. "And to the young it is enchantment."

Sourly, Raedler waved aside Lancome, who had moved around the table refilling the wine glasses. Canfield noticed that he had barely tasted the superb Romanée-Conti. He had eaten little, as if the food was distasteful to him; he alone at the table did not respond to the stimulants, the food, the great wine, to Sally's beauty and the aura of distinction and power that emanated unconsciously from Elizabeth. He had smiled feebly, unwillingly at Hayward's stories. All of these things threatened Raedler; his control of Elizabeth and of this house had slipped enough to permit laughter about this table, and good humour in the kitchen. He did not like it. It could even be, Canfield thought, remembering who were Raedler's masters, dangerous for him to have permitted things to have gone this far.

"To-morrow, everything will be as usual, Madame. I have a firm promise that two men from Sion will be here early in the morning—if not to-night, when they have come down from Montana. If it requires a work of any magnitude, the Zurich firm will have men here by mid-afternoon."

"*Quel dommage*," Elizabeth sighed. "We must enjoy our little escape into enchantment while we can."

They tried, and in a small way succeeded. It was not a brilliant company—Elizabeth was able to make only a small effort, and Sally was still too much in awe of her to take a lead. Hayward told his stories, but rather heavily. Apart from the wine, and the food of artistic subtlety, the dinner would not have been in any way remarkable if it had not been for the contrast to what they remembered of the night before. Now Elizabeth sat at the head of her own table, and her presence seemed a minor triumph over her body, which would betray her, and a triumph for the bid for independence she made from Raedler. It was very little, Canfield thought, and yet it was much.

Having failed for the moment with Elizabeth, Raedler made an attempt to win back control of the mood of the table through Canfield. Hayward had just finished telling of a wild night when he had attempted to entertain a young American author of the "cool" school and had found himself on the rounds of jazz haunts in London he had never even imagined had existed. "He kept calling me 'Daddy-o'," he ended. "I wasn't much of a success."

"But you have normal authors, Mr. Hayward?" Raedler interjected. "Authors who give you no trouble—many like Mr. Canfield here? Although I think," he added, as if the thought had just occurred to him, "that you have not previously published Mr. Canfield. I have not had the pleasure of reading Mr. Canfield's work, but the two volumes you sent Madame Devlin to peruse did not bear the Hayward imprint, did they?"

Here was one of the weak spots in the plan to get Canfield to St. Martin. Hayward was prepared. "Well, we wish they were all like Josh," he said quickly. "I mean—we haven't actually published Josh before, but we took notice of the reviews of his books, and when he published that piece on Dev in the *Opinion* I knew he would be our man for the biography, unless he was completely committed elsewhere. I made myself as persuasive as I could."

"A little piracy then, Mr. Hayward?"

"We never admit that we steal authors. It's bad for the morale of the trade. But authors are human. Isn't that so, Josh?—they like to be flattered a little, and they like to be paid. However, we find that we do business more easily with those who don't expect to be taken to jazz places."

Raedler spun around to Canfield, as if he suspected them of leading him off the subject. "And the biography of Monsieur Devlin will come—when?"

"That rather depends on Mrs. Devlin." It was delicate ground, and he didn't want to cause her to retreat again, as she had last night. But the cover had to be held to, and he had to act as if the Devlin biography was his only business here.

Everyone at table looked at her. She did not retreat, but she did not answer his question. "Yes, it depends, doesn't it?" she said. "It could be a long time—it could be never, that is, never from the official sources, which are his notebooks and his letters. I'm not sure that there should be a biography of Dev." She leaned back in her high chair; in the red robe with the slashed sleeves with her hair drawn back like a white cap, with the candle light flickering over the sharp prominences of her features, Canfield had, for a second, an uncanny feeling that he faced some medieval judge, weighted and deliberative with the power of office. The hand with the great ruby pointed to him almost accusingly.

"What kind of man will you make of Devlin?"

"I'm not sure I'll make anything of him. He may be impossible to write about."

She leaned forward, dropping the attitude of detachment. "Why do you say that?"

"Devlin had no enemies. He loved a life of adventure and achievement. He married a woman who had lived her own legend. He won a great accolade—and still he had no enemies. Who will believe in such a man?"

The hand with the ring hit the table sharply. "It could be your task, Mr. Canfield, to *make* them believe it. That is the truth of Devlin, and it must be told."

Canfield did not reply immediately. "If the truth about Devlin can be told," he began, "it must . . ."

A change came on the room. He halted. A dim brown light came grudgingly to the sconces and the three chandeliers. It flooded the room briefly, and then died. They looked at one another with some surprise, as if they had forgotten that there could be any light but the soft and kindly light of the candles. No one had greeted the one surge of electricity with any pleasure, no one but Raedler.

He got to his feet. "So . . . the electricians will be working. I shall go and speak to them." He began to walk towards the door, but before he reached it, it had opened and one of the young footmen stood there. Lancome hurried forward, but Raedler was there before him. The footman said something, and Raedler nodded. He left the room.

For a minute after he had gone there was silence. The great ruby winked with red fire as Elizabeth's hand moved to the stem of her glass. But she did not drink; she clutched it as Canfield remembered her clutching the brandy goblet the night before, a weapon, a support.

"Truth, Mr. Canfield," she said, "is a strange commodity. Those who deal in it learn its worth."

"Truth is what I hope to find at St. Martin."

The rubied hand stirred. "Keep searching. The truth is rarely revealed in one flash. It is gradual. Very few have been in the position of St. Paul on the road to Damascus."

"Like your bishop's motto, Elizabeth," Hayward said. "*Veritas Praevalebit*—but slowly, I take it."

"The full motto is *Magna est Veritas et Praevalebit*. From the Apocrypha. And it was not the bishop's motto, but Dev's."

"*Dev's motto?*"

"He never admitted it, but once he quoted it to me, and I took it and made it the motto of this house. For a writer, ultimately, there is nothing else but the truth. It is something he has wrestled with to find its essence."

"Dear Dev . . ." Hayward muttered softly.

"*That* is where your task may be impossible, Mr. Canfield. To tell the truth about Devlin." Elizabeth's hand motioned to each of them in turn. "All of us round this table think we know the truth about him. The fact is, we each know a separate truth. Your task would be to put those truths together, Mr. Canfield. You will fail, inevitably. But the failure must be an honest one. Are you able to fail on those terms, Mr. Canfield? You must be prepared to fail on those terms or not to begin."

"You place a heavy burden on a biographer . . . on any writer, Mrs. Devlin."

"The truth is always a burden."

The doors opened. Raedler stood there. Strangely, behind him, the Great Hall was revealed in a full blaze of electric light, so bright it seemed to hurt the eyes by contrast to the mellow dimness here. His slim dark-suited figure was silhouetted against the glare. He still held the knobs of each panel of the door, holding firmly, waiting until he had gathered the attention of all of them to himself. He looked at Elizabeth, his lips twisting in their strange smile. Even his grey façade of impersonality could not withhold the triumph, the declaration that he was assuming command once again.

"Madame," he said, "the messengers have arrived from the bank."

As he spoke the hand of the electrician on the main panel in the vault below had thrown a switch. From every source now, the light flooded on, momentarily blinding them. The room was revealed, too harsh, too stark, the reflection from the silver, the crystal, the old waxed wood were suddenly made mechanically brilliant and cold. Eyes blinked in the excess of light; the faces around the table seemed pale and drained.

They had not noticed Elizabeth rising. She stood, gripping the edge of the table. "The messenger? Now? He has come *now?*"

"There are two, Madame."

Hectic splotches of colour had leapt to her cheeks. She thrust the chair backwards with an uncontrolled movement that caused it to rock. She started, at half a run, down the length of the room towards Raedler, her eyes staring as if, suddenly, her guests had no existence.

"Pray do not disturb yourself, Madame," Raedler said. "They will stay the night."

She seemed to stagger, and clutched at the back of Sally's chair for support. Canfield sprang up to help her, but she had moved on with that strange half-run.

"You fool!" she said to Raedler; and her tone was a curse of anguish. "I will see them now—*now*!"

He bowed slightly, and let her pass. Before he closed the door he permitted himself a second or two to let his gaze rest on those still at the table. He had clamped his lips on the smile, but the air of triumph was not repressed; he did not mean it to be.

When he was gone, Hayward signalled to Lancome.

"Lancome, if we could have the lights . . ."

"Certainly, Monsieur." The old man hurried to press the switches.

But the room did not melt back into its own shadows any more. They had seen the place revealed in the sudden blaze of light, and all it had showed was that the darkness remained within the people themselves.

Lancome moved to serve the next course.

" We will wait for Mrs. Devlin," Hayward said.

" I would not advise it, Monsieur. It is unlikely that Madame will return to-night."

II

Sally quietly closed the painted door of her apartment, and leaned back against it, closing her eyes and no longer fighting the signs of dismay and depression she had held back for the last hour. The silence was very deep, almost complete; she felt the weariness of little sleep and the hours of high altitude up in the mountains. She felt the parting from Josh, brief and conventional, which had taken place under Hayward's interested eye. She felt what they all had shared when Elizabeth had left them and not returned—the sense of being shut out, the agonising search for the meaning behind the sudden arrival of two strangers and Elizabeth's reaction to them.

" Every month—every month since Monsieur Raedler has been here a messenger comes from the bank," Lancome had said quietly when he had served coffee. " Madame waits with great impatience. But this month he comes early—and there are two. And they stay here at the château, which also is a new thing."

They had walked on the terrace and discussed it briefly, and fruitlessly.

" I've known Swiss banks to do extraordinary things for their clients—but they do them at normal times of day," Hayward had said, fidgeting unhappily with his cigar. " And why would Elizabeth be so upset by the arrival of someone from her bank? Good lord, she doesn't *need* money. What do you think, Josh?"

" I think they have nothing to do with the bank. But we won't have any way of even judging that until we've had a look at them. And I would guarantee we won't be allowed to do *that* to-night. Lancome told me that Raedler had directed him to have rooms prepared on the other side of the house."

They had talked around the subject, and had finally dropped into silence, realising that conjecture was only that. The night was fragrant and soft, beneath them the lights of the village had begun to go off, the farms on the slopes were already dark, a train roared with a long snake of light down the valley, the river was suddenly silver in the pale illumination of the new moon that lifted itself above the line of the mountains. It should have been a peaceful night. But as they reached the end of the terrace and made the turn, each time looking up, they saw the lights in the long line of windows that Hayward said were the apartments that Elizabeth and Devlin had occupied. They had gone on walking, as if to outwait the lights. Finally, all the windows of the apartment but one had gone dark. They had stood and watched as someone had walked through and closed the curtains at each window.

"That's it," Josh said. "There's no sense waiting . . . we can't reach her to-night."

Sally pressed her head back against the door, and thought of the isolation of that one light, the loneliness. It had been the thing that had weighed on her most since coming to the château—the implication of loneliness that Elizabeth had lived through. She thought of the loneliness of the winter that each of them had lived through separately.

"We might have been together." For her, the loneliness had ended with Josh. Elizabeth still endured it.

A small sound in the dressing-room hit her like a blow in the stillness. She straightened, looking wildly round the room, remembering the manuscript she had hidden, fearing for it.

"Who is it?" she said loudly. "Is someone there?"

The door to the dressing-room opened; Marie stood there. "Forgive me, M'selle—did I startle you? I came to turn down your bed, and I waited to enquire if there was anything you needed."

Sally smiled her relief, and moved into the centre of the room. "No, Marie, thank you. There is nothing."

The woman looked about her. "Nothing? You are sure, M'selle. Not some underclothing to be washed?—a dress to be pressed? But no—all the young ones travel with nylon these days, and the drip-dry, is it not? Like Madame when she used to go on safari with Monsieur. But perhaps there is something . . ." Suddenly she flung out her hands. "Ah, listen to

Marie, like an old woman she is talking. Begging for something to do." She shrugged. " Fool I am that I can't take my ease when it is offered. But there is so little to do now . . ."

" You don't take care of Madame Devlin any more?"

" I take care of Madame's clothes. That is all. But the rest of it—the toilet, the dressing, the meals to her room . . . the other one, the nurse, does it all. I can no longer talk to Madame—nor she to me. Madame does not want to talk. I am troubled for Madame. She bears something great, which I do not understand."

The woman plucked distractedly at the starched frill of her apron.

" You forgive me for talking like this, M'selle? You are Monsieur's daughter. I said to Lancome that you will understand. We have tried to help her, but she holds us back. We have no one to ask, no way to find out what to do for the best. And to-night she will need help. She is shut up there, alone. All those great rooms empty but for her. She will sit in the room Monsieur used for his writing. Sometimes she speaks to herself, sometimes she weeps. I have heard her. It has always been like that whenever the man has come from the bank. I doubt that you will see her to-morrow, M'selle."

" In the room where he wrote . . . ?"

" Always. She spends much time there. It was a joke between them, that room. I hear them laugh about it—like young lovers. It was a joke because Madame had prepared a magnificent chamber for Monsieur to do his writing. Books to the ceiling—thousands of books. A desk with many drawers—the pencils and pens, hundreds, I think, cabinets for his notes. A secretary was engaged. Monsieur wanted none of it. He used the beautiful chamber a few times to please Madame, and the secretary sat outside and waited. And then Madame found that he was writing on scraps of old paper in a window-seat in a little room that was a kind of dressing-room for Monsieur in the apartments they shared. She laughed—she was so pleased that he cared to stay near to her. They moved a desk in there, a very small one. The big chamber stayed empty. It was the show place where they pretended he wrote. It was their joke. Now she clings to it, that little room."

Sally was silent for a while, pondering the idea of her father and Elizabeth sharing the process of his creation, the untidy ritual of actually setting down the words, sharing it deeply enough to be able to joke about it. It was nothing like the picture she had held of the two of them, nothing like her fiction of Elizabeth as a woman whose ambition had married a famous name, not the person of Devlin. She had been very wrong about that. But in a day she had learned how much she had been wrong about.

"Why," she said, returning to the immediate problem of Elizabeth, "why do they come—the men from the bank?" Twenty-four hours ago such a question would have been unthinkable. Now she, and all of them, were long past the stage of preserving the forms of conventional behaviour. They had lived a long time in twenty-four hours.

"Who knows? They did not come before. Nothing is as it was before. We cannot reach her—Lancome and I, we can touch her, but we cannot reach her. There has been no one else to try . . ."

Sally turned away from her and walked to one of the alcoved windows. The lights of Sion were there; it was strange that they were already familiar. It was as if she had been waiting for a long time to enter into this world, as if her heart already knew it in part. Why had she felt, she wondered, as if she had belonged with Elizabeth, that morning on the terrace? Why had she felt a strange protectiveness towards this woman who had, until finally seen, no need for anyone's protection, for anyone's help? The mask she had built for Elizabeth did not exist; the myth was shattered. Elizabeth was a woman, much like any other. What made her unique was that she had been loved by Devlin. Sally faced the thought with a sudden gladness that he had been able to love. Since the discovery of Josh, she would not have denied that knowledge, that experience to Devlin. She realised that until Josh was a certainty in her own life, she had never really known the fact of Devlin. All through the winter she had been groping towards him. Viewing him with Elizabeth, in the light of loving Josh, she had come to realise him fully. Whether he was alive or dead, the woman he loved had become of supreme importance.

She turned back to Marie. "Could *I* try?" she said humbly.

The woman's features quivered, and seemed almost to dissolve. She gave a soft, long sigh.

"If M'selle would . . ."

III

In the darkness the series of open double doors resembled a tunnel whose end was the lighted room towards which Marie pointed her.

"*Bonne chance*," Marie whispered close to her ear. Then she retreated.

She had been led there by the maid in a strange circuitous route, down a tight stone circular stair that broke off the one leading to her own room, then a modern wooden stair and a long corridor carpeted in drugget and linoleum, part of the servants' quarters, Sally guessed; then another ascent by a circular stair, within one of the jutting towers of the château. Here, Marie did not switch on any lights; they groped their way by touch and the uncertain light that came from the narrow slits in the walls. The way up seemed long, and Sally was assailed by coldness of the stone, and the feeling of being shut in, assailed by the feeling of doubt that this venture would accomplish anything, and yet knowing that for the sake of that small bit of insight, newly won this last day at St. Martin, as well as for Elizabeth's sake, she had to go on.

"Raedler will not know I am with Mrs. Devlin?" she whispered to Marie.

The older woman was panting slightly with the climb. She paused by one of the window-slits, where Sally could vaguely see her face.

"None of them will know. If you are quiet. The nurse and Monsieur Raedler have rooms across the passage from Madame.

So far she has resisted the woman sleeping in her apartments with her. *That* would have been an outrage to Madame. But they have ears like foxes for whoever goes in that way."

"Don't they know about this way?"

"It is possible they do not. You will see, M'selle, when we come to the end. This is a very old house, with many passages that go nowhere, and many doors that open on blocked walls. Much was changed when Madame rebuilt it to her convenience, but some of us remember the old days, as it used to be when it was a ruin. It is possible there are some things that Monsieur Raedler has not yet found out. I count on it."

"But *you* know these things?"

"I was born in St. Martin," Marie said. "I played, as all we children did, in the ruins of the château. It was Lancome who recommended me to Madame. St. Martin has Madame's interests at its heart." Her breathing was easy now. She gestured. "Come on, we must ascend."

Sally followed her up another turn of the stair until Marie paused again. "We wait a little, and move carefully. Raedler and the messengers and the nurse have left her alone. I must first make certain that none have returned. But they will not return once they are sure she is there for the night. Compassion is not for them . . . those ones." She put her hand on Sally's arm. "Careful, M'selle, and quiet."

She opened a small door outwards on to the stairs, so that they had to edge around it. They were met with a stuffy blackness within. It felt to Sally as if they were shut in a cupboard. And then, after closing it noiselessly, Marie opened a further door and gestured Sally forward. They were in a bathroom—a huge room that also, Sally thought, must have served as a dressing-room. In a room beyond it, a bedroom, a single table lamp burned, and its light was reflected in the glass and marble. The door through which they had come was part of a whole wall of similar mirrored doors, wardrobes, Sally thought, and even in the tenseness of the moment she was amused by the thought that not even Raedler could open every door of every room in such a house as St. Martin.

Then Marie had led her forward again, into the bedroom,

and had placed her where she could see the intervening rooms in their darkness, see the long tunnel of the double doors and the oblong of light at the end of it. "The little room at the end, M'selle." Then she had whispered her words of good luck, and was gone.

It seemed almost the longest part of the journey to traverse these rooms; and it also was a journey of self-knowledge. She looked about the bedroom first, not prying, but seeking to know. It was Elizabeth's room—a nightgown and robe lay ready across the chaise-longue; but it bore no resemblance to the room upstairs that Sally now inhabited, and which had been Elizabeth's before Devlin's coming. This was a warm room, and, for its size, an intimate room, softer, the pieces chosen for comfort not because they belonged in period. The room beyond it bore the same stamp. It was a sitting-room library. A door led to the outside passage, the normal way of entry to this suite, and it held one of the great stone chimney-pieces that were a distinguishing feature of the house. But the chairs and sofas were deep and comfortable, the books crowded into the shelves wore their strident modern wrappers; there was a clutter of tables and lamps. Sally paused here, and in the half darkness she felt a prickling of familiarity. It wore the look that all of Devlin's rooms had worn in the flat in London. It just escaped untidiness. It seemed still to be strewn with the things that Devlin might have thrown down there, his pipes, the loose change from his pocket, the book he was reading. It was a room that was well used. There were three impressionist paintings on the walls—the sun colours that Devlin had loved. This had been their home within a house. Sally knew now how Devlin had lived in this splendid museum; this had been his world within it, and as she passed she could almost see him, stretched out here in one of these half shabby chairs, having a drink with Elizabeth before they descended to the brilliant company gathering in the salon. What a fool she had been to think it could have been any other way, that Devlin could have lived in any other fashion. It was Elizabeth, not Devlin, who had changed in this marriage.

Then came another bedroom, a sort of extension of the

sitting-room, solid comfort, but no grandeur, again that inexpressible look of near-untidiness; Devlin's room. She moved across it to the lighted doorway.

"Who is it?" Elizabeth's voice said. "Is it you, Raedler?" The tone was abstracted. "Can I have no peace?"

Sally stepped fully into the light. Elizabeth sat at a small sturdy desk; she still wore the garnet gown which was strangely rich for this setting. The room was plain, small by the standards of St. Martin; it held two tables piled with books and papers, the desk, a row of cupboards. Only the light on the desk burned, and Elizabeth sat still with her head bowed over the papers before her.

"Well, what is it?" she said, without looking up.

Sally wet her lips nervously. "I came to say . . ." She didn't know what she had come to say.

Elizabeth's head turned to her, not quickly, as if she unwillingly broke her attention from what was before her. She stared past the pool of light on the desk, blinking rapidly. "Dev . . ." Then softly, "It's you, Sally."

They stared at each other in silence for a time; Sally, watching for the wary defensiveness, did not meet it. Elizabeth did not seem to challenge her presence there, nor even to be surprised by it. She sighed, and leaned back in her chair, placing both hands flat down on papers before her. Her face was shadowed and lined with weariness, and more than weariness; yet a kind of radiance lit it. She had the look of someone struggling back from some place that the ordinary voyager does not penetrate. Wherever she had been, she had brought back with her the grace of peace. For the first time since Sally had set eyes on her, there was no part to be played, no tense effort to produce an effect.

She pointed wordlessly to the chair that faced the desk. Sally came and seated herself, and again they waited, looking at each other.

"Your voice sounded like his," Elizabeth said. "I think I hear it because I'm always listening for it."

"I wish it could have been him," Sally answered slowly. "For your sake I really wish it could have been."

"For my sake?" Elizabeth's hands nervously stroked the papers before her. "What about you?"

"I learned to give him up—this last winter. The way I should have done five years ago, when you were married. What a waste it's been—you and I apart all this time. Feeling the same grief, but not sharing it. In five years I had a hundred chances to begin sharing, but I never took them. Even after your telephone call in October I made no special effort . . ."

Elizabeth struggled for recollection. "Yes . . . the telephone call. Yes, I remember—those first days are so mixed up in my mind. I put it through, and then I thought it was a mistake. That I didn't have the right to lay that burden on you. To involve you."

"That's what we've lacked, isn't it?—involvement? It seems extraordinary to me that this is the first time we have ever sat down like this, face to face—and more than five years have gone by—wasted. From the way I see it now, I wonder how I could have been so stupid."

"Aren't we all? In certain areas we are all blind. It's when people are blind in the same way that we begin to be alike. Races, creeds, the colour of our skins, create conditions which tend to make us alike. Similar prejudices are similar blindnesses. You and I, Sally—you and I have remained blind to each other and therefore blind to a part of Devlin. What we have lost we can only mourn. We can never get it back."

"I was young as well as stupid," Sally said. "But that's no real excuse. By the second and the third year I was beginning to *see* that I was stupid, but by that time my pride had stiffened.

"It was unrealistic to expect Elizabeth O'Mara Spence to keep extending invitations. Once I'd turned you down flatly, I shouldn't have expected anything but what I got. I've had five years of the sulks, and I got no more out of it than anyone ever did out of such stupidity."

"I avoided you," Elizabeth said. "I put it off and off—Dev knew what I was doing, and he was patient. He told me—how well I remember—that you couldn't believe that I might be afraid of you. That I had my own kind of jealousy. But you were young, and you couldn't know the torment that life can be. You couldn't forgive as much, or as readily as Dev could. I *was* afraid. I think I continued to be afraid right until this moment. You were Devlin's beloved, Devlin's beautiful Sally. I had had so little of love all my life—and now I had this Dev, this matchless Devlin, and I couldn't bear to share him. I didn't even know how to begin to share. I'd never had to before. He was so unexpected in my life, you see . . . I never imagined that there would be anyone like Devlin for me. It was so strange, and in the beginning I couldn't get used to it. I couldn't make myself believe it—or I was afraid to believe it."

Sally could see, on the grey and chalky skin of Elizabeth's face, that the beads of perspiration were beginning to stand out above the lips, at the edge of the hair-line. She wondered if she were in pain, or if the struggle to re-live the sequences of five years was beyond her present strength.

"Believe what?"

"It was obvious when I thought it through, but it took a long time before I discovered it. Of course, Dev wanted nothing of me but myself. I asked myself what there was I had that he wanted—or what I could get for Lawrence Devlin that he couldn't get for himself. And there was nothing—there was absolutely nothing! Money—that was what a great many men who had come around had been after—but Devlin didn't care about money. Devlin had enough, and the trappings of wealth were a joke to him. He prized freedom above everything else, so he had no use for power. He had won a great name for himself without me. I couldn't give Dev anything he hadn't got. There was only myself. You can't imagine how long it was before I could let myself believe that completely. I think it was the truth. I think so now. But all of my life until Dev came I had lived in a world where money and power counted, the goal always being to accumulate more and more of it. I had never conceived of the simplicity of a man who didn't want it and didn't need it. He didn't want anything for himself and he wasn't asking anything for you, either. He knew it was time you found your own life, and if it happened because of me, then that was the way it would happen. Dev was a realist, and he knew that no one is unflawed. The acceptance of the flaws is the beginning of love."

"I'm glad he found you," Sally said. "It was a real marriage, wasn't it? I've had such a time these five years, indulging my particular blindness—believing the public image of Elizabeth O'Mara Spence, imagining you running his life, and believing that it was all wrong for him. But it just wasn't so—and I wouldn't come here and see for myself. But then—I should have known him well enough—loved him well enough, I suppose—he just would not have existed within that wrong kind of marriage. I'm sorry, though—I'm sorry I had to wait until he was dead to find this out."

Again Sally saw the nervous rustling of the papers under Elizabeth's hand. The beads of perspiration grew more pronounced. She had lowered her eyes to the papers. The thin tall figure within the loose folds of the gown seemed to sway. Sally wondered if she was going to faint, and she leaned to her, half anticipating the sway and crash. Finally Elizabeth raised her head.

"He isn't dead," she said. "Dev is still alive."

Sally leaned close enough to grasp the desk herself. "Alive?"

Elizabeth nodded, her movement heavy and slow. "Alive."

The single word seemed as much as she could say. Sally sat, petrified, afraid to move. She watched as Elizabeth put one elbow on the desk, and her face rested in her outspread hand. She didn't know if there were tears. The shoulders did not move; there was something terrible and pitiable in this stillness, as if she had schooled herself in it, long past tears, long past the plea for compassion; past everything but the will to hold, to bear.

It was some minutes before she faced Sally again. There had been no tears; her eyes were dry and stony.

"Now I have said it . . . and you will have to know the rest. It's dangerous knowledge, and you will wish I had said nothing. But I have not talked . . . oh, God, I haven't passed a word in freedom and at ease since he went. Months . . .

like being locked in a tomb. May Dev forgive me . . . but I can't help it.

"His plane went down on the Soviet side of the border. An emergency landing, they said. God knows what happened. They say it went down, not shot down. A small, low-flying, unarmed aircraft like that—it could only have been accidental, whatever happened. He was hurt, but not badly. They were in touch with Moscow. In Moscow they knew his name. They made better plans for Lawrence Devlin than just to charge a border violation. And how quickly they worked. A few days—and they had him and they had me."

"They had *you*?"

"He is a hostage for my obedience." Elizabeth gave a short cry of anger and despair. "I've spent half a lifetime talking and writing against them, and here I am, finally their servant. They calculated that I would pay their price, and so far I have. They know now that where Dev is concerned, the obedience is unquestioned."

"But what?—what have you done for them?" The horror of the captivity was breaking on Sally. She looked at the other woman in a kind of awe, wondering how that fragile flesh could have borne it.

"Nothing. I have given them nothing but my silence. And they have given me his life. His life, and a return to health. Spared him the ordeal of one of their mock spy trials. From me they have had silence, and this withdrawal here at St. Martin."

"But why——?" Sally rose and leaned in close to Elizabeth. "*Why?*"

"Propaganda. Their best and least costly weapon. Oh, no——" She cut short Sally's objection. "It would be too crude just to say that Devlin was there and had gone over. They would have to produce him for a Press conference, and they know they could never force him to make that kind of statement. The confirmation is to come from me—in a few weeks I will make a statement to the Press. The act will appear to be voluntary. I will tell the Press that Devlin is in Russia, and that I am joining him. I have to say no more. That is all they need."

Sally just stared at her, for the moment dumb with shock.

"Other women have gone," Elizabeth went on. "I will not be the first to do it. There was a choice, and I chose to give this to Dev." Her hand went to her face again, distractedly. "In the beginning I wished I could die, right then, so that I need not make the choice. But if I died I could win nothing for him. If I died before this was done perhaps Dev would die too. Once the decision was made I wanted to go at once. But I learned who was master. *They* will dictate the time. The time is quite soon." Her voice had grown faint, as if she were slipping off into the fog of her pain and dilemma, retreating again.

Sally broke at last through her own numbness.

"How do you *know* he's alive—for sure? How do you know that they didn't find him dead, and they have concocted this story in the hope that you would believe it? Once you make that statement, they've won. They don't need Dev."

Elizabeth made no reply. She looked at Sally with glazed eyes, closing out the question, closing out the hope of relief that the doubt might bring.

Urgently now, Sally leaned across to her and took one of her arms firmly, holding it hard so that Elizabeth should be forced to feel the contact with another human. The withdrawal had to be broken.

"*Why* do you believe it?"

Elizabeth blinked, and some life, some sense of reasoning seemed to flow back. "You think I didn't ask?—demand? As if I could *demand* anything. I asked for proof. They gave it to me. They produced the things he had in his pockets—the watch I'd given him—that old pocket knife he always carries with him."

"He could have been dead," Sally insisted brutally, knowing that the truth would be brutal in any case. "They could have found him dead and taken the things just the same. It might have been worth a try—in the hope that you would believe it."

"Could I risk not believing it?" Elizabeth demanded. Suddenly the dead and apathetic look was gone from her face; her eyes blazed with a curious passion. "Would *you* have risked it? If I had shrieked to the world that they had him, it would have been easy for them to deny it. He would simply have . . . disappeared. Finally, and for ever. That would have been the end of Devlin. I waited. I had nothing to lose—perhaps something to gain . . . for him."

"You waited?—for what?"

"They promised me proof. They promised me that when he was recovered I would have proof that he was alive. And they gave it to me. They keep on giving it to me. So the pressure is constantly renewed. I can never forget that he is there, alive—and his life depends on me."

"What proof? For God's sake, what proof?"

Elizabeth spread her hand on the papers before her.

"This," she said very softly.

Sally's hand reached for them. "Show me."

Elizabeth did not immediately give them up. "He's writing," she said. "Do you hear that? He's writing—magnificently—like an angel. The best work he's ever done. It seems to flow out of him. And through it he laughs at them—he laughs at captivity and oppression. He's telling them that tyranny cannot be supported for ever . . . that it comes to an end, however long it takes."

"They let him write that—about them? Show me," she demanded again.

She still did not give up the papers. "It isn't about *them*—it's an allegory of tyranny. He's saying that essentially it's the same wherever it's met, in whatever country, whatever circumstances. He's gone back to the history of his own people to tell it. It's a novel about an Irish family—the Devlins—it has to be them, because he writes as if he lived it. His grandfather, and his father—how they fought against the British. And his father dying in the Easter Rebellion—exactly as Dev told me it happened. His grandfather losing everything because he wouldn't take an oath of allegiance. It's there—his whole belief in freedom, the shout against tyranny. It's everything

Dev felt that crystallised during the years when he was writing about African independence. It's the heart of everything he learned about the struggle for freedom, for a man's right to determine what he would do with his own future, his own life. And he's found a way to express it here, in this story of his grandfather, his father and himself. It's the best thing that Devlin has ever done. Magnificent!—astonishingly sure and confident and real. Once I saw it, there was no more choosing. I *knew* what I had to do. I had to buy time for Dev—time and a place where he could work. He's got all his past to dig into as he's done here. He's got himself to fall back on. What I've got to spare him is the brainwashing, and the mockery of a trial, and one of those repentant statements they seem to be able to get. I've got to spare him a prison camp, and being slowly done to death by imprisonment. This is the only thing I have ever been able to give Dev, and I mean to give it."

Slowly she put the papers into Sally's hand, jealously, as though to leave go were a hurt.

"When it is published the world will know—surely everyone will know—that the man who wrote that has not given up on freedom." For a moment still she held on to the pages. "You will tell no one about this—not Hayward or Canfield. It is dangerous for Dev that even you know about it. But something is due to you. I owe you this. I will find a way for you to read all of it. This is only the part they brought with them to-night."

Sally sat down again. For a moment she could see nothing because the paper shook with her trembling hands; she felt a mist of tears blur her eyes.

She looked down and read the words before her and knew that she almost did not need to read them. Remembered phrases leapt out of the manuscript, memory recited the sequences to her, paragraph following paragraph. She remembered the months of being haunted by the feeling that the papers were being looked at, but never taken. They hadn't needed to take the originals; a camera could have done the work for them. What lay in her hands was an exact tracing of the original manuscript that Devlin had been sending her, the last half of which she had kept locked in the desk at Tyne and Townsend, a tracing of Dev's impossible handwriting. To the eyes of someone who had never seen it before it would appear as an original.

Sally looked across at Elizabeth; she rested the papers in her lap. "You don't want to read it?" Elizabeth said, wonderingly.

Sally didn't reply directly. "Is this all the proof? The only proof?"

"What more could you want? No one could fake this—this is the way Dev wrote, the way he thought. I couldn't be deceived about that."

Sally shifted forward to the edge of the chair. "But they gave you nothing beside this? Nothing at all?"

"I didn't need more than that—but yes, there is something else." She reached into the top flat drawer of Devlin's desk. "This . . ."

Sally took the photograph and looked at it carefully. It showed Devlin standing in a wood with deep snow. The leafless white birches rose behind him in a pattern of stark beauty. He wore boots and a parka, with the hood slipped back. It was Devlin, his expression serious, but the wit and humour written there. They had worked on it so that the hair revealed the grey that had developed in the last decade, and the lines of his face were deepened to what they had become. But Sally knew the picture. It had been taken about eight or nine years ago in Canada—or was it the Alaskan part of that journey? She had slipped it into the photo album with all the others, and forgotten it. And they had taken it, worked on it, and delivered their new version back to Elizabeth, to feed her hope.

Sally got to her feet, thrusting the manuscript back at Elizabeth. "Wait," she said. "Please just wait. Don't do anything—or call anyone. I have to bring something to you. Don't talk to anyone."

At the doorway she turned. "You will wait?"

All she got was a half nod from Elizabeth, a puppet-like movement of one accustomed to obedience.

Sally raced then through the darkened rooms, heading towards the light in Elizabeth's bedroom, and from there to the great marble bathroom. She opened two of the mirrored doors before she found the right one. The blackness of the stair waited for her.

"Marie?"

There was no reply from the darkness below her. It seemed to take an eternity to feel her way down the circular stair, the rough stone biting at her hands, making herself take careful, cautious steps, knowing that Elizabeth waited, and that a fall in the darkness would mean a delay past endurance. She reached the hall of the servants' quarters finally, Marie was not in sight.

"Oh, damn—where do I go now?"

She found the straight stairs they had descended together and ran up them. She was panting now. She began to think about Raedler. Marie had said he had left Elizabeth, but she had not said that he had himself gone to bed. She was afraid of his seeming ability to be everywhere, and now was horribly aware of her own danger, the danger in which she had placed herself and the manuscript. She froze for a moment before emerging from the little stairway that joined the one leading to her own apartment. She was breathing heavily from her run, but she was conscious of being sucked into the vortex of physical fear. What if Raedler met her now?—what if he met her on the journey back to Elizabeth? She had told Elizabeth nothing, she had told Josh or Hayward nothing. If Raedler should suspect what she was carrying back with her, her danger would be as great as the pains they had gone to to contrive this whole deception. If she could be prevented from reaching Elizabeth, the deception would continue. It would be as if she had never come to St. Martin. There was no time to think of it now. She ducked out of her concealment, and raced up the last remaining steps to the double painted doors.

They gave to her touch, and she had an instant's terrified premonition that Raedler was here before her. Had he somehow entered Elizabeth's apartments while they had been talking, heard her tell Elizabeth to wait? Had he raced her here, taking the quicker route by the main staircase? Fear had given her imagination a dizzying thrust. Only silence and emptiness greeted her. Raedler was not there. She raced to the hiding-place.

The enormous porcelain stove gave back its contents, the plain buff envelopes with her typed manuscript and the original of Devlin's last work. She took only a minute to flick through it, tracing the paragraphs of the pages that Elizabeth had shown to her, making sure, as she had to do, that they were completely identical. She could not add to Elizabeth's torment the cruelty of doubt about this. But they were exactly as she remembered, exactly as Elizabeth's manuscript had been. She thrust it back into the envelopes.

The return seemed longer, the three staircases, the long corridor. The deadening quiet that she hated was on the house, so that her footsteps seemed magnified on the stone. There was still no one in the servants' corridor; a light under two of the doors, but no sound; did no one play a radio, hum a tune, take a bath in this house? Did no one live here? The last, the narrow spiral staircase seemed without an end; she was hampered by the large envelopes and the darkness; again the stone scraped the tips of her seeking fingers—fingers that sought, and missed. She knew the moment of absolute terror she had dreaded when a final upward step slammed her violently into the body of a man.

A scream was stifled as a hand clamped against her mouth. She felt another about her waist, holding her, keeping her from the backward plunge down the stairs.

"*N'ayez pas peur, Mademoiselle.*" The voice was a whisper, young, soothing.

Gradually, the hand came down from her mouth, though she was still held closely as she swayed on the edge of the triangled step.

"*C'est Pierre.*"

The arm still held her. In an instant a flashlamp clicked on. He directed it so that she could see his face—one of the footmen who attended Lancome. But the blond handsome young face had lost its well-trained detachment. He wore a half smile, conspiratorial; she might have imagined it, but she thought that one of the eyelids flashed down in a wink.

"*Doucement, Mademoiselle . . . doucement.*"

She had regained her balance, but he still held her tightly, and continued to keep his arm about her waist as he guided her back down a few steps, and the flashlamp revealed the doorway that she had missed. He opened it, and finally his arm left its place.

"I guard, Mademoiselle." The words were halting, and heavily accented. "Proceed." She smelled again the familiar stuffiness of the cupboard, but she left Pierre with a certain reluctance. It would have been a comfort to feel the presence of that eager young man behind her as she made the journey back through those rooms. But if Pierre appeared, Elizabeth would retreat. She must leave him behind. She smiled her thanks; he watched until she closed the mirrored door.

The way was clear; no one in Elizabeth's rooms, no one in the sitting-room. She paused momentarily to listen by the door that led to the main corridor, but there was no sound from it. She moved on with more confidence, the lighted doorway at the end of the suite now was like a beacon.

She was a few feet from it when Raedler suddenly placed himself in the door-frame, his figure silhouetted darkly. She checked.

"You!" She took a backward step.

"Is there something wrong, Miss Devlin?"

"No . . ." Another backward step.

"You were coming to see Mrs. Devlin?"

She didn't answer. Then he himself stepped backwards. The gesture of his hand was an invitation to enter. "Please—come in," he said smoothly.

She was acutely aware of the envelopes she carried, and of Raedler's eyes on them, aware of the subtle menace of that invitation. She knew that if she entered that room, it would be to deliver the manuscript into Raedler's hands, not Elizabeth's.

It was the cry from Elizabeth that released her. "Sally—go! Go now!"

She turned and ran back through the sitting-room, and out by that door to the corridor. Momentarily she was confused about the direction she faced in; the sound of a door opening diagonally across from Elizabeth's sitting-room decided her. She sped away from it. She could hear Raedler's voice behind her. He spoke in German—probably to the nurse. The passage took a bend, and in front of her was the open space of the gallery above the Great Hall. She gained the middle landing where the stair took its opposite fork up to the other side of the house, and for a moment hesitated. Almost all the lights were off in the Hall below; it was deserted. She took the flight up to the principal guest suites. In the midst of her frenzy to escape Raedler, and the terror that she might not yet have escaped him, a feeling of triumph had accompanied her on this flight. The memory of Elizabeth's shouted command to her to go, the defiance of Raedler, the end of his dominance; for an instant Elizabeth had broken free; had acted to warn her, Sally—acted to protect her.

She reached the door of Josh's room and flung it open.

"Josh!" Silence and blackness. She groped frantically for the light. It revealed the empty room, the empty bed.

"Oh, God!"

Before she slammed the door again she went to the bell beside the bed and jabbed it three times quickly, urgently. That would bring someone—anyone. It was what she should have done up there in Elizabeth's apartments—that, and screamed for Pierre.

She went back to the stairs again. As she reached the gallery she saw Raedler at the top of the other fork, turned sideways to her, leaning over and looking down into the Hall. Before he straightened she had gained the middle landing. He started down towards her.

"Miss Devlin . . . ?" For once his voice did not carry a command; was it possible he had hoped to get her back up there?

She didn't stop, or even look around at him. She wondered why he had delayed up there. Afraid, in case his suspicions were not correct, to finally reveal himself?—perhaps to call the nurse to Elizabeth?—perhaps to summon on the telephone the two that he had described as the messengers from the bank? But whatever the reason, it had given her two minutes' start, and it had got her clear. She ran across the Hall, her heels clattering on the stone floor.

Before she reached the salon Lancome emerged from the service door, struggling into his jacket to go to answer the summons from Canfield's room.

"Lancome—stay there," she called. "I shall need you." She jerked her head towards Raedler, who had stopped short of the end of the stairs. The butler looked across the Hall at the other man, sizing up what he saw, Sally's flight, Raedler's defensive menace. His old head came up like a fighting cock. Without taking his eyes off Raedler he swung open the service door behind him again, and shouted, "*Jean—toute de suite!*" There followed a stream of shouted orders, in a French too rapid and too altered for Sally to follow.

The doors of the salon were flung open and Josh came out. "Sally—what is it!" Behind him in the distance she saw Hayward, half risen from his seat, the cognac glass tilted crazily.

"Quickly—I need you upstairs. With Elizabeth. Don't ask questions. Just come."

As they started back across the Hall Lancome and his helper, Jean, fell in with them. "Madame's apartments," Sally said. Behind them Hayward called a question; when he got no answer he ran to catch up with them.

Raedler had waited until Lancome and Jean had fallen in line with her and Josh. Then he turned and started up the stairs again, not running, but his long athletic legs taking three steps at a time. He had disappeared from the gallery before they reached the foot of the stairs. Sally remembered his delay in following her, and fear seized her again.

"Lancome—where are the men from the bank? They must not come up here."

"The rooms on the north side, M'selle. But three of my men already watch there. They will not take a step beyond. I guarantee it."

They had gained the level of Elizabeth's apartments. Hayward was struggling for breath. "I say, Sal! . . . what is this?"

"You'll see . . . you'll see. Just take no notice of Raedler. Whatever he says. He's not to stop us getting in to Elizabeth. No matter what."

For an instant, as they ran from the gallery to the passage that led to Elizabeth's rooms, Josh held her back.

"You're sure about this, Sal? You're *sure*. This will mean he'll know why we're here."

"I'm sure. This is the end of it for them." She jerked from his hold and started to run again. "It's finished, Josh. It's all over."

Then she stopped short as she ran up against Raedler himself, who was placed squarely in the doorway to the sitting-room. Everything about him was ordered and calm; he spoke calmly.

"I'm sorry, Miss Devlin. It is now too late. Madame cannot be disturbed to-night."

Sally gave an incredulous laugh, "You surely don't think you're going to keep me from her now?"

He spoke to her alone, as if there was nothing odd about the presence of the four men behind her. He even brought out his strange, mechanical half smile; he had the air of a man patiently endeavouring to calm an over-excited child.

"Perhaps in the morning, Miss Devlin. Madame is suddenly unwell. The nurse is with her."

"She is not so unwell that she can't hear what I have to tell her. I have something that she must see. I will," she added, matching his weird smile, "guarantee her rest once she has seen this."

"Regrettably, Miss Devlin, that is impossible. I am here to guard Madame's privacy as well as her health."

Sally noticed that Raedler's glance kept going past the men behind her, watching the passage, she thought, for the appearance of the two men whom Lancome's action had sealed off. The discovery reassured her; he was playing for time without knowing that Lancome's watch extended to every part of this house, and that, when it had direction, it was formidable. She could already taste the victory.

"Please stand aside, Mr. Raedler. All this trickery is finished—over. Let us not upset Mrs. Devlin more than is necessary by having scenes."

"Under no circumstances let us have scenes, Miss Devlin. You have been stupidly meddlesome—and the responsibility will be yours."

"Yes, it is mine——"

The words and the flash of triumph froze. She had not paid attention to the smooth movement of Raedler's hand into his coat, but Josh had. She found herself thrust out of the way as Josh lunged forward. But Raedler had prepared for the action and he had retreated into the room beyond Josh's reach. Sally found herself staring with terrified fascination at the polished steel of the gun Raedler held.

"Keep your distance, Mr. Canfield. As you may—or may not know—in this contest we engage in, violence is the last resort. But too often it has been used."

"No violence, Monsieur Raedler. Drop the weapon, or you are dead."

For a second Raedler permitted himself to turn to the direction the voice came from. The tall young figure of Pierre stood silhouetted by the light from Elizabeth's bedroom. It was not possible, in that second, to tell if his hand held a gun. But Josh used that time to cover the distance, and his hand closed on Raedler's wrist. The gun dropped to the floor, and Lancome darted to retrieve it. Then as Pierre advanced into the light cast into the sitting-room from the hall, Sally saw that he did hold a gun, a revolver much larger than Raedler's, clumsy-looking beside it, but lovingly, carefully cradled. Pierre's face was split with a smile. "*Eh, bien, Monsieur . . .*"

Lancome, Pierre and Jean bunched about Raedler; his expression did not betray dismay. His shoulders came together in the slighest shrug that might have been an attempt at bravado, or the gesture of a realist who acknowledges defeat.

Josh had turned to Sally. "Elizabeth——?"

"This way." She signalled Josh and Hayward to follow her as she went quickly through the sitting-room and Devlin's bedroom to the little study.

Elizabeth appeared not to have moved; she was seated still as Sally had left her. The nurse was there; on one of the side tables she had a small bag opened, and Sally could see a cotton swab and a syringe and a small sealed bottle laid out on a towel. The woman turned.

"Out," she said roughly. "Madame must have privacy."

Sally moved close to Elizabeth, between her and the nurse. "You don't have to take it. It's a sedation, isn't it? They were going to put you to sleep so that I couldn't see you."

Elizabeth opened her mouth, but no sound came; her body seemed numbed, as if she had no power of movement or decision. Sally, putting her hand on Elizabeth's shoulder, felt her whole frame rigid.

"You don't have to," she said again. Briefly she jostled for position with the nurse, who was trying to brush her aside.

"Go, please," the woman said, "I must attend Madame."

Josh called back to Lancome. "Bring Raedler here."

The nurse stepped back, her attitude hesitant. As Raedler appeared and she saw the guns in the hands of Lancome and Pierre she laid the syringe down on the towel again with a dull reluctance.

"Tell her to go," Josh said to Raedler.

Raedler merely jerked his head in the direction of the door. The woman shrugged, much as Raedler himself had done, and packed the instruments again into the bag. Josh and Hayward parted to give her passage, but Lancome barred the way.

"Monsieur?—we let her go?"

Josh nodded. "What can she do now? Just see that she keeps to her room."

"And the others? The ones from the bank?"

"The same."

Unwillingly Lancome gave way. He jerked his head to indicate to Jean that he should go with her.

With the woman dismissed, the eyes of all of them went back to Elizabeth. Although Lancome and Pierre stood behind

Raedler at the entrance to the room, she had seen the guns, had seen Raedler under guard, had recognised the import of the nurse's withdrawal. She looked all around at them, her grip on the arms of the chair so tight that the knuckles showed white. Her gaze rested finally on Sally, her eyes despairing.

"What have you done? I trusted you and you have told them—Dev will die. They told me if I communicated with anyone, that Dev would die."

"Dev *is* dead."

Elizabeth shook her head. She unclenched one hand from its grip on the chair to lay it protectively on the papers on the desk before her. "No . . . Dev is here. Dev wrote this. Alive . . ."

"Dev died in the crash," Sally said softly. "This . . . this work they've been giving you has been finished almost a year."

"Finished . . . ? No! This is not finished."

"You don't have all of it." Sally laid the envelopes on the desk and began to take out the contents, to spread them before Elizabeth. "And it's my fault that you don't have it all. I've been stupidly, selfishly late in giving this to you. Dev meant it for you, but I held on to it. I think, probably, you understand why—but that's past now. All I can say is that I'm sorry, and that isn't enough. There's no way I can make up to you for what you've suffered needlessly because I delayed . . . But Dev meant it for you."

It felt strange to be giving it up—not only giving it physically, but giving up her claim to it. The manuscript had been Devlin's gift to her, the gift of her own past, her own family. But Elizabeth needed it—as much as she, Sally, had needed to be able to give.

"Finished?" Elizabeth said again. Wonderingly she touched the new manuscript, Devlin's original and Sally's typescript—touched it tentatively, ready to reject it. She bent her head to read, and as they watched, a feverish activity gripped her; she began to search through the pages, looking at chapter beginnings and endings, reacting to the familiarity of the words and sentences with little sounds of pain and pleasure. Sally leaned across her and found the place where Elizabeth's own manuscript had ended.

"This is as much as they gave you," she said. She flicked to the beginning of the next chapter. "*This* is what they would have brought to you the next time."

Without speaking Elizabeth continued on through the manuscript—the first and last page of each chapter, seeking the continuity, squinting over the illegibility of Devlin's handwriting, comparing it to Sally's script. During this time no one in the room spoke or moved. Raedler stood there motionless; Lancome and Pierre crowded the doorway, refusing to be left out of the climax they had helped bring about.

Finally Elizabeth looked up. "How?" she said. "How has this happened?"

"The manuscript has been with me in London," Sally answered. "Dev has been sending it to me in pieces almost since the time you were married. I was typing it as it came. He said . . . he said it was to be completely finished before you saw it. It was . . ." There was a slight check in Sally's flow of words. "It was to have been a surprise for you. The part that I'd finished typing before Dev died I left in the studio. The rest of it was at the office. They didn't know about the part at the office. It must have been a piece of luck for them"—here she looked over at Raedler as if to confirm this—"to find a whole continuous manuscript. I expect they were planning to dole out to you bits and pieces of things Dev had written years ago. Lord knows, I had enough of them there. Fragments . . . But to get a whole manuscript, not published! They must have known, from finding the original with it, that no other copy existed, and that you wouldn't have seen it. It must have been quite a risk, that first time they tried it on you, to see if you had heard about it from Dev, if you knew it had been in existence before the crash. But you accepted it, and knew they were safe. They had you for as long as the manuscript lasted . . ."

"Sal——" Hayward broke in, "didn't you *miss* this material? Good God! A whole book of Dev's! It seems damned careless to me."

"She didn't miss it," Josh said, "because it was never taken. They didn't need to. All they needed was a camera and some time to work. And we gave it to them. All the time they needed. The only mischance was my seeing Kogan at Devlin's flat. But what they didn't get that time they must have got later. And in any case, Sally's studio turned out to be a much better cache."

Elizabeth appeared to have paid small attention to what had passed between them. Her face wore a look of bewilderment; her fingers plucked at the scattered pages of Devlin's handwriting.

Sally looked again at Raedler. "You know us very well, don't you? All of us—even me. Were there dossiers on Devlin and Elizabeth?"

He performed his strange, slight bow, as if complimented on the efficiency of the service. "Naturally. Preparations are made for many eventualities. Lawrence Devlin fell into our hands. It was not felt necessary to say he was dead. A chance was offered and used. We are not without some skill and imagination."

"And God-damn it, it worked because we let it work!" Josh exploded. "We knew something was happening, and we stood aside and let it happen. If we had had the sense to bring it out in the open, to *say* what we suspected——"

"If all of us had come into the open——" Sally broke in. "If I had told someone that I thought the studio was being entered. If I had come here——" Once more she looked at Raedler. "You knew us *very* well, didn't you? You knew that there was more than a fifty-fifty chance that I wouldn't get in touch with Elizabeth when the news came that my father was missing. You knew I wouldn't act—because I had never chosen to act before."

"In our business, Miss Devlin, a fifty-fifty chance is an excellent one," he answered. "And what was there to lose? A small period of waiting, to see how you would act, a little time to gather material. Madame Devlin was easy to hold under restraint. We also knew how *she* felt about Lawrence Devlin. As long as you and Madame Devlin did not come together, did not talk of Devlin's work, the chances grew better than fifty-fifty that our plan would work. And if it did not . . ." He shrugged. "Was Madame Devlin going to announce to the world that she had allowed herself to be blackmailed by a foreign power in order to save her husband's life. Is she going to tell the world that *now?* Of course not! We should merely deny it. Our denial would be accepted . . . and I think we should have co-operation from all the Governments involved. There are more pressing bargains to make for living men, rather than to fight over those who are already dead."

Then he added, as if he were loath to leave the beauty of the completed plan. "Ah, but think of what would have followed success . . . if she had made her statement. Think of the reputations that she could have taken with her, the trail of scandal and doubt and suspicion she would have left behind her. It had great potentiality . . . a pity Miss Devlin here had to spoil it."

"But you allowed us to come to St. Martin," Sally said.

"We were almost compelled. But in taking that risk we also pulled more fish into the net. The publicity of a Foundation established in the name of a man who no longer believed in the worth of the West, a number of prominent Britons associated with the Foundation and claiming great friendship and devotion to Lawrence Devlin, as we heard so movingly at the memorial service. The more that could be dragged in, the better. We planned to use what came our way, so we took the risk of the visit to St. Martin. It seemed, even if Miss Devlin and Madame had talked together privately, it would have meant little without the existence of goodwill. Without goodwill there would have been no sharing. We saw no evidence of goodwill." Once again the clinical smile puckered his lips. "You seem, however, to have forged it."

A movement now from Elizabeth brought their attention back to her. She had sat as if frozen while the dialogue had gone on, someone acted upon, as she had been since the time Raedler had come to this house. She leaned back in the chair, and for the first time withdrew her hands from the manuscript.

"We have forged goodwill," she repeated. "Almost too late. One neglects to cultivate what is right and just and human at great expense. I wrapped myself in Dev to the exclusion of the world—the world that also was Dev. In your own fashion you also have done it, Sally. I haven't very long to cherish my lesson. The principal benefits will have to go to you. But, yes . . . finally we have forged goodwill."

She nodded towards Raedler. "Now go. I have no need to listen to a further catalogue of my frailties. Yes, I would have done it. I would have given far more than my life for a sight of Dev. I was going to go to him, and let the thunderbolts fall on whom they would. I had to believe—I did believe that in the end what Devlin wrote would point to the truth about him. Devlin alive was what I believed in. An emotional —a woman's—belief. I am not ashamed of it. I do not retract it."

They were silent. Lancome and Pierre seemed to have understood little of the conversation; but the words that stayed with Lancome he rejected fiercely.

"Madame means him to go—to go *free*?"

"Free—who is free?" she said wildly. "What can they do now." Again she put her hand on the manuscript. "The power lay here—in Devlin, living. Without him, they have nothing. Violence serves no purpose, Lancome. Let him go."

Canfield watched, as, despairingly, Lancome lowered the gun, and signalled Pierre to do the same. The bewilderment in the young man's face was almost comical; Lancome's expression was anguished. Raedler gave, incredibly, his slight, formal bow, and turned and walked out through Devlin's bedroom and the sitting-room, to the lighted hall. He must have wondered, Canfield thought, what had become of the two men they had sent to reinforce him here at St. Martin. He would wonder that, but he had other things to wonder about. Elizabeth had said that violence served no purpose. It was true that it no longer threatened those in this room. But Raedler had still to account to his masters for failure.

IV

Marie appeared in the doorway of Devlin's room, where Raedler had stood. But now there was a domestic tranquillity in the squat figure of the maid, her arms piled with sheets.

"Madame sleeps," she announced to Sally, Josh and Hayward, who had waited there. "She has taken pills, and will sleep until morning." She added, her tone strongly possessive, "Now she gives in to fatigue, and it will be possible to rest. She has had so little rest . . ." She shifted the sheets and said briskly, "Now I will make up a bed for myself in the sitting-room—to be near Madame. The other one—the nurse—will not show herself again, I think."

When she was gone Hayward said, "They're back in control again, aren't they?—Marie and Lancome. Elizabeth at least will have some peace. You really don't think, Josh, that something ought to be done about Raedler?—even tipping off the Swiss authorities quietly."

"Nothing," Josh answered. "Even the quietest information could cause a leak. For Elizabeth's sake, they must leave here as if none of this has ever happened. In the morning they'll be gone, you'll see. They know the ropes . . ."

He was perched on the edge of Devlin's desk lighting a cigarette. Sally's hand strayed towards the packet, and then drew back. She sat down on the rather shabby leather sofa, swung her legs around and stretched out fully, her head finding the comfort of a soft, old pillow. The pillow and the sofa seemed to be saturated with the smell of tobacco; Dev also had smoked too much.

Josh and Hayward had waited here when she had gone with Elizabeth to her room. After Raedler had left, Elizabeth had said almost nothing; her body had seemed to slump in the chair with a degree of weariness that had silenced them all, as if the abrupt withdrawal of the need to brace herself for effort and control had left her without will or strength.

But before she had risen to take Sally's arm for the journey to her bedroom, she had spoken briefly.

"Is it enough now to say that I'm glad he's dead? Can you

all understand that? I'm glad he died the way he did, and not because of them. Selfishly, I'm glad that I no longer have to live to keep him alive—or to do what I thought I could do."

That was all she had said.

There had been a final "good night" to Sally when Marie had come to help her undress. In its off-handedness Sally found a degree of acceptance. Goodwill had been forged, as Raedler had said, but not yet intimacy; perhaps there never would be intimacy. It hardly mattered. They had achieved what had been needed. Sally was content to have it so.

She thought, though, as she returned to Devlin's room, that by to-morrow she would have had to strengthen her fiction about the manuscript being kept from Elizabeth as Devlin's idea of a surprise. To-morrow Elizabeth would be rested, and her critical powers stronger. To-morrow she, Sally, would have to lie very well indeed to make the story ring true. Elizabeth would not accept a gift out of pity. So to-morrow she, Sally, was going to have to blacken herself a little more so that Elizabeth could believe that the manuscript was truly hers. She would have to believe that Sally had clung to something that was not hers. It was not, Sally thought, what she wanted to do, but everything cost more than you expected, and you'd better have the price. There was never a cheap way out that was worth buying.

They had lingered on in Devlin's room. Lancome brought coffee to them there. It was very late, but they had hung about like people who had at last found the place where they wanted to be. For all of them it was like entering Devlin's final citadel; none of them wanted to leave quickly.

Lancome, too, had lingered, plumping up pillows, emptying ash-trays. Finally, with no further reason to stay, he had spoken. It was to Sally he directed his words, as though to indicate that he understood what she had assumed this night.

"We have guarded her, and watched," he said. "Until to-night we did not know what we guarded against." Then he wished them good night, and went.

"Odd old chap," Hayward said. "Completely devoted to Elizabeth—you don't find much of his sort around any more.

I remember Dev telling me that he fought in France with the Maquis during the war. Something feudal still about the way he has everyone in this household and half the village lined up. Well, at least he'll have that to hold on to when Elizabeth . . ."

He poured himself more coffee, and was silent for a while. He paced up and down the room as he drank, and then with the coffee cup put aside, wandered over to the shelves, taking down books and various objects there, examining them, fondling them, almost. To him they were Dev.

Suddenly he exclaimed, " Look at this!—look here! It's the Peace medal from the Academy in Oslo—Dev's Peace medal! I found it here, just in this box here on the shelf. Typical of old Dev. Damned casual . . . I wonder where the citation is . . . ?"

" I suppose," Josh said as he studied the gold disc, " that most Victoria Crosses wind up in a drawer somewhere. If you're the kind who wins it, you're also the kind who doesn't display it."

Sally looked at it for a minute, turned it over, then replaced it on the velvet. She closed the box decisively and put it back on the shelf. When he had first won the award she had been hurt that Devlin hadn't brought it to London for her to see. He had probably hoped that at some time she might arrive at this detachment.

She went back to the sofa, and this time Josh came and sat beside her. They watched as Hayward fidgeted with a cigar, pierced it, took a minute or so to get it properly lighted. Then abruptly he turned to the two of them.

" But I don't understand!" he burst out. " Damn it, I don't! All that talk in there from Raedler. How were they going to pull it off? Dev was dead!—she would have found out as soon as she got there."

" But she *believed* he was alive—she really believed it," Josh said. " She wasn't just taking their word for it. She had proof. No one but Dev could have written that manuscript. So she had her proof, and she was ready to do what they wanted of her. No statements that she was a Communist or that the

West was wrong, or any of that kind of thing. No—much simpler, and easier for her to do. Just the statement that Devlin was alive and had gone to the Sovet Union, and that she would join him. The implication would be that Devlin had defected, and of course the Russians would have been expected to produce him for a press conference, the way they've done with the others."

"But they *couldn't*," Hayward protested. "Dev was dead!"

"Elizabeth wouldn't know it. She would make her statement and go to join him. After *Pravda* had had enough play out of the story, there could have been a regretful announcement of a sudden death, or some such thing. The Russians are very good at that. And a splendid State funeral for a hero in the cause of peace. They would have managed it, and all the time Elizabeth, whatever her doubts, still would have gone on believing that Devlin had actually been alive, and in Russia, since last October. She probably would think they had killed him rather than produce him for the Press. Whatever she thought, she couldn't retract her action or her statement, and the damage would have been done."

Josh's head tilted back and his eyes surveyed the ceiling for a moment. "And just think," he said, "of those she would have taken over the dam with her. Guilt by association. It could have thrown the Allies into an absolute uproar. Think of the people who've stayed at St. Martin—the people who've associated with Devlin and Elizabeth. Think of Whitney Spence. Most of all, think of who her brothers are. It scares you, doesn't it? There you have the American Under-Secretary of Defence, and the Chairman of the Senate Foreign Relations Committee nicely pulled into the net, the biggest fish, I suppose, in a catch that could have included hundreds of big names, names very vulnerable to this kind of taint. It doesn't matter how much the whole business was questioned, some mud would have stuck. Can't you just see the Senate enquiry in which *both* O'Mara brothers were called to testify in their own defence?—it would have been a Roman circus of suspicion and accusation and denial, with all the Right-wingers in America having a field day."

"Why have they waited?" Sally said. "Why so long? She said a few weeks now."

"Well—they needed time to convince her that Devlin really was alive. They couldn't produce a bundle of manuscript and claim that he wrote it all in a month. And then, in the state Elizabeth is in, time works for them. Being shut up here, ill and isolated, has been a virtual brainwashing. Every month here alone, Devlin becomes more important to her, the only thing, literally, on earth that she cares about. And the shorter her life, once the statement was made, the better for them. If it was to have been in a few weeks' time, then I suspect it would have come at the moment that Defence Ministers met in Paris. Secretary of Defence Spauling is recovering from an operation, and Jim O'Mara will represent the United States. The meeting is crucial—on the matter of nuclear arms for Germany—the last thing Russia wants. This would have been a spanner in the works of gigantic proportions. It would be my guess, right now, that the meeting would never have taken place. Look—last year the British Government was nearly brought down because of the Profumo Affair—the indirect connection between the War Minister and a Russian. The chief value to them of Burgess and Maclean wasn't the information they might have passed on, but the mistrust of British Security that the whole business produced in the Americans. They understand propaganda very well, and of course an open society with a free press is a relatively easy tool to manipulate. Every newspaper in the West would have joined the clamour—anti-American, anti-German, anti-British. Almost anti-anything you like. Oh, yes, Elizabeth O'Mara Spence could have taken a great deal over the dam with her when she went. I don't think, at this stage, she is entirely a responsible person—but, she did know what she was doing. It's a hell of a situation to be in . . ."

"How cruel it's been," Sally said. "I'm sorry for her. And that's the last thing I ever thought I could feel about her."

"And *this*," Hayward said, "is the last that should ever be said on the subject. It's closed now. It nearly succeeded, but it didn't. No one will ever hear it from me. I intend to go ahead with the Foundation, and I know Elizabeth will agree. We have even more reason than before to create the kind of memorial to Devlin that he deserves. He so nearly had another kind—an infamous one.

"So, it's over," he added, "and he can rest."

It wasn't completely over, Josh thought. It never would be. There were those in London for whom the file on Devlin could never be closed. They were never going to know now, absolutely and completely, that Devlin had not been implicated in Fergus's murder in Beirut, and the disappearance of the cypher book. They would never know whether the border violation had been accidental, or done on purpose, and on schedule. There were those in London who would say that they had been waiting for Devlin, and that the crash of the plane was all that was accidental. These were the questions that had first led the official minds in London to the quest for the truth about Devlin. The official mind never accepted the half answer; the non-answer was more their line. They would end the file on Devlin with a question-mark.

SIX

Sally stirred and blinked and tried to hold on to sleep. She had left one of the windows with the curtains drawn back for air, and now the pale, opalescent quality of the light that filtered in, the grey not yet fully gold, told her that it was still very early. She turned in the bed and tried to bury her head in the pillow, but the sound rose, as it had the morning before, maddening, insistent. The swish-and-tap, swish-and-tap of Raedler's skipping rope. Still in the fog of sleep she was stirred to a kind of awe of him, the purposeful discipline of a man who could stand aside from the wreck of his plans, and maintain a purely physical routine as if nothing had changed. And yet everything had changed for Raedler. He had failed to carry out his task. She wondered, dully, what kind of punishment that would bring. How serious was the punishment for that kind of failure? Was it prison, or was it being sent to the lowest management level in a power station in Siberia?

As she thought of it, she knew Elizabeth's overwhelming sense of relief that Devlin was dead, and that no fate of their devising would wait for him. She thought of Devlin dead in the plane crash, and it seemed a clean and orderly death, right for him, right for the way he had lived. What was unthinkable was Devlin as their captive, obeying their rules, living to their routine. That would have been death to him, the worst kind, the slow and unnatural death, where spirit died before flesh.

Her thoughts went back to Raedler, and to his masters. She was aware then that the swish-and-tap had stopped; she wondered suddenly if this was the moment of Raedler's leavetaking of St. Martin. Would he, as most others would, pause for a minute on the terrace, look up and down the valley, to the great circle of the mountains about him, the moment weighted by the knowledge that he would never stand in this precise place again, never see this exact aspect? Or did Raedler belong to the species who had no such thought, who was never swayed by feeling. A kind of blind curiosity impelled her from the bed and over to the window from which she had been able to see Raedler's terrace the morning before. She had never encountered anyone like Raedler; she hoped she never would again. In a sense it was a moment of leavetaking for her also. But when she leaned from the window the figure on Raedler's terrace below her was not the man in the grey track-suit of yesterday morning. Moving through the french doors back into the house she caught the last glimpse of blond hair and the white jacket that Lancome's helpers wore. Raedler had gone, then, and there had been no pause for leavetaking. And by sending a servant, to assist his departure, Lancome was giving him no time for such pauses.

She went back to bed, and pulled the blanket almost across her eyes.

When she woke again Marie was there with *café au lait* and croissants. "An English breakfast later downstairs, M'selle. On the terrace. But late, since the sleep was so short last night. This morning Madame will not attend. She still sleeps. It is most necessary that she rests. Madame has little strength to call on, and it is almost exhausted."

The little maid's face was shadowed as she bent over the tray. Sally wondered if she had guessed what it was Elizabeth faced in the future; the premonition was there. But they could be glad, at least for the peace that could yet attend this house.

Marie brought the big coffee cup to the bedside.

"Raedler—and the others?" Sally asked.

"Gone, M'selle. Gone—thanks to God. Packed up and gone this morning before anyone was stirring. Monsieur Raedler leaves all his baggage behind, but that is nothing." She shrugged. "If he does not send for it, someone in the village will be the richer."

Sally thought about it as she sipped the coffee. Had it been so early when she woke?

It was midday before Hayward, pacing in the sun on the big front terrace, came to rest at the parapet to look down over the slope of the vineyards. It was he, therefore, who first saw the crumpled shape in the grey track-suit lying across the smashed vines. The men who went to him found a skipping rope tangled about his feet. There were many lacerations to his face and body from the fall, but the doctor gave the opinion that he had died when his spine had snapped at the neck.

II

"I wish you'd take me up to some high place, Josh. Up there somewhere," Sally had said, looking at the mountains above the château. In the late afternoon light they had driven through Sion and taken the road up to Crans-Montana, past the apricot and cherry trees, past the highest line of the vineyards, into the deep spring grass of the high pastures. It was softer country they travelled through than the road to Evolène, this south slope of the mountains that descended to the Rhône. It was wider and more open, more friendly. Every turn of the road that brought them into the mountain face eventually swung them round again and they saw not just a deep ravine, but the whole shining panorama of the Rhône valley. The villages here did not press so closely to themselves. The modern chalets began to appear. It was the tourists' country, the skiers' country.

"I'm glad we came this way," Sally said, as the high towers of the hotels and apartment houses of Crans began to appear. "I couldn't have taken any more of those brooding mountain villages living with the feeling that an avalanche could come down on me any minute. I've had my avalanche."

The avalanche, Josh thought, had also come for Raedler—or he had created his own. For the sake of ease, the police and magistrate would probably decide that his death had been accidental; it had been demonstrated that it was perfectly possible, if Raedler had tripped on the rope, or had had an attack of dizziness, to have fallen over the low parapet. He may have chosen to forestall his masters, to have prejudged the harshness of his punishment, to have carried out his own execution. It was possible that the two men who had come to St. Martin to aid him had received their orders and had, themselves, become his executioners.

Then Sally spoke. "I saw him."

"Saw who?"

"I don't know. Someone on the terrace—Raedler's terrace. I heard him skipping, and I looked out—but Raedler wasn't on the terrace. It was someone else—someone wearing a white jacket. It looked like . . ."

"You didn't see anyone, Sal." He didn't turn to her, didn't take his eyes off the road. He said it very quietly, without force.

"I didn't see . . . ? Josh, what do you mean?"

"Just that, Sal. You didn't see anyone on Raedler's terrace. You didn't look out. You heard nothing."

"You mean . . ."

"Rough justice, Sal. It's not our way, but we can't undo what's been done."

"I see."

The police would make their enquiries, he thought, and no one would say anything. The routine would be followed in respect to Raedler's passport, but Josh doubted that anything would ever be uncovered about the true identity of Hans Raedler. He thought it unlikely that anyone would ever claim Raedler. He would remain one of the anonymous grey men moving in the shadows of the grey war they waged on each other. He would probably even be buried at St. Martin, for lack of any other place. Elizabeth would pay for his burial; the parish priest would give him the benefit of the doubt, and there would be some prayers for him, for the sake of charity. It might well be the first and last charity Raedler had ever received. The very greyness of the past and the future of the man made Josh long for the tangible proof of the thing that had given his own life this sudden warmth and joy. He reached for Sally's hand on the seat beside him.

"I love you," he said. The words were strange on his tongue; it was a long time since he had said them to anyone. They created a wholeness in him where there had been an empty space before. For years now, the world had existed in terms of himself; suddenly it had been transformed. He had begun to see it in terms of someone else; it had grown immeasurably in dimension.

She turned to look at him, smiling slightly, the marks of strain of the night and the day still there on her face, but the peace was gaining. The avalanche had come for her also, but the rumble was dying and the disturbed terrain was settling to stillness once more; the new growth on the places swept bare could be slow and painful for her, but it would be a richer growth, he thought.

As if she spoke for him she said, "Everything is wider, Josh—suddenly I'm seeing things straight on, not looking at them out of the corners of my eyes. Because I love you, I have some left over for Elizabeth. I can afford to give something away. That's the richest I've ever been."

"It's the only kind of richness that will take you somewhere. Otherwise you stand still, the way I've been standing still for so long."

He drove until he found a place where the road was wide enough to let him pull off. They got out and walked down the slope. The grass was green with the moisture left by the retreating snow, dotted with the yellow and blue flowers that would die in the dryness of the summer. They found an outcrop of rock to sit on. The cow-bells tinkled as the cattle came home for milking; at the other end of the meadow, on the path leading to the barn, a little girl whose flaxen hair shone in the sun, waved to them. They waved back.

"Are you going to stay here, Josh—to work on the book? Elizabeth will help you now. I think she'd let you see any of the papers you wanted. And there are stacks of them back in the studio. . . ." She broke off because he was shaking his head.

"I'm not going to write the book about Devlin, Sally."

"Why not?"

"I was never meant to, in the first place. It was a necessary lie to get me to St. Martin."

"But it made sense—so it wasn't a lie, Josh. You could write it. You could write it very well. Hayward thinks so—he's such a bad liar he couldn't even have played that part without believing it. *I* think so."

"No, Sal. It's not for me. A year ago I would have given almost anything I possessed for a chance like this." He shook his head. "What am I talking about—a year?—a month ago I would have jumped at the chance."

"What changed it?"

"You."

"I don't understand," she said in a small voice.

"Don't you? You have to understand, my darling Sal, that I couldn't begin to interpret Devlin to the woman I'm in love with, because she happens to be his daughter. Look, Sal, it's time to stop this kind of inbreeding. You and I are beginning something fresh. Let's not keep harking back to the past. Devlin was a great man. Let's go on believing that, quite simply. And let's stop there. There'll be biographies of Devlin—of course there will. But there won't be a Canfield biography. I want to love you—simply, freely. I don't want to love the overtones of Devlin. We don't want Devlin beween us. And he wouldn't want to be there, either."

She nodded. "Yes, I see. What you're saying is that it's

time we moved on, isn't it? Away from Dev, into our own life." She twisted on the rock, sudden urgency in her movement. "Are you going back to them?"

"Them?"

"Whoever you work for. I don't even know what they're called."

"They prefer not to be called anything. And I'm not going back to them. I don't work for them any more."

"Why not?"

"I suddenly realised to-day that I'm free of them. I've been looking for a way out, and not really finding a reason for it, until you provided it. But that isn't *why* I'm finished with them. It happened automatically. Once the other side knew that Josh Canfield was in any way involved in what happened at St. Martin, involved in the failure of their plan, I automatically ceased to be of use to my own people. You see—well, if the whole situation at St. Martin had been innocent—if there had been nothing to find out, I would simply have been there as Josh Canfield, the writer. Now, in their minds, and in their dossiers, I'm Josh Canfield who is also something else. If I'd gone under an assumed cover, as a different person, I might still have been of use as Canfield. But as Josh Canfield I'm marked. I'm finished. It's as simple as that. Wherever I go from now on, I'll be going for myself. It's a funny feeling, Sal, to possess yourself again. One slips in gradually, and before you know how it's happened, or why, you belong to them. So I'll go back to being a landlord, and a writer, and I'll stop blaming them for whatever goes wrong. There'll be no more scapegoats. Not you with Devlin and Elizabeth. Not me with them."

She was silent for a time. He watched her plucking at the tough short grass that grew from a fissure in the rock. The sun fell on her hair as if it struck amber liquid; the sheen and glow of it made him want to touch it, to stroke it, to run his fingers through its disorder.

"I wonder if it's the altitude that makes me light-headed," she said. "Or is it going without cigarettes."

"The altitude . . . it always affect——"

She cut him short. " I'm only talking for the sake of talking, Josh. What I'm trying to say is that I have to stay here. I have to stay here with Elizabeth."

He nodded. " I know that." It was said with great finality. There would be no argument.

" I'll have to stay for as long as I'm needed. Perhaps she doesn't even know that I'm needed. Perhaps she won't even be very pleased when I say that I'm going to stay. But I have to, and she'll know it, eventually. I'm all there is left of Dev, and she should have whatever I can give her. It isn't very much, but it's something. It's something that's given willingly, and it's something she can't buy or command. I don't want to stay, Josh. I'll be impatient until I can come to you. But first I have to do this."

" Yes," he said.

" And will you come when I ask you to?"

" Any day you ask it," he said. " Any hour."

" I'll live with that, then. And for that time."

She got to her feet. " We'll have to go back now. This has been a little escape, but what we both have to do has to start right now."

They didn't speak as they walked back to the car. The sun was still warm, and it gilded the snowfields on the heights above them, though the shadows had flowed into the valley. As he held the car door open for her, she paused.

" I'll have to wire to have Tim sent here."

" Tim?"

" My cat. I left him with Robert. Robert never liked him in the first place . . ."

He remembered that big grey and white striped tom, standing in the studio, his back humped, spitting at the intruders. They had deserved it, of course.

" He'd better come and live with me," Josh said. " We'll have to get used to each other."